JAMES Y. BARTLETT

Death from the Claret Jug

A HACKER GOLF MYSTERY

This Yeoman House softcover edition of Death from the Claret Jug is an original publication. It is published by arrangement with the author.

This is a work of fiction. All of the events, characters, names and places depicted in this novel are entirely fictitious or are used fictiously. No representation that any statement made in this novel is true or that any incident depicted in this novel actually occurred is intended or should be inferred by the reader.

Cover Design: YH Studio
Printed in the USA.

ISBN **978-0-9852537-1-4**

Library of Congress PCN: **2018941048**

To Susan

"Sometimes, reaching out and taking someone's hand is the beginning of a journey.

At other times, it is allowing another to take yours."

– Vera Nazarian

Prologue

Carl T. Abercrombie roused himself and his wife Priscilla early that morning. Priscilla groaned: Having been married to the man for thirty years, she knew that when he had a schedule to keep, she would not be able to sleep late.

Schedules, plans and checklists ruled Abercrombie's life. He was a partner in the bluestocking Wall Street law firm of Somerset and Soames. His life was lived according to schedules. Daily, he caught the 6:12 train from the station at Dobbs Ferry, debarked at Grand Central at 6:55 (unless it was raining or some wino had decided to sleep on the tracks and get run over) and arrived on the 44th floor of the office building at Broadway and Exchange Place no later than 7:30 sharp. His mug of coffee and a neatly folded copy of the day's *Wall Street Journal* would be waiting on his antique walnut writing desk. At eight, the ever-faithful, ever-efficient Mrs. Patterson would enter the office and they would begin the daily routine of working through Abercrombie's checklist. Everything on his schedule was numbered, and he never varied how he tackled his tasks: Item Number One was taken care of first, followed by Item Number Two, and so on.

The rest of his life was similarly ordered. There were their two children, a boy and a girl. The golden Labrador retriever. The fund-raising and cultural events that he and Priscilla attended every year. Charity galas at the country club. The holiday schedules: Thanksgiving with his family; Christmas with hers. The February vacation to the Caribbean; they rented the same villa on St. John every year. August spent at the family cabin on the lake in the Adirondacks. And in May, the golf vacation.

Usually the Abercrombies went with friends to the Greenbrier resort, in the West Virginia mountains, because they liked the way that place never seemed to change. They counted on booking the same suite, seeing the same bellman, greeting the same golf professional, and ordering the same roast duck with blueberry compote in the same immense, rococo dining room.

But this year the other couples in their golf group had dropped out. Charley Pyle's company had been acquired by some French conglomerate and he was spending an inordinate amount of time shuttling back and forth to Lyons. The Chesters had divorced, an event not entirely unexpected given Ken Chester's well-known wandering eye. And Barton Pickwick III, known as Trippy, was on an extended stay at the federal prison at Fort Dix, New Jersey, due to some unfortunate insider-trading events involving his hedge fund. He had *not* been represented by Somerset and Soames.

So Abercrombie, abandoned by his golfing pals and by fate, had decided to strike out, uncharacteristically, on his own this year, breaking new ground. He had decided to take his wife to visit the Home of Golf: Scotland. Mrs. Patterson had called a tour company and made all the arrangements. They had started with a few days at Gleneagles, driven up to the north to play Nairn along the Moray Firth and Royal Dornoch in Sutherland, and then made their way back down to the Kingdom of Fife for a visit to St. Andrews, which is where they had awakened that morning. They were staying in the Old Course Hotel, in a lovely suite on the golf course side, overlooking the dogleg of the famous Road Hole on the Old Course. Carl had played the Old Course, which he didn't warm to, thinking it rather flat and featureless; Carnoustie, where he had shot an embarrassing 97; and the American-designed course at Kingsbarns, which he liked because they allowed him to ride in a cart. Priscilla, who was an unenthusiastic golfer at best, had played only the latter course; the rest of the time she shopped, walked and, while reading English mystery novels, drank herself into an afternoon stupor every day in the hotel's quiet and well-appointed bar.

Abercrombie wanted to get an early start on the day because they were driving back across Scotland to the Ayr coast, where he had a mid-afternoon tee time at Old Prestwick. They would then stay at the Turnberry Resort for a long weekend before heading home.

"C'mon, Pree," he said, throwing the covers back and heading for the bathroom. "They say there's a lot of history in this old town. We've got to visit Young Tommy Morris' grave, spend an hour at the Scottish Golf Museum, and take a tour of the Castle."

Priscilla turned her throbbing head back into the pillow and tried to ignore him.

It was a blustery day with the sun ducking in and out of fast-moving clouds. The wind ranged from very hard to ridiculous gusts that threatened to carry away anything not bolted down. "Good thing we're not playing in this, eh old girl?" Carl said as they wandered down Market Street towards the towering transept that guarded the churchyard, where row after row of monuments and weathered headstones leaned against the howling wind. Priscilla noticed that the green of the grass—such a deep, lovely green!—was dotted with tiny white daisies with yellow eyes the size of BBs. She smiled—they really were pushing up daisies here!

They found Young Tommy's marker, an elaborate Victorian memorial set against a brick wall. "Dead at twenty-four," Carl mused, standing there with his hands in his pockets. "They say he perished of a broken heart after his wife died in childbirth. He'd already won the British Open three times by then. Imagine how many more he could have won if he'd lived." Priscilla could only think of the poor dead wife and the poor dead baby. She wanted a drink. Carl read the inscription aloud: "Deeply regretted by numerous friends and all golfers, he thrice in succession won the Championship belt and held it without envy, his many amiable qualities being no less acknowledged than his golfing achievements."

"'Many amiable qualities,'" Abercrombie mused aloud. "Isn't that an interesting thing to say about someone?" Priscilla wished for an amiable quality, but all she really wanted was to get out of the infernal wind and knock back a couple fingers of one of those golden whiskeys they knew how to make in this otherwise godforsaken place.

They wandered back into the town and on a busy corner ducked into the humid warmth of a Starbucks. Perhaps Abercrombie was hoping to hear a friendly

American voice, but he knew, when he saw the rosy red cheeks of the curly haired lass behind the counter, that there were no Americans working here. He ordered a latte, and a chai tea for Priscilla, and they sat near the window looking out at the street. Carl heard the two men sitting at the next table talking about golf, and when he was sure they were Americans, he leaned over and spoke to them. Before long, the three of them were rehashing shots and courses and exchanging cards and planning a late-summer get together at one or all of their golf clubs back home. Priscilla picked idly through a worn copy of *Horse and Hounds* she had found on one of the tables. *If I lived the kind of life these people do, all tweeds and leather and romping about in manure and windy moors, dogs underfoot everywhere, I would kill myself,* she thought to herself.

"Right," Abercrombie said when the coffee was done and they were standing on the sidewalk again. "It's getting late," he glanced at his watch. "We only have time for either the golf museum or the castle. Which would you rather see?" He looked at Priscilla, who was gazing longingly at the Central Pub across the street.

"I guess the Castle," she said, wondering why "none of the above" was not a possible choice.

Abercrombie, reverently holding a city map in front of himself like it was Dante's *Guide to the Seven Circles of Hell,* led the way through the twisting, narrow streets past some of the quadrangles of the University of St. Andrews, down the hill and out to the rocky promontory on the sea, where the crumbling ramparts of an ancient castle clung to the edge of a cliff. What had once been a moat was now a grassy depression that followed the walls around, with a heavy wooden plank bridge leading through an arch carved out of the thick stone wall and into the inner courtyard.

Abercrombie paid the admission fees and purchased a souvenir booklet giving the history of the ancient castle and the occupants who had lived and died there. Built around 1100, when St. Andrews was one of the ecclesiastical centers of the British Kingdom, the Castle had been the home of the powerful bishops and archbishops of the day. The ruined walls, green lawns and one towered parapet were all that remained after the Protestant Reformation in 1560 temporarily eliminated the power of the Roman church in Scotland.

They climbed the parapet and looked out at the cold gray ocean until the wind chased them back down the roughhewn stairs. Priscilla suggested they visit the dungeons, thinking they, at least, would be out of reach of that cold, relentless wind. They learned that the castle was undermined by two tunnels that had been carved out of the rocky base during one or another sieges from centuries past. The attackers had carved out one tunnel to get into the castle, while the defenders carved out one just a bit higher to surprise the first group. Abercrombie, who had a slight case of claustrophobia, shuddered at the thought of all that digging and hacking and crawling around underground in the dark.

Just before climbing the stairs back to the courtyard, they entered a triangular chamber and peered down into the entrance of the Bottle Dungeon, a 24-foot-deep hole in the rock below. A plaque on the stone wall said that the dungeon, carved out of the rock in the shape of a bottle of claret, had held prisoners during the Reformation, including most likely the unfortunate Protestant preacher George Wishart, burned at the stake by Cardinal Beaton in 1546 at the height of the religious wars. Abercrombie leaned over the thick metal grating and peered down into the hole, where a single light bulb illuminated the dankness of the stone cave. Priscilla, feeling a bit dizzy in the close air, did not look.

"Humph," he said.

Up in the courtyard, where the thick stone walls blocked the worst of the wind, Abercrombie spotted a man wearing a phosphorescent neon slicker with reflective tape markings. He had been in the country long enough to know that this uniform signified some kind of official. He went up to the man and tapped his shoulder.

"It's none of my business, of course," he said, "But I think if you're going to put a figure in the dungeon, you should make it easier to see. It's awfully dark down there and there's no lighting at all. Can't you get more light down there?"

The man, who was a waste services engineer, which is to say the garbage man emptying the trash bins, looked at Abercrombie as if he were mad. "I dinnae unnerstan' wha' y'mean," he stammered.

"The dummy ... the figure ... the *mannikin*," Abercrombie said, enunciating his words carefully and pointing down the stairs toward the dungeon. "In the bottle dungeon. It's too dark down there to see the figure of the prisoner. That's all I'm saying. Just my opinion."

Luckily for the poor man, one of the museum docents was walking past on her way to the office and overheard Abercrombie. Seeing the rank confusion on the face of Willie McTavish—the garbage man—the woman stopped.

"I'm sorry," she said. "There are no figures in the dungeon. We used to have some, but took them out long ago—they tend to get moldy down there."

Abercrombie stared at her. "What are you talking about?" he said. "I was just down there and saw one with my own eyes. Though it's really too dark to make out much detail. That's all I'm saying..."

Priscilla, embarrassed, tried to pull on her husband's arm, to get him to come away and forget all this nonsense about figures in dungeons. *The things that get into Carl's head*, she thought. *Once lodged in there, they never come out.*

The woman, who had worked at the castle museum for years, long enough to have ages ago gotten sick and tired of pushy, self-righteous Americans, decided for once to do something. She crooked her finger at the man standing there, red in the face. "Come along then," she said, "We'll just go have a wee look."

Abercrombie followed the woman back down the stairs to the dungeon. Priscilla decided to take a look through the gift shop. She wished she had thought to slip into her purse some of the tiny bottles from the well-stocked minibar in their suite. One or two of those would have helped the morning immensely.

When Abercrombie reached the small low-ceilinged chamber to the dungeon, he stood out of the way, and allowed the woman to pass by. She smiled at him grimly, bent over the edge and peered down through the grating into the dank, dark chamber below.

"Good Lord," she said.

Chapter One

I PULLED THE door closed on the Vauxhall Omega, inserted the key and turned it on. I clipped my seat belt in, adjusted the mirrors all around and revved her up. As with most modern-day cars, instead of the deep throaty growl I was looking for, the Vauxhall responded with a whiny, tinny sound in protest. But I didn't care. In my sleep-deprived and over-imaginative state, it sounded just like an Aston Martin.

I glanced over to my left at Mary Jane Cappelletti, who was holding a cardboard cup of coffee and looking confused, trying to figure out why the steering wheel and pedals were on the wrong side of the car. It took her a moment or two before she remembered we were in Scotland. They make the cars backwards here.

It was a little before seven in the morning in early July, and we had just flown into Glasgow on the overnight from Boston. The weather was like it always is in Scotland: brisk, showery and due to change in a moment's time. In a little over a week, my presence was required in St. Andrews, when the Royal and Ancient Golf Club would once again stage the tournament to decide "the Champion Golfer of the Year." To the rest of us, it is known as the British Open. Or just The Open, as the snobby Brits prefer.

I'd be there chronicling the action for the readers of my paper back in Boston, most of whom would be more interested in how many games behind the Yankees the Red Sox were, or whether the Patriots would sign their high-priced, newly drafted running back before training camp opened in another month. But I've long since gotten used to writing about golf in our baseball- and football-crazy town. There are still enough newspaper readers left who like to get in 18 holes before the Sox come on TV to keep me employed, if just barely. How much longer, I have no idea, what with the number of newspaper readers declining faster than John Daly's bank account after a long weekend in Vegas.

But this year, I had invited Mary Jane along. I have discovered that traveling with her is far superior to traveling alone, even if I occasionally have to wait a few minutes for her to "put on her face" or perform one of the other mysterious ablutions that women seem to have. There is, of course, the warm body to snuggle with at night. But it was more than just that with Mary Jane. She had rather quickly become a constant presence in my life, and it felt more right being with her than not. Once again, Mary Jane had been able to get someone to look after her precocious ten-year-old daughter Victoria; this time with some cousins who were spending the summer at their camp on a lake in Maine. The idea of Vickie spending a couple of weeks in the fresh air, swimming and boating, and having a gaggle of kids to hang around with overcame the knowledge that the family she was staying with was part of The Family. Victoria's grandfather is the *capo* in Boston's Italian North End, and many of her uncles and cousins are your typical bent-nose hoodlums. Victoria, thankfully, had never really known her father, now dearly departed, who had been a small-time leg-breaker and your basic bum, despite his impressive parentage, and had finally bought it one fine morning in the hallway of a dingy Charlestown tenement.

I revved the car again. Mary Jane cocked an eye at me sleepily.

"Hacker," I said in my best Sean Connery brogue. "James Hacker."

"Are you sure you know how to drive this thing?" Mary Jane asked, doubt creeping into her voice. "And when did you change your name from Peter?"

"Miss Moneypenny never doubts her man," I said.

"Miss Moneypenny died a lonely spinster," Mary Jane said. "There's a moral there somewhere."

I threw the car into gear and eased out of the parking lot. I had specifically requested that my rental come with manual transmission, because I know of few things more fun than driving along Scotland's twisty roads, shifting up and down the gears, imagining SMERSH agents hot on my trail. I know: I should grow up. But I can't help it.

After negotiating a series of roundabouts getting out of the airport—there wasn't much traffic this early in the morning, so I could zoom through them a bit too fast, which is always fun—I slowed down and followed the signs onto the M8 motorway that took us past the sooty gray downtown of Glasgow and onto the A80 heading to the north. I like driving on the "wrong" side, and shifting with the "wrong" hand. It's fun. And because everyone else is doing it too, it's not too hard to get with the flow.

For Scotland, it was turning into a pretty nice day. It was a little cool for the month of July, but then, Scotland is always a bit chilly. If it wasn't for the saving grace of the warm Gulf Stream, Scotland would have the same climate as Labrador, and you can often feel that menacing background coldness in the air. The collection of gray-bottomed clouds that had just crossed the Atlantic with us blew across the sky in an energetic following wind, alternately hiding and releasing the warming sun. The pebbly surface of the macadam on the roadway—the road-building process had been invented by and named after a Scotsman, John Loudon MacAdam—had been darkened by one of the frequent showers released by the clouds and when the sun came back out, the reddish surface of the road sparkled happily.

I am Scottish neither by ethnicity nor heritage, as far as I know, but I have always felt instantly and strangely at home here. Some might say that I was probably a Scot in a previous life, and I suppose I could claim to be the reincarnation of William Wallace, Robert the Bruce or some other great warrior hero of the ancient and misty past. Others may think that as a golf writer, of course I feel an affinity to the place where the game was invented, Dutch, French and Chinese claims to the contrary notwithstanding. But that doesn't explain that deep inner feeling of being home whenever I arrive back in Scotland. I don't try to explain it, it just is.

Mary Jane had drifted off to sleep. Neither of us had slept very much on the overnight flight. The cabin had been crowded, noisy with caterwauling children and too hot, and just as I was beginning to nod off a bit, the flight crew had thrown on the lights and began serving us breakfast, a mere two hours after they had cleared away the dinner. I knew that I would be sleepy soon, but had learned over the years to fight off sleep on the first day in Europe as long as possible, to get my internal clock adjusted to its new time zone.

I clicked on the radio and found one of the many BBC channels, which was playing some kind of retrospective of Frank Sinatra, the Columbia Years. Frankie launched into "The Lady is a Tramp" and I motored along with him, swinging up the A80 and merging onto the M9 signposted for "The North."

We weren't heading too far north. I had arranged to spend the first couple nights of our trip with an old friend of mine, Duncan Taylor, a longtime rules official and golf professional who lived just past Glendevon, down the road from the Gleneagles resort. I had met Duncan years before at the U.S. Open, where he had been imported to help with rules adjudication, and we saw each other annually after that. He had spent some time in Boston, where I had taken him to some of our good local courses, and he had issued a longstanding invitation to visit with him and his wife Vivienne in Scotland. We were taking him up on the offer.

The local Scottish version of the BBC interrupted Frankie's singing at the top of the hour, and I listened to the news announcer telling us of a work stoppage in the Borders, a football fans "incident" after a heated match in Inverness, and the weather report, which called for the usual strong gales across the Orkneys.

"And in sport," the announcer said, "The world's best golfers will gather next week in St. Andrews for the Open Championship. But they may find a reception not to their liking from one group. Jane Harrison reports from Fife…"

Jane Harrison, whose Scottish brogue was as thick as the Argyle sweater she was probably wearing, told us that a group called Eliminate Golf, or EGo, was planning a series of protests and marches in the Auld Grey Toon during the week of the Open championship. This organization was apparently down on golf, holding that it was a rich white man's game that discriminated against minorities and women, desecrated the environment and diverted attention and especially funds from the world's poor, who were more important, said Jane's interviewee, "than this group of coddled, spoiled, overpaid leeches who do nothing, really, for the benefit of the world."

The speaker, a male with a deep, dramatically theatrical baritone voice, continued. "Just take this one week, Jane," he said into the microphone. "It will cost more than three hundred and fifty million pounds to stage this tournament here in St. Andrews next week, and that's not counting the time and talent of the local residents here who will be displaced, delayed and disgusted by the many thousands of visitors who will traipse through our city. Imagine what good could be done with three hundred and fifty million pounds among the poor, the disenfranchised and the hungry. And if you ask yourself, 'Is it worth it?' I think you'll come to the same conclusion as EGo. Not by any reasonable standard of the Western world today."

"And that's the opinion of Dr. Cecil Knox a professor of sociology at the University here in St. Andrews, and chairman of EGo, Eliminate Golf," Jane said, wrapping up her piece.

I laughed, but you had to admire the man's brio. To stand on the street in St. Andrews, the Home of Golf, and diss the game took some fairly large onions. I made a mental note to go find this Knox guy next week. He might make an amusing sidebar for my readers back home.

As we left the flat valley behind, the hills began to rise on both sides of the highway. Soon we passed by Stirling, the gateway to the Highlands, with its impressive fortress castle atop a forbidding and rocky escarpment. I would not want to be the general in charge of storming that castle, nor would I want to be the foot soldier to whom it fell to climb that cliff while fending off hails of arrows or buckets of boiling oil.

North of Stirling, the Ochil Hills rose on both sides of the road. Too small, really, to be called "hills," they were not yet mountains either. They rolled up dramatically in smooth, rounded lines, almost totally devoid of trees, and filled only with the heather and gorse, a billion or two white dots of grazing sheep, and the whistling of the ever-present wind.

In another half hour, I pulled off the motorway at the Auchterarder exit. To the left, the road led up to the famous Gleneagles resort, a 1920s-era railroad resort hotel that was probably the classiest, and most expensive, golf resort in Scotland. I have been there many a time, both for pleasure and to cover the occasional Scottish Open staged on one of its three courses, and never tired of the place. Especially when someone else was picking up the tab.

I turned instead to the right, crossed the railroad tracks, and followed the road through a narrow valley and into the dramatic cleft in the hills known as Glendevon. Over the millennia, the River Devon had etched away the rocky hills and created an east-west passage, bounded on both sides by the steeply rising terrain. I reached over and nudged Mary Jane awake. It was too pretty to miss.

"Wow," she said as we began driving through the glen, the twisting road following the rushing torrent of the river down below. "Where the hell are we? I have to pee."

Oh, yeah. That was another thing about traveling with Mary Jane. The woman has a bladder the size of a thimble. Luckily, I knew there was a pub and cafe not too far down the glen, and in short order, we pulled in, and Mary Jane scurried inside to take care of business. I got out, yawned and stretched in the cool sunshine of the morning. I could hear the river rushing through the rocks, and meadowlarks singing in the hills above. Above the tall forest of pines, I saw a pair of hawks riding the thermals way up high, and hoped that they—the hawks—had as much fun doing that as it looked from down below.

"Right then," Mary Jane said as she came out of the restaurant, looking refreshed and combed, and holding two cups of to-go coffee. "Where are we?"

"Glendevon," I told her. "Just passed Gleneagles, where I'll bet we're playing golf tomorrow. Duncan's place is just down the road, maybe ten miles or so."

"It's pretty," Mary Jane said. "The air smells fresh."

"Aye," I said. She looked at me, a smile playing about her lips.

"Are we talking pirate?" she said, giggling a little.

"Nae, lassie" I said. "Scottish."

"Oh," she said. "Well, me hearty brawny lad, let us hie away forthwith. And is that a claymore 'neath your kilt or are you just happy to see me?"

"Shut up and get in the car," I said.

She reached for the passenger door, realized it was the driver's side, cursed under her breath and walked around. I smiled.

Chapter Two

Duncan Taylor's home was in the village of Pool o'Muckhart, which was a village only in the sense that there was a group of about four buildings comprising a bank, a gas station, a pub and the local farm supplier who sold tractors, tools, feedstock and Lord knows what else. I didn't see a pool and didn't really want to know what a 'muckhart' was.

We came out of Glendevon, still following the river as it spilled out of a reservoir near the end of the valley and headed toward the Firth of Forth. Now on the south-eastern slopes of the Ochil Hills, the land faded away and flattened to the east, towards the capital of Edinburgh on the southern banks of the Firth, with the Kingdom of Fife and St. Andrews to the north.

Duncan had sent us detailed directions, and it wasn't hard to find his place. We motored slowly through the village, took a fork to the right off the main road, turned right again at the brown fence and continued up the road until we came to Duncan's house. It was a pretty little whitewashed stucco cottage with a steep tiled roof, sitting back from the road on a small rise and surrounded by a small green lawn and a garden in the back. The sweep of the hill rose off in the distance beyond the house.

I pulled in and honked and Duncan came bustling out to greet us. He was in his sixties, short and round, with a mass of snow-white hair and dramatic eyebrows that stuck out like the prow of a ship. He was delighted to welcome us, made a fuss over Mary Jane and ushered us inside.

"Viv is out doing the marketing," he said. "But I think I can manage a cup of tea. Sit down, sit down! How was the trip? You must be exhausted! Would you like to nap right off, or are you going to fight to the bitter end?"

I laughed and led Mary Jane as we followed Duncan out to an enclosed sunny porch with floor to ceiling windows on three sides. It brought the garden and the looming hills into the house. The windows magnified the sunlight and made the room warm and bright. Vivienne had all kinds of things growing in pots tucked here and there on the floor and on shelves of the sunroom, and they apparently liked this warm, sunny spot, for the greenery spilled out and several plants were in gorgeous bloom.

Duncan came out from the kitchen carrying a tray with teapot and china cups and a plate of cookies and set it down on a side table. He poured three cups of steaming tea, made sure we had the proper additions of sugar and milk, and finally sat down with us.

We chatted idly about golf while we sipped our tea and munched on the lemon cookies. Duncan was always full of good gossip about the golf scene on his side of the Atlantic, as he often was called to work as a rules official for many of the European PGA tournaments, as well as all the big Scottish amateur and junior events. It gave him an excellent view of up-and-coming talent, and he always had several names that he predicted would be heard from in the years ahead.

"So," I asked him, putting my cup down. "Any dark horses likely to rear up on the Old Course next week?"

His eyebrows jumped up and down energetically. "You mean, can anyone beat your American chaps?" he said, chuckling a bit. "That's always the question, isn't it? Even now that Tiger Woods has left the scene, there are always two or three more threatening to dominate." He sipped some tea. "We used to have a complex about you Yanks, but now there are plenty of golfers on this side of the Pond that can put up a good fight. Padraig Harrington has been playing well this year, Poulter always seems to be on the verge, but I don't think Justin Rose has quite rounded into top form this year." He paused and nibbled the edge of a cookie.

"But I know of two young men who might surprise some people next week," he continued. One is Willie Dalgleish, who plays out of Helensburgh, just over the mountains from here," he gestured vaguely to the west. "Fine player, long, straight and seems unflappable, like so many of the young men coming along these days. But if you wanted a longshot, I might suggest the Irish wonder, as they're calling him, Conor Kelly. When you watch him play, I swear you can hear poetry and music in the air."

Mary Jane, who had been sitting quietly sipping tea and listening to us talk, laughed softly. "Yeats or Joyce?" she asked.

Duncan smiled fondly at her. "Makes a difference, doesn't it?" he asked. "Hearing the voice of James Joyce when watching a golfer play might not be so good, with all those run-on sentences and jagged use of language. No, my dear, Kelly's play is more lyric and flowing, like William Butler Yeats."

"'Things fall apart, the center cannot hold,'" Mary Jane recited. "'Mere anarchy is loosed upon the world/ The blood-dimmed tide is loosed, and everywhere/ The ceremony of innocence is drowned. The best lack all conviction, while the worst are …'"

"' …Full of passionate intensity,'" Duncan finished. "Yes," he said, nodding, "That's it exactly. He plays with passionate intensity, although he's far from the worst. It's quite a thing to watch."

I stared at Mary Jane. "Poetry?" I asked.

She smiled. "I was an English major at UMass before I got pregnant with Victoria," she said. "The Irish poets were my favorites."

We heard a car pull up the drive. Duncan jumped to his feet. "That will be Viv," he said.

Vivienne Taylor was the model of a Scottish housewife. She was short and plump, with jet-black hair pulled back in a bun, and wore a plain cotton dress under an old blue sweater that hung down to her hips. She wore sensible black square-toe shoes and a pair of spectacles dangled from a chain around her neck. She also had an impish smile and a wonderful sense of humor.

Mary Jane and I jumped up to greet her and offer help loading in the groceries, but she shooed us away back to the garden room while she put things away and puttered in her kitchen, and finally came out with her own cup of tea to join us.

"Lovely day tis, yes?" she said, plumping herself down in a soft chair. "You poor people must be tired after that long flight. Duncan, why don't you take these young people out for a walk? The fresh air is reviving after traveling."

"Yes, m'dear," Duncan said, smiling. "I thought I'd let them relax a bit, take them out for a bit of lunch and a wander and we'll let them catch up on their rest tonight."

All this talk about being sleepy was making me sleepy. I poured myself another cup of the strong dark tea. Mary Jane launched into her conversation starter, a sure-fire gambit designed to get others talking so she didn't have to.

"So," she said, smiling at Viv, "How did you two meet?"

"Oh, my," Viv said, glancing over at Duncan and blushing a bit. "That was so many years ago, I think I've almost forgotten. I believe it was Duncan's cousin Hugh who suggested that he give me a call. I had just broken up with another lad, and he thought Duncan would be amusing for me."

"What?" Duncan sat up. "There was someone else before me?" He sounded outraged, although we all knew he wasn't. "I thought I was your first!"

Viv chuckled softly. "Oh, you old coot," she said. "You knew about Harold."

"So was he?" Mary Jane said.

"What is that, m'dear?" Viv asked, giving her husband a fond glance.

"Amusing?"

"Oh yes," she said, smiling to herself. "He was amusing and interesting and handsome, all at once. I think I knew in the first ten minutes that we would be married."

"And never a doubt since!" Duncan trumpeted.

"Oh, I wouldna say that, old man," she said. "I wonder sometimes when I hear you talking to the news presenters on the telly. Imagine," she said, looking at Mary Jane for feminine support. "A grown man talking to the box!"

Mary Jane smiled. "I'd say you only need to worry when he tells you the telly is talking back," she said. We all laughed.

Duncan helped me lug our suitcases into the house, and showed us to the guest room in the back. Mary Jane and I looked longingly at the bed, covered with a thick down duvet and soft pillows, but we changed into blue jeans and sweaters and climbed into Duncan's car.

He drove us down to the Muckhart Golf Club on the other side of the town and ushered us into its rickety wooden clubhouse, a Victorian-era building with some elaborate gingerbread highlights. In the back there was a small dining room and bar overlooking the last hole, and we could see a four-ball of women, pulling their trolleys behind them, trundling up the fairway. Duncan was a member here and something of a celebrity, judging by the way he was greeted and backslapped by everyone. We sat down in a sunny corner and ordered some soup and toasties—basically a grilled ham-and-cheese sandwich and one of Scotland's true culinary delights. Even though we'd had two meals in the last six or seven hours, I was ravenous.

People came and went throughout our lunch, stopping to chat with Duncan and shake our hands. When the four ladies we had seen on the 18th hole finished putting out and came inside, I saw that they were all well into their seventies, with grandmotherly white hair and rosy red cheeks. They parked themselves off in a corner, ordered gin and tonics all around and began a spirited discussion of who, actually, had won the match. It reminded me again of the egalitarian spirit that informs golf in Scotland. In almost all of the rest of the world, golf is an elitist game, played mainly by the upper classes who are the only ones who can afford steep greens fees and multi-thousand-dollar private-club dues. In Scotland, it's quite the reverse, and the game is played and embraced by virtually everyone. Kids play after school. Grandmothers play in the morning, have a quick lunch and a few G&Ts and go home. A couple of elderly gents, both trailed by their dogs, will blast around a course on foot in two hours. Sure, there are some fancy and upscale places in Scotland where the great unwashed aren't much welcomed—Muirfield and Royal Troon and Loch Lomond spring to mind—but for the most part, golf is viewed as a birthright of the Scots, and its cheap, accessible and accepted for almost everyone. It would have been rude of me to ask Duncan what his annual club dues were, but I knew they could not be more than about $200 a year. Probably less.

Towards the end of lunch, I felt my eyes getting heavy. It might have been the excellent local lager I had ordered with my lunch. I wanted to have another, but Duncan looked at me, smiled and said "I have a place I want to show you before I let you sleep. It won't take long."

He drove us back up towards Glendevon, then took a side road barely wide enough for his small sedan that groaned as it climbed up the hill in a series of switchbacks. We heard Mary Jane, sitting in the back seat, make a little gasping sound. "Don't look down,"

Duncan chuckled. "You're not afraid of heights, are you?"

We reached the top of the first part of the swelling hills, where the road descended onto a broad plain for a time before beginning to climb again. But Duncan turned off at a sign which said "The Lookout," and parked in a gravelly area beside the road. "It's not far," he said, "And the path is mostly level. Worth the walk. I think it's one of the best views in Scotland."

We followed him on the narrow dirt path that wound through the waving, wind-ruffled grasses. In about ten minutes, we came to the Lookout on the edge of the hill which dropped precipitously down into the valley below. To the left, the reservoir behind the dam sparkled deep and blue in the sun and reflected the wispy clouds still streaking by overhead. The spillway of the River Devon dropped down to the valley floor to the right and snaked its way through farm country, with the green, rectangular blocks of fields visible as far as the eye could see. Away in the distance, we could just see a hint of the North Sea, and the inlet of the Firth of Forth.

"On a good day, you can make out Edinburgh Castle," Duncan said. "But I'm afraid there's too much moisture in the air today."

Mary Jane sighed. "That green and sceptered isle," she said, mostly to herself, and reached for my hand.

"Yes, quite," Duncan said. He pointed to a smaller hillock just below where we were standing. "Down there, the archaeologists found a circular village that they have dated to the time of the Picts, who were here before the Gaels and the Norsemen. We don't know much about the Picts, unfortunately."

"We know they must have enjoyed the view," Mary Jane said. "How could anyone not fall in love with this?"

"Quite so, child, quite so," Duncan said, smiling.

Chapter Three

MARY JANE AND I awoke the next morning in Duncan's sunny guest room after booking in about twelve hours of sleep. We had napped for an hour or so after returning from our visit to The Lookout, roused ourselves long enough to enjoy the delicious leg of lamb and roast potatoes that Viv had prepared, and fallen back into bed before nine. The next thing either of us knew, it was morning, and I could smell coffee percolating in the kitchen.

I left Mary Jane still sleeping to take the first shift in the bathroom, tossed on some pants and a sweater and set out in search of java. Duncan and Viv were sitting in their large kitchen, reading the morning newspapers and nibbling on toast and jam. A big gray cat was napping under the kitchen table, and a huge red painted appliance dominated one side of the room. It looked like an oven on steroids.

We exchanged morning greetings. A pot of coffee sat atop one of the burners on top, and I grabbed a mug from the nearby island and poured myself a waker-upper.

"What is this thing?" I asked, motioning at the appliance.

"It's an Aga," Duncan said. "Combination cooker and home heater. Lovely warm things. The cat will sleep under it at night in the winter."

"It's amazing," I said, looking over the heavy steel cooktop and the bulging ovens in the front. And it was emitting a comfortable warmth that filled the room. "I wonder if they have these things in the States?"

"I should think so," Viv said, turning the pages of her newspaper. "Don't they have everything in the States?"

I grunted noncommittally. "Everything except good stuff," I said.

Duncan laughed and motioned me into a chair on the other side of the table. I looked out the window into the back yard. The sun was shining and the sky appeared to be blue.

"Looks like a nice day," I said. "We going to tee it up?"

"Absolutely," Duncan said. "In fact, I have something of a surprise lined up."

"You mean, you're finally going to give me strokes?" I smiled.

"Never in a million billion years," Duncan said, grinning back. "You told me that Mary Jane liked to play," he said.

"Yeah, but she's fairly new at the game," I said. "And she gets all nervous about holding better players up. When we play, I try to find the time and places where we aren't playing with the crowds. So she doesn't like to play with others too much."

"Perfectly understandable," Duncan nodded. "So I called Sir Hamish to come play with us. It is physically, mentally and metaphysically impossible to remain nervous in his presence. First of all, he never stops talking. Second of all, he may well be Scotland's worst golfer. Third of all, his stories are world-class. I'm certain that she will have an unforgettable experience with the man, no matter how she plays."

"No matter how who plays?" Mary Jane exclaimed as she came into the kitchen. Freshly showered and dressed, she looked gorgeous and when she came over to my side, she smelled better.

"You," I answered, wrapping my arms around her and inhaling deeply. "Duncan has arranged a game for us with some duke or earl or something."

"Oh," she said. "That's great." Her tone of voice conveyed exactly the opposite, and she shot me a look that said I would be hearing about this privately at some point in the very near future.

Vivienne had poured Mary Jane a cup of coffee, and she came over with it to the table, chuckling softly. "Now, my dear, you mustn't fret. Sir Hamish Cavendish is a delightful old coot and the most patient man I have ever met. You will simply adore him, I promise!"

"And without having seen you play," Duncan said drolly, "I daresay the chances are pretty good that you can beat him straight up. He is a miserable excuse for a golfer. But he doesn't care a whit about it and manages to have a jolly time anyway."

Mary Jane took a sip of coffee, then she grinned. "Okay," she said. "But I warned Hacker that I didn't want to hold up anyone. I'm still learning the game."

"Aren't we all?" Duncan said, and we all laughed.

"So what is Sir Hamish a sir of?" I asked. "If that's the right way to put it, which I'm certain it's not."

Mary Jane looked at me with undisguised pity. "You really need more coffee in the morning before you try to use the language," she said.

"His is an honorary title from the Queen," Duncan said. "Not a land title. He was honored because he happens to be one of the foremost Scotch whiskey makers in the country. The Cavendish family has been making good malt whiskey for almost three hundred years now."

"I like him already," I said. "Does he pass out free samples?"

"If he takes to you," Duncan said, "You may get the royal tour of the distillery or an invitation back to his country house, which is quite something."

I stood up. "In that case, I'd better go get cleaned up. Want to make a good impression on the Duke of Hootch."

I volunteered to drive, since the Boston *Journal* was paying for my car. Duncan told me to head back through the glen the way we had come the day before.

"Normally, I never play Gleneagles," Duncan said. "They have priced themselves well out of my league. In fact, they're out of everyone's league except for visitors from the States, Germany or the Arabs. But I told them that I was bringing a noted American journalist and they offered to let us all play for free."

"All hail the power of the press," I said. "How much do they get for a round these days?" I was thinking a top-rated golf resort like Gleneagles must be charging Pebble Beach-like rates.

"The last time I checked, it was nearly a hundred quid," Duncan said, shaking his head at the monstrosity. "Plus another forty for the caddie."

"In U.S. dollars that's nearly…" I tried to do

the math while simultaneously driving on the left and found it all too much.

"Just about $250 all told," Mary Jane said from the back seat. She is better at head math than me.

"And that's per person!" Duncan was aghast. "For one round of golf! Totally ludicrous."

"Word of advice—don't ever play at Pebble Beach. If you think $250 for a day of golf is ludicrous, you might have a coronary at Pebble. How much do they charge at your club for a visitor?" I asked.

"It's been twenty quid for the last ten years," he said. "And we do quite well. We even purchased a new flat-screen television for the lounge with last year's profits. But then, we're not a multi-national hotel company with a staff of more than a thousand souls, either."

I was pleased, however, to have another crack at the King's course at Gleneagles. It had been one of the first courses I ever played in Scotland. Back when I first started coming over, the Scots laughingly referred to "the milk run" for the thousands of golfing tourists from the States who came over every year to experience "Scottish golf"—a stop at Gleneagles, a drive down to St. Andrews to play the Old Course, and a final jaunt across to the Ayrshire coast to stay and play at Turnberry. Three fine courses, to be sure, but hardly representative of the true flavor of Scottish golf.

The King's course, designed by James Braid, a former Open champion and one of the Great Triumverate of British stars at the turn of the last century, was not a links course at all, but a hilly parkland course with blind shots, devilishly placed bunkers, and, in my view anyway, one of the toughest par-three holes in the world: the sixth. It's not long, at around 160 yards, but the green sits atop a small tabletop plateau and the terrain drops off severely all the way around. It's a true hit-and-hope kind of shot, and I had rarely scored less than a six on the damn thing.

Gleneagles has two other courses for guests as well. The Queen's course, another Braid design, is quite a bit gentler than the King's, but it's also a lovely walk through the countryside—lambs gamboling in the adjacent fields and pheasants skittering about here and there—and I've never had a bad time playing it. Then there's the newest course, which was designed by Jack Nicklaus, who bulldozed over the holes that had once been called the Prince's course and created one of his usual mounded, tricky, long and hard layouts. And he had designed in concrete cart paths, apparently in the belief that his course would inspire the Scots nation to abandon walking when they played and get them to clamber inside motorized golf carts, which are as rare in Scotland as a native who admires the English. The ploy didn't work. Local kids loved to ride their bikes and skateboards on the cart paths, but only the American tourists occasionally shelled out the cash for a cart. In Scotland, as nowhere else, golf is still a walking game.

We drove past the gilded sign at the entrance to the resort, and soon pulled in to the parking lot next to the golf clubhouse. The stately gray stone edifice of the main hotel building perched regally atop the hill beyond, a giant blue flag with a white diagonal cross—the so-called St. Andrews Cross, the national flag of Scotland—fluttering in the wind atop a tall pole in front.

Duncan organized the unloading of our clubs, and as we were taking off the travel covers and unpacking our shoes, we heard the bleating of one of those car horns from the Roaring Twenties: *ahh-ooo-gaaa*!

"Ah," Duncan said, smiling. "That will be Sir Hamish."

A tan-colored Mercedes Benz convertible sedan, circa 1975, pulled into the space next to my Vauxhall. The door opened and out popped Sir Hamish Cavendish.

"I say," he said happily. "It's always a good day when I can toot my own horn!"

Mary Jane laughed out loud.

He was tall and aristocratic looking, with slick dark hair and an aquiline profile. But he was also wearing a canary yellow sweater and a pair of tan checked plus-fours, with red-and-black plaid knee socks. It was as if he had never got the memo that was issued at the end of the 1980s that said golfers should no longer wear outlandish clothing on the course. He leaned into his car and clucked a few times, and out jumped a wiry black-and-white border collie, who tore into the middle of the parking lot, made three fast circles and then trotted back to sit calmly at the side of his master. The dog stared at us with limpid eyes, head cocked as if to say "And now?"

"What a beautiful dog!" Mary Jane exclaimed, and came over to pet the dog's head. "What's his name?" The dog gave her hand an appreciative lick, tail wagging furiously.

"Her official name is Queen Elizabeth McCorkle Penzance," Sir Hamish said. "But I call her Queenie so when I kick her at night, I can feel like I'm striking a blow for the Scottish nation."

Mary Jane giggled, and bent down to give Queenie a hug around the neck. "Oh, poor Queenie," she said. "He didn't really mean that."

Sir Hamish stuck out his hand. "You must be Hacker, the famous American journalist," he said. "Welcome! And this is your lovely lady. What fun. It's a grand day for golf, no?"

I shook his hand and told him that I was anything but famous.

"That's not what I hear," he said, smiling at me. He turned and clapped Duncan on the back. "Right then Taylor," he said, "Are you giving me strokes today?"

"As many as you'd like Sir Hamish," Duncan said with a smile.

"Excellent!" he trumpeted. "Come along, Mr. Hacker, let's have a wee bracer before we set off. You, Queenie…" he looked down at the dog. "Stick close to that woman at all times and make sure she doesn't cheat!" He smiled at Mary Jane. "Actually, she's very good at retrieving balls from the woods. If we don't finish the day with more balls than when we started, I'll buy the house a drink!"

"You'll probably do that anyway," Duncan said under his breath.

"Just what I've always wanted," Mary Jane said. "More balls."

"Hah!" Sir Hamish exclaimed, leading us up the walk towards the clubhouse. "A woman with verve! I like that. Oh yes, m'dear, we're in for a good time. I can see that!"

He ushered us all inside, sent Mary Jane and Queenie off to the ladies locker room to get ready and tried to lead Duncan and I into the lounge. "I'll just go and make sure they're ready for us," Duncan said and he slinked away downstairs to the pro shop. Sir Hamish and I walked into the lounge area, a broad, tiered room decked out in red carpeting with large windows overlooking the finishing holes of both the King's and Queen's courses.

Sir Hamish led me over to the brass-trimmed bar and nodded at the bartender. It must have been a secret code, for the man immediately took an old dusty bottle down from the top shelf behind the bar, twisted off the top with a nice corky pop and poured two fingers of whiskey into each of two glasses. He laid out two cardboard coasters and ceremoniously placed the glasses in front of us with a small bow. Sir Hamish reached for a nearby pitcher of water.

"Old Cavendish A'Gloamin'" Sir Hamish said, nodding at the glasses holding a dark amber liquid that shimmered in the lights above the bar. "Forty-five-year-old single barrel. My grandfather supervised the making of it. There're only about twenty cases left in all the world. This place has one of them."

He poured a tiny dollop of water into both glasses.

"Just a wee drop of Highland water to open up the pores," he said. "Lets every bit of 45 years of history come flowin' out on the tongue. It's not just a whiskey, m'boy, tis a religious experience."

He handed me a glass and took up his own. Indeed, I had a flashback to Communion Sundays of my youth, with all the solemn ceremony and ritual words before the gulping of the wine. But we clinked glasses and I sipped the whiskey. The first taste was sweet, not unlike the sensation of biting into a juicy fresh peach, but as I swallowed, the fiery part of the whiskey kicked in. But it was not harsh, just a smooth golden fire that coated my throat as it worked its way down, and then finished with a smoky tang on the palette. I swore to myself at that moment never again to drink a cheap blended Scotch.

"Wow," I said.

"I can tell you're a writer, m'boy, from your eloquence," Sir Hamish said, cocking one of his eyebrows at me wryly. "Most people can only gasp after their first taste of A'Gloamin'."

I laughed, and he joined me. He asked me questions about my plans for the next week, and I asked if he was going to be at the Open next week.

"Oh, yes," he said, nodding. "I try never to miss the Open. I'm staying with Johnny Cheape at Wormwood. I always stay with Johnny when the Open's at St. Andrews."

"Ummm...Johnny who?"

Sir Hamish blinked and shook his head apologetically. "Of course, what am I thinking? Lord Cheape is a distant cousin of mine, don't ask me how distant—I have no idea really. His family's lived in Fife for five or six hundred years at least. Has a nice place outside of St. Andrews...old family seat and all. I stay there ... yes, well, I said that, didn't I?"

He tossed back the rest of his dram. "That should help get the old noggin back in gear," he said. "Interesting thing about Johnny, he actually owns the land upon which the Old Course is built."

"Really?" I said. "I thought it was all owned by the local government in St. Andrews."

"Well, yes and no," Sir Hamish said. "Parliament passed an Act back in the 1970's that set up the Links Trust to operate and maintain the golf courses for the public benefit on behalf of the local council of Fife—roughly equivalent to the county government back in your country. The Trust handles all the maintenance, runs the new public clubhouse and takes in the greens fees for the seven courses in the town, counting that new one up above town to the south. And while the

Act specifies that these certain parts of the seaside can only and forever be used for golf, the actual title to the ground, as from ancient times, belongs to Lord Cheape of Wormwood."

"That's pretty cool," I said. "The guy who owns St. Andrews. Can he play anytime he wants?"

Sir Hamish laughed. "I would certainly hope so," he said.

We strolled out the back door into the sunshine. Duncan was talking with a well-dressed young man in a suit and tie, holding some kind of packet in his hands. I immediately ID'd him as the PR guy for the resort. *Oh well,* I thought: *Such is the price of admission.* I walked over and Duncan introduced me to the young man, who pumped my hand enthusiastically and passed on the press kit he was holding. It weighed about three pounds. I pretended to be delighted at receiving all this wonderful information and promised I would read every last word immediately upon completing our round of golf. Satisfied that his job was done, the PR guy wished us a good game and, bowing and scraping towards Sir Hamish, made his exit. I looked around for a trash bin. Sir Hamish took the packet out of my hands. "Handled with the aplomb of a veteran journalist under attack by the flacks," he said approvingly. "One of our Fleet Street jobbos would have told him to fleck off and then hacked his phone." I laughed. He turned to one of two men who had suddenly materialized with our golf bags over their shoulders. "Will," he said, "Could you find a place to file the propaganda for us?"

"Aye, guv," Will said, tugging at an imaginary forelock, and he took the package inside.

"I arranged for Will and Tommy to caddie for you and the lady," Sir Hamish said. "They're experienced lads. I would listen to their advice very carefully, except if they try to give you tips on the ponies or ask for a personal loan."

Mary Jane was over on the putting green, going through her usual mysterious appraisal of the greens. Queenie the border collie lay on the grass just off the green, watching her every move. Mary Jane is convinced that she can read the slope and speed of the greens better by using her feet instead of her eyes, and prefers to "read" a putt by walking the line to get a feel for the slope. On the practice green, she also likes to roll a few balls with her hand, like bowling, to get a sense for the speed. I'm quite sure that this technique is neither included in Hogan's *Five Lessons*, nor in Nicklaus' *Golf My Way*, but I understand there is a certain holistic sense to her technique, and I have come to believe that in golf, if not all else, "whatever works" is as good a strategy as any other. Queenie, whose limpid yet alert eyes tracked every move Mary Jane made, was sitting on her haunches at attention as though every part of her being wanted to chase the balls Mary Jane was rolling across the green grass, but she stayed where she was. I'll bet if the ball had baa-ed like a sheep, she'd have been after it like a shot.

We wandered over to the first tee where another foursome was just walking off down the fairway. The first hole on the King's course is a fairly innocuous par-four with a wide flat fairway that runs out about 270 yards before climbing straight up a steep hill to the green perched on a nearly hidden plateau. Will had picked up Mary Jane's golf bag, a nice powder-blue one with beige trim and straps. He opened up her ball compartment and began tossing out all the sleeves I had packed in there for her for this trip.

"Och, Tommy," he said mournfully to his fellow looper, "She's trying to kill me, the lass is!"

"Stuff it, Will," Tommy said back. "You could use the exercise. Been spendin' a wee bit too much time doon th' pub, ain't ye?" But he took a look inside my bag, and, seeing just the two or three sleeves of new balls I had in there, he nodded with approval. Will packed Mary Jane's extra balls in a plastic bag and handed it to the starter to keep until we came back. Duncan had said he preferred to carry his own bag, which was small and light; and Sir Hamish had the latest trolley, or what we in the States inelegantly call a "pull cart."

"Right then," Sir Hamish said. "What game are we playing? How about the young lady and myself against you two brutes for drinks? We'll play thirds."

Mary Jane shook her head. "I can't do that," she said. "I'm still a new golfer. You don't want me on your team, and probably I should just wait in the clubhouse and let you gentlemen have at it."

"My dear lady," Sir Hamish said, swinging his driver back and forth to get loose. "I can guarantee without the least hesitation that you and I shall win whatever match we devise."

"How?" she asked, looking overly stressed.

"Because I am the scorekeeper and I cheat at every opportunity! Isn't that right, Will?"

"O, aye, lass," Will said. "Ye need not worry aboot yer game. Sir Hamish here will make sure it all works out."

Mary Jane laughed and then walked over to Sir Hamish and gave him a kiss on the cheek. "You are a strange and dear little man," she said.

He looked nonplussed. "Heavens," he said, "I think she likes me!"

"What is 'thirds'? " I asked. I had never heard of that particular game.

Sir Hamish looked at me sideways. "Never you mind, laddie," he said mysteriously.

We all laughed. The starter, who had been watching the group in front of us progress up the hill towards the green, announced that the tee was ours. Duncan and I flipped a tee, and I won the honor. I was feeling relaxed, so I asked for the driver from Tommy and sent one flying down the fairway. It's pretty hard to mess up the first shot on the King's course, with its large, flat and open landing area. Duncan followed suit, and then Sir Hamish sent his ball skidding along the ground, off to the right. Mary Jane's forward tee wasn't that far forward—Scottish courses rarely give women much of a break on the tee box—and she managed a pretty good shot, though a little high and also to the right.

And so we were off. Duncan and I walked together, trailed by Tommy with my clubs. Sir Hamish and Mary Jane, dutifully followed by Queenie, who by now seemed to have adopted her, walked together followed by Will the caddie. In due time, we climbed the hill and reached the first green. Duncan and I managed to get our approaches near the green. Mary Jane flubbed one, hit the next halfway up the hill and then powered one over the green. It took Sir Hamish three swings to reach the base of the hill and then three more to get to the edge of the green.

My approach had been a bit too long, and I was faced with a delicate chip downhill on the large green that tilted back towards the fairway. Perhaps because the jigger of A'Gloamin had rendered me slightly numb, I powered my chip shot past the hole a good thirty feet.

"Go in," I said as it continued to roll away from the hole. The caddies thought that was amusing.

Duncan managed a par, I finished with a bogey, Mary Jane did well to card a seven and Sir Hamish took three putts from the fringe to finish with a nine. He seemed uncommonly happy when he pulled his ball out of the cup.

"Excellent!" he exclaimed, as we walked up to the second tee. "Nine for a three. We're one up."

"How's that?" I asked.

"The game is thirds," he said. "Highest score on a hole is reduced to a third. My three takes the hole."

"I think I'm gonna like this game," Mary Jane said with a broad smile.

We stood for a moment on the second tee, waiting for the group ahead to get out of the way. The fairway dropped away down the ridge we had just climbed. The majestic slope of the Ochil Hills rose in the distance, dotted with the shadows of the clouds scudding across the sky. The mountains in the distance covered the entire horizon and they were blissfully empty of buildings or roads or anything human. It was like looking out at a wilderness totally devoid of civilization.

"Who owns all that real estate?" I asked, nodding at the vista in the distance. "The Queen? The Lord of Gleneagles?"

"Bloody Arabs," Tommy grunted. He spat once for emphasis. "Saudis."

I looked at Sir Hamish. He nodded. "Yes, it's true," he said. "Several of the Saudi princes have bought up a great deal of land in the Highlands. You could say they've turned their oil into solid earth, just as the sheep are out there now, turning grass into wool. There's probably a lesson in there, but don't ask me what."

"Bloody wankers," Tommy growled. I guess we knew where his Scottish heart stood in the geopolitical debate.

We continued our way around the course, enjoying the warm sunshine of the day. There was a steady breeze, but it was not blowing so hard as to make golf impossible. With Sir Hamish chatting away a mile a minute, Queenie following dutifully along, available for a pat every now and then, and the nice day, Mary Jane seemed to be relaxed and having a good time. I would hear her girlish peals of laughter from time to time, and even when she had a bad hole, she delighted in counting every stroke to have her score reduced to a third at the end. It was quickly obvious that Duncan and I had no chance against the magical power of illegal division, so we just played our own game and enjoyed the beautiful day, the gorgeous views and the companionship of friends.

We eventually made it to the tee of my personal bête noire, the sixth. A sign on the tee announced the name of the hole: "Het Girdle."

"What the hell does that mean?" I asked, unable to keep the whining out of my voice. "And don't tell me some old dame lost her girdle on this hole or something."

Tommy looked at me like I'd gone suddenly mad. "It means 'hot griddle,'" he said. "Like a frying pan. Describes the shape of the green, aye?"

"Maybe an upside down griddle," I said, looking at the flat round green atop the hill across a deep valley from the tee. The terrain fell away on three sides 40 feet or more. "I hate this hole."

Nevertheless, for once in my life, I managed to put a good swing on a six-iron, cutting it up into the wind and watched with amazement as my ball dropped onto the putting surface, maybe twenty feet right of the hole. Mary Jane and Sir Hamish both hit their shots down into the abyss, while Duncan caught a bunker on the left. I was happy to finally walk off the green with a par. If nothing else happened today, I had finally conquered the Het Girdle.

As we walked down a wooded path to the next tee, we flushed two pheasants, who scurried into the underbrush. Queenie went on full point, her eyes alive, her body quivering with barely contained excitement. The male was a gorgeous bird, with multi-colored feathers. We all stopped until they had disappeared.

"What do you call a group of pheasants?" Mary Jane asked.

"A bouquet," Sir Hamish told her. "A bouquet of pheasant."

"I call 'em dinner," said Will laconically, and we all laughed.

After teeing off on the 11th, an impossibly long par three, we detoured over to the snack shack, a log-cabin type structure positioned to serve golfers on both the King's and Queen's courses. Mary Jane ordered a bottle of water and a Snicker's bar to go, Duncan and I had a beer and Sir Hamish, with a wink, pulled out a silver hip flask and upended it. "Ahh," he said, smacking his lips, "Nectar of the gods, it is." The caddies had asked for a bottle of Irn Bru (pronounced 'iron brew'), a bright orange Scottish-made energy drink. They each took a long swig. "World's best hangover remedy," said Will. "Irn Bru, Made from Girders," Tommy said with a smile, reading from the label. Mary Jane was busy sharing her water with Queenie, whose body shook with pleasure.

We sat outside on the patio for a few moments, enjoying the sunshine and the views across the broad valley.

"I say, Taylor," Sir Hamish said, turning to Duncan, "Have you heard about Colin Kinkaid?"

"Indeed I have," Duncan said, shaking his head. "Quite a thing, isn't it?"

"Who is Colin Kinkaid?" I asked, draining the last of my can of lager. It was slightly warm, but still tasty.

"He was until recently an executive of the Links Trust," Sir Hamish said. "And he was found in a dungeon cell at the Castle in St. Andrews two months ago."

"Do not tell me he was murdered," Mary Jane said.

"He was indeed, m'dear," Sir Hamish said.

"Crap," Mary Jane said, "There goes the vacation." She got up, sighed with deep displeasure and headed for the green, first shooting me a look of warning. Queenie followed her, tail wagging happily.

"I'm not sure I understand," Sir Hamish said, looking befuddled and a bit upset at Mary Jane's obvious mood swing.

"It's me," I said apologetically. "Ever since Mary Jane and I have known each other, I've been getting caught up in the middle of murder cases. Not my fault, you understand. It just sort of happens. But she thinks I like crime busting and sticking my nose in."

"Ah, I see," Sir Hamish said, nodding, as we followed Mary Jane over to the green to putt out. "Well, not to worry. I think the authorities have this one under control."

"So who dun it?" I asked, a natural question, I thought.

"I've heard that the police have questioned Conrad Gold," Duncan said.

"*The* Conrad Gold?" I was surprised. "The hotel and casino Conrad Gold? Why would he want to kill someone from the Links Trust?"

Sir Hamish sniffed. "There's apparently been some bad blood between them for many years," he said. "The police haven't made an arrest yet, but I hear they're really bearing down hard on the gentleman."

Duncan chimed in. "It goes back to when Gold first opened his hotel near St. Andrews," he said. "He and the Links Trust got off on the wrong foot and it has never been completely forgotten."

I smacked my head. "Of course!" I said. "I remember now. I was there!"

Chapter Four

Conrad Gold was already an international celebrity when he came to St. Andrews to open one of his "Gold Standard" hotel properties. His glistening bald pate and gold-colored bow ties made him instantly recognizable, as was his ability to turn any conversation around to being about how great he, Conrad Gold, was. His hotels, resorts and casinos were not just good, they were the "best ever." His many business ventures were not just savvy and timely, they were the result of Conrad Gold's ability to rise so far above the competition, that "there really isn't any competition, literally, no one else in the world has the quality and value that we do."

Any amateur psychologist could tell that this strange little man was overcompensating for something. And anyone with more than a passing familiarity with a balance sheet could also tell that Conrad Gold was leveraged up to his eyebrows and that his persistent self-promotion was born of the need to stay one step ahead of the debt collectors.

Yet he somehow managed to get away with it, braggadocio and all, year after year. The media ate up the guy's patently obvious self-serving nonsense, fawned over the movie starlets he liked to date, shook their heads in amazement at the ratings his idiotic reality TV show pulled in (viewers loved it when he stared at some hapless fool and snarled "You suck!" before tossing them off the show) and pretended that he had some political influence in the Republican Party.

He was not even a self-made man. His father had purchased and built several hundred nondescript warehouses and small manufacturing buildings in post-war Los Angeles, and as that city grew into the behemoth it is today, the value of the Gold real estate skyrocketed into the billions. Conrad had taken over from his father, re-mortgaged most of his property and immediately launched himself into higher visibility projects. He built his first Gold Standard resort and casino at the far end of the Las Vegas Strip, and waited for the city to grow towards him. When it did, he began opening new casinos in New Jersey and Puerto Rico, each one financed by a hefty second-mortgage on the last. Then he started building a network of private golf facilities supposedly catering to the high-end market, called the Bullion Clubs. The press always showed up for the grand opening galas at these pleasure palaces, but never seemed to follow up a year or two later to see if the Bullion Clubs had actually attracted any members. Few of them did.

So when Conrad Gold announced that he was bringing the Gold Standard roadshow to St. Andrews, the nominally quiet Calvinists didn't know what to make of him when he promised to build a hotel and resort in the Auld Grey Toon that would transform the place into one of the tourism meccas of the modern world. In typical Conrad Gold fashion, he had never thought to ask the people of the town if they really wanted to become one of the tourism meccas of the world.

He purchased one of the rambling old manor houses, situated way up on the ancient bluff that extends northeast from the old town, a bluff which happens to afford a nice view of the tidal plain that contains most of the golf courses in St. Andrews. He spent more than a year dumping several of his mortgaged millions into the place to transform it from a dumpy and drafty old pile, originally built for some 19th century jute merchant from nearby Dundee, into one of the Gold Standard-brand hotels. It was all ostentation, with acres of marble, miles of brass, armies of white-gloved servants, every imaginable service and amenity known to mankind, and not an ounce of character or soul.

When the time finally arrived to open the place, Gold pulled out all the stops. He arranged to stage an exhibition match on the Old Course between Tiger Woods—then the top player in the world—and Sergio Garcia, then the top man in Europe. Only Conrad Gold had the pull and the deep pockets to get Tiger to appear for a promotional grand opening, something Woods never, ever agreed to do, unless it was for a product or promotion that Tiger himself owned. To make sure he got the maximum amount of press coverage, Gold scheduled his event to take place a few days after one of the Ryder Cup Matches was played at the Belfry in the English Midlands. Then he invited the entire international golf press corps to journey up to Scotland on an antique steam engine-driven train, with sleeper cars and Art Deco-decorated public lounge cars, where the booze would flow freely, the food would never stop and the ever-present Golden Girls from Vegas would be paraded around.

Who could say no to something like that? I told my idiot editor back in Boston that I was taking a few personal days after the Ryder Cup and signed on for the ride. I've been to quite a few press parties in my day, but this one was over-the-top in a Caligula-in-Rome kind of way. The train left Birmingham at nine p.m. and arrived in Edinburgh early the next morning, and almost no one aboard bothered to use the sleeping cars. There was a buffet car, complete with linen-covered booths and liveried servants bearing never-emptied carafes of champagne. There were several lounge cars with full bars dispensing alcoholic beverages, all gratis, of course, including one entire car reserved only for serving the finest Scotch whiskeys. That one also contained a cigar bar where the thick smoke made it difficult to see more than three or four feet in front of you. There was a music car with a live cover band where the Golden Girls, bedecked in full feathery regalia, encouraged the guests to dance. Most of my fellow myrmidons of the press box didn't need to be asked twice.

And Conrad Gold strolled up and down the aisles of his hedonistic love train, meeting and greeting, backslapping and joke-swapping, clearly in his element. *Look at what I have done,* he seemed to beam outwardly, emanating all the trappings of wealth and power, cigar in one hand, one of the very fetching Golden Girls in the other.

We all rolled off the train in Edinburgh at dawn, bleary-eyed and hungover, or perhaps just inebriated and sleepless, and rolled onto a series of streamlined coaches that were waiting to whisk us north to St. Andrews. An hour later, we stepped off the buses and were handed keys to our suites—the Gold Standard hotels do not have mere "rooms"—and told to report back to the lobby at 2 p.m. to catch the buses that would take us down to the Old Course to watch the golf match between Woods and Garcia.

But that's when the doo-doo hit the fan. When a hundred or so grumpy, sleep-deprived and now hungover journalists began milling about restlessly and undirected in the marble lobby, I sensed something was up. And it was. It turned out that Conrad Gold had somehow neglected to obtain the one thing in the world that money apparently cannot buy: a tee time on the Old Course.

Everyone knows the Old Course at St. Andrews is a public golf course. It is not owned by the Royal & Ancient Golf Club, whose imposing clubhouse squats regally behind the first tee, nor by any of the other four or five private golf clubs in the town. The golf course, and the six others in and around town, is 'owned' by the people of the town and the surrounding shire of Fife and administered by the Links Trust, a quasi-public organization set up by Parliament to keep the grass mowed, the burrowing rabbits kept to a minimum and to collect the money for and arrange the distribution of tee times. Some of those tee times each day are reserved for the members of those private clubs, while a few others are allotted to the hotels and B&Bs in the town or to the tour operators who reserve blocks of times for their travelling customers. But a certain portion of each day's play sheet is meted out on an egalitarian, first-come, first-served system called The Ballot. Anyone who wants to play the Old Course can put their name in for The Ballot and every day at 2 o'clock in the afternoon the next day's tee times are assigned to the lucky few. It used to be that names were literally drawn out of a hat, but these days it's all done by computer, and the next day's starting times and their owners are faxed and posted to all the hotels in town every afternoon. It is supposed to be a completely blind drawing, so it doesn't matter if you are a homeless pauper or if you are Conrad Gold—the computer spits out the chosen names and that's that.

Apparently, someone in the Conrad Gold organization had just assumed that the Links Trust would gladly go along with the hotel magnate's plans to stage an exhibition match between two of the world's greatest players. After all, it was just one two-ball on an autumn afternoon, even if that two-ball would be followed by a horde of photographers and reporters and a few thousand other interested souls. And this was Tiger Woods versus Sergio Garcia, sponsored and hosted by the great and worthy Conrad Gold in person! How could anyone not leap at this once-in-a-lifetime opportunity? But the Gold team had overlooked the British love of proper procedure, of paper to be filled out in triplicate, of the importance of precedence and the supremacy of the bureaucracy.

In any case, the request to use the Old Course had not been properly submitted, the required papers had not been duly authorized, procedures and channels had not been followed and, therefore, permission to use the course had not been granted. In what must have been a huge shock to Conrad Gold, the 2 p.m. start time on the Old Course that day had been assigned to a foursome of mechanics from British Airways and that's who would have the tee. Gold's people tried to flash some rolls of cash at the mechanics, who were on an annual toot to the north for some golf and drinking, and were told to "sod off."

Gold tried to use his prodigious network of business and political contacts to convince the Links Trust to bend their policy just for one day, but that just put the back up of the bureaucrats and the officials of the Links Trust and they, too, told the magnate to go piss up a rope. In the most polite, bureaucratic language they could muster. So Conrad Gold's grand opening event was pretty much ruined. He did the best he could in the circumstances. The Woods-Garcia match was quickly moved to a nearby parkland course, Ladybank, which was more than happy to have the two golfers and world's golf press invade for an afternoon, in return for a nice fee. The course was short and pretty easy and the shaggy greens were running about six on the Stimpmeter, which provoked some raised eyebrows and then some outright laughter by the two golfers. But they were good sports and probably figured since they had already been paid a few hundred thousand dollars just to show up they might as well make the best of it. A few stalwarts walked the entire eighteen with them, but most of us caught a bus back to the Gold Standard and frittered away the afternoon either in the bar or taking the steam and a massage in the hotel's spa.

There had been another wild banquet that night in the cavernous meeting rooms at the hotel. The Golden Girls were back in full feathers and not much else, and this time there was a 30-piece orchestra belting out show tunes, while a lineup of Conrad Gold's Hollywood buddies appeared on stage to do their usual schtick, sing a song or tell us a story about how great a human being Conrad Gold was.

I was, by this time, getting close to reaching the limit of acute alcohol toxicity, but I clearly recall hearing, on my way to the loo, Conrad Gold dressing down one of his underlings in the back of the room.

"I will never forget this day," I heard him say, his voice low and cold and almost shaking with barely controlled rage. "I will never forget what those bastards did. And if it takes me the rest of my life, I will get even. Those snooty, stuck-up bastards have not heard the last of Conrad Gold."

Even in my malt-induced fog, I heard the resolution in the man's voice, and that made me very, very glad I was not one of the snooty, stuck-up bastards who were now squarely in the sights of one of the richest men in the world.

Chapter Five

I KEPT MY mouth shut for the rest of the round at Gleneagles, as the four of us followed the gently descending fairways down and around a central ridge line before the last hole dropped like a ski jump dramatically down to the clubhouse, with the magnificent edifice of the Gleneagles Hotel off to the left. Sir Hamish kept up his amusing patter, but I could tell Mary Jane was still brooding over this new murder case, worrying that I would jump in with both feet, get into trouble and possibly endanger both our lives. Again. So I asked no more questions about the dead guy in St. Andrews, and instead kept the conversation on golf.

Sir Hamish's scorekeeping was brutally effective in keeping Duncan and I down in the match. Sir Hamish developed a hitch in his backswing that kept sending his ball flying wildly off the tee—first to the left and then the right. After his tee shot on the fifteenth went skittering wildly off into the wild gunch, a shot which we all watched in dismayed silence, my caddie Will spoke up. "You do realize, guv, that ye've paid for the right to utilize the fairway?"

We all laughed.

After we finished and bid a fond farewell to Will and Tommy, after pooling our pounds Sterling to give the lads their just reward, we ducked into the Dormy House for dinner. Unlike the grand rococo dining hall of the big hotel, this clubhouse restaurant was informal, quiet and far less fussy. I ordered a steak, Mary Jane opted for a seafood pasta special and the two Scotsmen ordered roast lamb. Sir Hamish, who apparently knows everyone in Scotland, made himself the center of attention—his favorite place—by asking after the families and pets of the various wait staff. It was not coincidence that everyone who worked in the restaurant seemed to be hovering, waiting for Sir Hamish to ask them to do something for him.

Mary Jane, who said she had actually enjoyed the round of golf, watched the act with a bemused look. "I can't decide if everyone actually loves you, or if they're just sucking up because you're a rich guy," she said to him when our orders had been placed and we were temporarily alone. I was a little embarrassed by her question, and hoped Sir Hamish wasn't offended.

"An excellent question, m'dear," he said. "I don't know the answer. But these are my people—" he swept his hand out across the room to indicate not only the restaurant, but the country outside. "Here in Scotland nobody pays too much attention to the social class thing," he said. "I genuinely like these people. All people, in fact."

"No enemies?" I asked, smiling.

"Oh, well, that's another question," he said. "I'm sure the chaps at Chivas Regal don't think too highly of me, since our margins are higher, our customers more loyal and our whiskey far better. But then, if any of them were here tonight, I'd stand them a wee dram anyway. Life's too short for enemies, really."

"Tell that to Colin Kinkaid," Duncan said. "He had one enemy who stuck him away in the bottle dungeon."

"Aye, a sorry state, that," Sir Hamish said, his bushy eyebrows darting up and down and a frown circling his red face. "But we don't want to talk about that…" He cast a worried eye at Mary Jane, who smiled and reached over to pat his hand.

"That's OK," she said. "You can talk about the murder if you want. You can take the boy out of America, but you can't take the newspaperman out of the boy. It's in his blood." She looked at me with what I hoped was fondness.

"Thanks," I said, and meant it. I turned to Duncan. "So tell me what happened."

"Well," he said, "I don't know if you've ever been to the Castle?" He looked at me, and I shook my head. I'd seen the ruins perched on the rocks just down the hill from the old cathedral churchyard, but I'd never had the time to go wandering through the place. "Well, there's actually not much left of it after all these centuries," he continued. "It's really not much of a castle, although you can still wander around the ramparts and see where the moat once was. It was really more of the grand house for the bishops and archbishops of the Cathedral. It was destroyed during the Reformation—old John Knox had it in for the papists. But one of the few parts that's still there is the bottle dungeon—it's hacked out of the bedrock, and the chamber has the shape of a bottle of claret. They'd drop the prisoners straight down through the neck cut in the floor of one of the cells. You look down in the hole and you can see the rocks below and the moisture seeps in with the tides, and it smells old and musty and dank. You can just imagine being tossed in there and having no hope of escape, ever. Quite a shocking thing, actually. But they have a metal grate across the top now and it's always padlocked. I guess tourists like to throw coins down into the hole for good luck, so I suppose someone has to go collect the change now and again. But it's always locked up tight when the place is open for tours."

"So how did the body get in there?" I asked.

"No one quite knows," Duncan said. "I would guess that the killer must have obtained the key to the padlock, which had been refastened after the body was dropped in. But I don't know how many copies of the keys there are."

"And the police are convinced that Conrad Gold is the evil-doer?" I asked.

Mary Jane looked at me with a small frown. "Evil-doer?" she said softly. "Where have I heard that before?"

"Well," Duncan continued, "The Fife Constabulary asked Gold to come in for an interview, based on the fact that he had expressed severe displeasure over his treatment at the hands of the Links Trust in general, and with Colin Kinkaid in particular. The men were said to have been in something of an ongoing feud since the day of the hotel's grand opening. Gold later complained that his hotel was not getting enough access to tee times on the Old Course, and Kinkaid said that was completely untrue and they frequently made somewhat disparaging remarks about the other in the pages of the newspapers, which, of course, encouraged the feud between the men."

"Of course," I said, nodding. "Makes good copy. Part of Gold's general schtick."

"Quite," Duncan said. "Gold cooperated fully, flying into Scotland for a lengthy interview about two weeks ago. But the constables have not yet pressed any charges against Mr. Gold, who claims that he was not even in the country when the unfortunate event occurred. Of course, Conrad Gold is wealthy enough to arrange for someone to murder one of his enemies. The newspapers said he was questioned for several hours. There has been no word of any other suspects, officially at least. The case is still under investigation."

"How was the victim killed?" I asked. "And where?"

"The police haven't released any details yet," Duncan told me. "But he seems to have managed to get his neck broken. We don't know if that happened before he was dumped in the dungeon, or because of the fall down the neck of the bottle."

"So we have a body killed somewhere by person or persons unknown, somehow dumped into a locked dungeon, and the one possible suspect with motive has a good alibi," I summed up. "Sounds like someone needs to call Agatha Christie or P.D. James and get some ideas flowing."

Our dinners arrived, so we stopped talking about the case. But it kept running around and around in my head. Mary Jane is right. I can no more stop being a newspaperman than I can stop breathing.

Chapter Six

WE HAD ABOUT five days to kill before I was due to show up in St. Andrews for the Open, so the next morning Mary Jane and I bid a fond farewell to Duncan and his wife and headed north into the Highlands. If there is a more gorgeously scenic road than the A9 heading up the spine of Scotland, I have yet to find it. Mary Jane had brought along a CD of the Boys of the Lough, an Irish folk group, and we listened to the ancient Gaelic melodies all the way to Inverness, where we stopped for lunch.

This ancient city sits at the eastern end of the Great Glen, the geologic fault line that bisects Scotland from southwest to northeast, ending at Loch Ness and the Beauly Firth at Inverness. We refreshed ourselves at a little pub and then continued north again over the Black Isle, round the Cromarty Firth and finally over the bridge at the Firth of Dornoch and on up into the town.

Dornoch has become the in-crowd destination for American golfers in recent years, which is too bad, since an influx of loud and obnoxious American golfers is almost a guarantee of ruination for a place. Blame Tom Watson and Greg Norman for talking about it too much. I've been coming to Sutherlandshire for decades now, first drawn to see the place where the golf course architect Donald Ross grew up, and to play the course from whence much of his inspiration was drawn: Royal Dornoch. I've watched the place grow from a tiny outpost on the North Sea, with one pub, one restaurant, one small hotel (disguised as a fake turreted castle) and maybe a dozen residents (for which blame the first Duke of Sutherland who had most of his people cleared out in the 19th century to be replaced with sheep). One can hardly call Dornoch a city even today, but these days it boasts a coffee bar, several bed-and-breakfasts, about six good restaurants and two or three new hotels. At least the town still has its one bookstore, and a good one at that. A good bookstore is always a welcome indication of advanced civilization.

We motored slowly through the quiet streets, past the old Cathedral that was really not much more than a parish church with some history, made two quick turns and passed by the clubhouse at Royal Dornoch, positioned at the top of a hill looking out at the sea. I decided not to stop in to see Andrew, the pro and an old friend, and instead carried on along the ridge that runs alongside the first hole to the small place called the Wayward Inn, where I liked to stay.

Mrs. Gunn the owner was waiting for us, and after she made a fuss, insisting we sit down and have a cuppa with her, we managed to carry our bags upstairs to our room, which had lovely picture windows looking out at the golf course and North Sea beyond. And the public campground tucked in next to the golf course, filled with RVs, campers and passels of kids. Scotland is an egalitarian country in so many ways. I pulled the heavy drapes back from the window and inhaled the view.

"So what do you say?" I asked Mary Jane when she had finished her visit to the loo and her usual quick inspection of the premises. "Wanna go play a quick nine before dinner?"

"I have a better idea," she said smiling. "I'm feeling wayward at the Wayward Inn." She pulled the drapes closed again, grabbed me around the waist and kissed me. The kiss turned into a clinch and then we fell down together on the soft duvet-covered bed and then I determined that wayward was a much, much better idea than a quick nine.

Several hours later, after naps and long hot showers—Mrs. Gunn makes sure there is always plenty of hot water, another reason I love her place—we decided to walk into town and have dinner. Mrs. Gunn told me about a relatively new place that the townspeople had decided was quite good, just across the back street behind the cathedral. On our way into town, I took Mary Jane over to a small, neatly kept little cottage where I showed her the witch's plaque. It commemorated the spot where, in 1727, Janet Home had been burned at the stake, the last woman in Britain to be executed for the crime of witchcraft. Mary Jane paused a minute in silent prayer for the poor woman then looked at me with a smile.

"I'm suddenly ravenous for a nice grilled steak," she said. "Well done."

I laughed.

We found the Stornoway Café right where Mrs. Gunn said it was, the doorway and frame on the ground-floor of the street of terrace houses painted a cheerful purple and yellow, with a slateboard on the sidewalk chalked with the day's specials. Roast lamb, grilled sea bass and Angus steak were the listed entrees. "Bingo," Mary Jane said.

We went in. It was a smallish place, with perhaps ten tables, six of which were occupied with diners. The tables were covered with white tablecloths, a single burning candle on each, and a small vase filled with summer flowers. The yellow walls were covered with cheerful paintings; a mix of landscape scenes and modernistic swirling. Soft jazz could be heard coming over the sound system, and the atmosphere was pleasant, warm and welcoming.

A pretty young woman with flaming red hair, dressed in a denim skirt and long-sleeved white blouse, came out to greet us, and ushered us to a table near the front windows. She handed us menus, told us her name was Fiona and whisked away.

I had already decided to do the lamb—it's always good in Scotland—while Mary Jane took her time reading everything on the menu. I watched her concentrating, biting a corner of her lip as she read, her blue eyes reflecting the golden light of the candle. It had been a long time since I had felt so happy. I was in Scotland, I was with someone I dearly loved, I was within about a seven-iron of one of the best golf courses in the world and I was about to have what would surely be a great meal. What else—other than world peace and a bank account crammed with money—could any man possibly desire?

She must have felt, or heard, my inner sigh of contentment, because she glanced up at me and smiled, her eyes going soft.

"You look incandescent," I said.

"Not luminous?" she said. "I was feeling rather luminous."

"Nope. Pretty much incandescent."

"Do you writer guys always bring out the forty-dollar adjectives to impress the ladies?"

"I dunno," I said. "Does it work?"

"Well," she said, fanning herself with the menu, "Thinking of myself as incandescent does make me kinda hot."

"I rest my case," I said.

Fiona came back and took our orders. Soup to start, the steak for the lady and the lamb for the gent. How about a bottle of wine? And why not? I asked Fiona to bring us whatever she felt would be best. She nodded, pleased and went away, returning a minute or two later with a nice Spanish rioja that was as smooth as butter and had a lovely spicy finish. Fiona must have sensed something because she unbidden brought us an appetizer plate, filled with grilled scallops, boiled shrimp, bacon-wrapped somethings and what looked like spring rolls as thick as my wrist. I started to protest that we hadn't ordered this when she put the plate down between us, but she just smiled and said the chef had sent it out with his complements because he thought we looked hungry.

"Not incandescent?" Mary Jane asked as she popped a shrimp into her mouth.

"Beg pardon?" Fiona said, confused.

"Please tell him we appreciate it very much," I said. Then a thought occurred to me. "That is, if he's a he. I was just assuming ..."

Fiona laughed. "Oh, he's a he, all right," she said. "Wouldna ha' married the lad if he were not!"

"Right on sister," Mary Jane said, and they both laughed.

The chef must have been prescient, because the appetizer plate was gone in minutes: everything on it simply delicious. Then came the soup course, a homemade leek and potato which was exquisite, and the dinners, which were sublime. We were so busy eating, that we barely exchanged a word for the next forty minutes. Mary Jane merely reached over and tapped her wine glass with her steak knife, and I refilled it.

When Fiona finally came out with two demitasse-sized cups of black coffee and a plate with thin chocolate mints and asked if we cared to have any dessert, we both just looked at her with bleary eyes and groaned. In unison. She laughed.

"I take it that's a 'no,'" she said.

"Does your husband have time to come out and say hello?" Mary Jane said. "I'd love to meet the man who can cook like that. But I have to warn you, I may kidnap him and offer to have his babies."

Fiona nodded wisely and smiled. "I'll tell him to come out, but armed with sharp knives."

A few minutes later, as we were finishing the coffee, a tall and brawny man dressed in his white chef's coat and black-and-white checked pants pulled a chair over backwards to our table and squatted down. He held out his hand while his large face, wreathed in curly red hair, beamed a warm smile at us.

"Eamon Higgins," he said. "You're welcome. I hope you enjoyed your meal with us."

I shook his hand, introduced myself and Mary Jane. "You're Irish," I said with a note of surprise.

"That's OK isn't it?" Eamon said, feigning alarm. We laughed. "What gave me away?" he asked, "The hair, the name or the accent?"

"Actually," I said, "It was 'you're welcome.'"

"Beg pardon?" he said, this time not pretending to be puzzled.

"It's the phrase you used," I said. "It's an Irishism. When they want to say 'how are ya' or 'nice to see ya' they… you…say 'you're welcome' which is what we say after some says 'thank you.' So, you see…."

"Hacker," Mary Jane said. "Please shut up."

"Right," I said. Eamon was laughing out loud by now, shaking his head at us.

"Well I can tell you both are crazy Americans," he chortled. "What brings you to Dornoch…the golf?"

"Yeah," I said. "We're killing a few days before I have to be in St. Andrews to cover the Open."

"Ah, lovely," he said, nodding. "A journo, eh? Who do you favor going in? I plan to go down the betting shop and lay a quid or two."

I shrugged. "I have heard some good things about a countryman of yours…Conor Kelly. I'm not that familiar with his game."

"Oh, Conor is a lovely man," Eamon said, nodding. "Plays a lovely game, he does. Dunno if he's quite ready for the Open, though."

"He plays like a Yeats poem," Mary Jane said. "That's what a friend of ours said."

Eamon smiled at her. "I wouldn't know about that," he said. "I'm more into onions and potatoes than poetry."

"Not if the meal I just had is any indication of your cooking," she said, smiling at him. "It was stupendous."

Eamon nodded at her, pleased.

"But how did you land here?" she asked. "It seems a long way from anywhere."

"Indeed," he said. "Fiona and I heard about this place a couple of years ago and came up for a look. Fiona grew up not far from here, so it's mostly home for her, and I liked the vibe of the place. Sure, it's a bit quiet in the winters, but then we open only on weekends and cook mostly for our friends and neighbors. And we take three weeks in Morocco doing nothing but lying on the beach. During the summers, we get loads of American golfers and other tourists. So it works out pretty well."

"Where else have you cooked?" Mary Jane asked.

"Well in fact, my last job was in St. Andrews at the Gold Standard hotel," he said. "I was executive chef there for about four years. Before that, some hotels in Dublin and London, with a side trip to Prague."

"So do you know Conrad Gold?" I asked.

"Oh, yeah, of course," he said. "He's the kind of micro-manager that insisted on going over every menu, adding things he thought would be good, taking off things he didn't think people would like." He laughed softly, to himself. "Yeah, we had a few good battles, Conrad and I. Pretty good bloke, though, in the end."

"I hear he's in a bit of trouble with the law," I said. Mary Jane threw me a warning look across the table.

"Aye," Eamon said, shaking his massive mane of curly red hair. "But I don't believe it for a minute. Conrad Gold can be hot-headed but he's about as much a killer as Fiona, and she still weeps when she has to swat a fly."

"Yeah," I said, "I've met the man and I have to agree with you. But you never know," I said, remembering the tone in his voice the night of his grand opening fiasco. "Man's capacity for evil is pretty deep. It can surprise you sometimes when and where it comes out."

"Okay," Mary Jane said, "Enough with the murder talk. Eamon, I have a question. When you go home after a night like this, do you cook anything for yourself? I've always wanted to know what chefs do."

He laughed. "Yeah, maybe a big bowl of Frosted Flakes," he said. "Or an apple."

"More likely he'll have me scramble him some eggs," Fiona said, as she rushed by. "He does get a wee bit lazy when he gets home. And I don't mean to interrupt, but Charlie is ready to go home."

Eamon shrugged the shrug of a man who knew it when he heard a spousal order. We shook hands, thanked him again for a wonderful meal and headed out into the still twilight of the Scottish evening.

Chapter Seven

We played Royal Dornoch the next morning. Or rather, I played and Mary Jane mostly just walked along with me. There are times when the golf spirit simply doesn't inhabit her, and this morning was one of them. Maybe it was the late night, or the early rise, maybe it was the weather, which was overcast with a cool wind blowing in pretty hard from the sea. Or maybe she just didn't care that she was playing one of Scotland's classic links courses, one whose lineage could be seen at any of a couple hundred Donald Ross-designed courses spread throughout North America. I suspect all of the above, with a healthy helping of the last.

No matter. After she scraped it around helplessly for about three holes, she just smiled at me and said "I'll watch you for a while," and picked up her ball. Even on a cloudy day, Dornoch was a pleasant spot to go for a walk. Nestled in its grassy stretch along the beach, hemmed in by the long ridge of dunes to landward, where the marram waved in the steady breezes, the ceaseless drumming of the surf on the long sandy beach was the only sound one could hear. I could see about four other groups on the course.

Dornoch is a joy to play, unless your score really matters to your sense of self-worth. With the exception of the first two and last two holes, and one small detour on the front nine, the course is your basic long, flat, nine-in and nine-out, side-by-side golf links. In today's wind, the onshore breezes helped shots on the front nine, while always pushing them a bit to the left, while coming home was a brutal fight all the way. When the wind turns against you, all you can do is try to hit the ball solidly and without extra effort. It's hard to gear it down and swing with ease in the face of a three-club wind, but that's the best strategy. Anything hit with sidespin is doomed. Shots that are cut to the right begin to sail away as if the ball is riding a windsurfer, while hook shots often dive like a hungry pelican into the gunch. But a shot hit squarely on the screws will overcome the wind and somehow find a way to bore through it. So I tried to slow it all down and club it way up. Most of the time it worked pretty well, like the approach on fourteen where I hit a smooth little half-power seven iron about 95 yards directly into the freshening breeze and watched it hit and stop about 10 feet short of the flag stick.

We walked together and talked some, but Mary Jane was fairly quiet during the round and seemed a bit preoccupied. She decided to play the last two holes up the hill back towards the clubhouse, and once inside asked me to order her some soup and coffee and said she needed to call home. She tried to call home every day while we were away, but hadn't had time during yesterday's travel day to talk to her daughter, Victoria. I figured the mother genes had kicked in that morning, which explained much of Mary Jane's demeanor.

She came back to the grill room smiling, though, always a good sign. "Victoria caught her first fish," she reported. "A pickerel. Five inches. She wanted to have it for dinner, but her grandfather is going to have it stuffed and mounted." Victoria's grandfather, the *capo dei capi* of the North End mob in Boston's Italian neighborhood, could make things like that happen with the snap of a finger.

"Did she say she missed me?" I asked.

Mary Jane smiled. "I told her you had just played golf and she sighed and said 'golf, golf, golf…is that all he ever does?'"

I laughed.

Later that afternoon, we drove back south to Nairn, where we stayed a night in a little B&B inn in the town I had discovered years ago after a recommendation by a friend at the British Tourist Authority. It was a real Miss Marples kind of place run by two delightful gay men with all the dramatic swish and eccentricities one would expect from a couple of drama queens who had escaped from London's West End theater scene. The inn even had a small auditorium with stage, proscenium and theatre seating, where, in the cold and drab winter months, the hosts invited their old friends to come up for long weekends and staged "theatricals." Our room was chockablock with chintz, flowers and mirrors, but the food was outstanding and the dinner table conversation, led by the two owners and enthusiastically joined by the rest of the guests, was at turns hilarious and edifying as it played out at a high level of erudition.

After procrastinating as long as possible over breakfast of rich Kenyan coffee and fresh-baked croissants, we headed south over the rolling hills of the Grampians and into the beautiful Spey Valley. Here, the scenic road followed the twisting river past fields of barley, thick forestry tracks and through narrow rocky gaps in the mountains that began to rise on both sides. All along the road were signs pointing the way to one or another of Scotland's most famous whiskey distilleries, all of which utilized the sparkling cold and fresh waters pouring down off the rocky hills above to find their way into one of the famous "Speyside" malts: The Macallen, Grants, Glenlivet and Cragganmore, to name just a few. I've always preferred the darker peaty malts made in Scotland's west and islands over the clear amber fire of the Speyside whiskeys, but a good whiskey is a good whiskey, and I've never said "no" to an offer of a dram of good malt from anywhere.

In a few hours, we cut off the main A-road to Aberdeen and headed east to the small seaside town of Cruden Bay. Once upon a time, around the turn of the last century, a busy schedule of trains brought golfers and other tourists out to this gray little village. The long sandy beach attracted walkers and birders and the Cruden Bay links has long been my favorite Scottish course. When I first started visiting, the clubhouse was a threadbare shack that seemed to shudder in the wind as if about to fall down in a tired heap. Just a few years ago, the membership tore down the old building and replaced it with a sturdier modern structure that boasts a nice grill room overlooking the broad plain of golf below, a fancy new pro shop and men's and women's locker rooms that were actually heated and carpeted. I figured I was looking at the collected profits of thousands of American golfers who had come to play Cruden Bay over the last decade or so.

I knew another quaint little B&B in the town, which these days is pretty dingy. Our room had a tiny slice of a view of the sea, and if you looked hard to the north and squinted, it was just possible to make out the hulking ruins of Slains Castle, a mile or so up the beach. When it was still occupied, the Gothic towers of the place were said to have inspired Bram Stoker when he was writing his book about Count Dracula.

We had burgers and soup in a pub in the village that night, and turned in early. The next morning was bright and sunny and we teed off around nine. The first few holes play to the north until the course reaches the narrow, sandbar-filled Cruden Water, then turns and heads back across the wild corrugated landscape of dunes, gorse and wee burns. A smaller and shorter course, called St. Olaf, is contained inside the routing of holes of the big course, which clings to the towering dunes pushed up over the millennia by the ceaseless tides and winds.

After a long uphill climb on the eighth hole, the ninth plays alongside a farmer's field, with a blind tee shot and a gradually descending fairway. We putted out and then walked over to the tenth tee.

"Holy cow," Mary Jane said.

"This is probably the best golf course view in Scotland," I told her.

We were standing at the edge of a precipice that dropped down into a hidden niche next to the sea which was just wide enough to contain four holes. Beyond, the perfect arch of the empty beach curved off into the distance, broken only by some rocky outcroppings. The surf was crashing, the foam was flying, the sun was ach-ingly bright. It felt like we were alone at the end of the world, standing at the entrance to Shangri-La, and the good news is that it had golf holes to play.

I had packed some cookies and extra water in my golf bag, and we stopped here and had a snack, drinking in the view.

"Not too shabby, eh?" I said.

How am I ever gonna play Hingham Muni again?" Mary Jane asked. "Compared to this, every other golf course is crap."

We played our way down into the valley, back and forth over its holes, and climbed out again with a few holes so hidden by the mammoth dunes that one had to ring a large ship's bell after putting out to signal the all-clear to the golfers waiting on the tee. Even though there were no golfers behind us, I rang the bell loudly. It's part of the fun.

We finished the round, had a cheese toastie in the clubhouse and packed up the car for the ride down to St. Andrews. Vacation was over. It was time to get back to work.

Chapter Eight

I ALWAYS FEEL a quickening of the pulse whenever I approach the 'Auld Grey Toon,' also known as St. Andrews, and it was no different this time. We made pretty good time blasting down the coastal highway from Aberdeen to Dundee, skirting past Carnoustie and several fine links courses that lie along the Firth of Tay, before zipping over the river and into the Kingdom of Fife. Once past the little village of Leuchars, the road curves around the Eden Estuary and then flattens as it approaches the ancient city.

Coming in from the northwest, the view is unspectacular. Off to the right, the terrain rises gently to a line of higher ground and what must have once been the shore of an ancient sea, while to the left lie acres of fallow linksland left behind over the eons: wet, flat, sandy, gorse-filled, overgrown windblown emptiness. As one gets closer to the town, however, you begin to see golf holes carved out of the waving grasses, with red and yellow flags snapping at attention in the wind. It was along this stretch that Sam Snead, on his first visit to play in the Open Championship, looked out and wondered aloud "What crappy little course is this?" It was, of course, the Old Course.

Round a final corner, the spires and steeples of the town came into view. That's when the tingles hit. I was hoping Mary Jane would have the same feelings, but she was asleep. She finally awoke when I began braking and turning in the roundabouts on the edge of town as I made our way into the old town and navigated through its narrow streets to our rented apartment, located within walking distance of the Royal & Ancient clubhouse.

As with any other major sporting event in the world, accommodations are both hard to come by and ridiculously expensive at the Open Championship. Most of us in the American press corps learned long ago to save money by pooling resources and sharing space. I usually roomed with three guys: Brad Pennington from the Miami *Herald*, Brett Conte from the Denver *Post* and Mario Cassio from the New York *Daily News*. This year, however, Brett's wife was having a baby and he had dropped out, a story the rest of us suspected might be a cover for the fact that the Post, like many newspapers these days, was cutting back expenses and had told Brett he couldn't go to the Open. But since I had Mary Jane along, it all had worked out.

The apartment, owned by a professor at the university in St. Andrews who didn't mind at all moving out for a week in July in return for a fast thousand quid, wasn't large, but it had two bedrooms, four beds, a nice bathroom and a full kitchen, so we could cook our own meals and save some cash that way. And it took all of about seven minutes to stroll down to the press tent next to the first tee. I knew from past sorry experience that both Brad and Mario were heavy snorers, so it was good that they would share their own room.

The guys were already there when Mary Jane and I staggered in with our suitcases and golf clubs. They had made a run to the local market, where it appeared they had purchased mostly canned beer and crisps, and they were watching a cricket match on the telly and arguing about the rules of that impenetrable game. They stopped arguing along enough to stand up and greet us. "As you were," Mary Jane said with a smile. "And who's got a beer?"

They both relaxed and looked relieved to know that having a woman in the house wasn't going to cramp their style.

"They just said this guy was the 'rear square leg,'" Brad said, waving at the television. "Is that a position or a disease? What kind of crazy sport is this?"

"Yeah," I said. "Just try and figure out the scoring, too. At the end of the day, the announcer will say something like 'And today's result is 156 over 22, not out.' What the hell does that mean? I think they just make up some numbers and figure everyone watching is so far gone into their gin and tonics that they're dead asleep in front of the telly."

Mario shrugged. "Hey, in Afghanistan, the biggest sport is this thing where they ride around on horses fighting over the carcass of a dead goat," he said. "I imagine they'd look at our football and wonder why everyone is running into each other all the time. While dressed like some kind of spaceman."

"Which proves what?" Brad asked.

"Which proves it's a big weird old world."

"I need more beer," Brad said.

I glanced at my watch. "I think I'm gonna go down and sign in," I said. I looked at Mary Jane. "You want to come? It shouldn't take me that long."

"No," she said. "I think I'll take a shower. Do they have enough hot water here?"

"Oh yeah," Mario said. "We put that in the rental contract. Can't be taking cold showers in bloody Scotland."

Our place was in a small terrace on a side street up behind the University. I walked into town, crossed South and Market Streets and then followed North Street down towards the Marine Hotel and hung a right on Golf Place, which ended in the plaza behind the 18th green of the famous Old Course. As usual, there was a crowd of people just standing alongside the white railed fence stretched along The Links bordering the 18th fairway staring out at the golf course. There was no one playing a practice round coming down the fairway, but people stared anyway. Several huge grandstands had been set up behind the green and down along the first fairway, and banners and pennants were flying everywhere. The big yellow scoreboard, still operated by hand by a crew hidden within, dominated the skyline, and there were a half dozen huge video screens waiting to show the highlights of the tournament to come. The air held the usual supercharged tension that seems to descend on a place when a major golf tournament is staged, a mixture of anticipation and history and excitement that seems to make the atmosphere almost palpable.

I wandered around the sandstone edifice of the R&A clubhouse, sitting frumpily on its plinth behind the first tee, and entered the first large tent beyond it. I showed the security guard my access pass and, inside, almost ran right into Bernard Capshaw, the genial press secretary for the Open, dressed in his official R&A blazer and gray flannel slacks.

"Hacker!" he said, stopping to pump my hand vigorously. "How good to see you again! I trust all is well in fair Boston?"

We chatted for a while as I went through the process of checking in, getting my press packet of information, statistics, history and the like, as well as the first of several small gifts that some of the sponsors had provided for the media in attendance. It was the usual swag package of golf balls, hats, a towel or two…the usual crap they hand out at these things in a vain attempt to curry favor with us. I keep the balls and give the rest away to the kids that are always waiting outside in hopes of getting an autograph from one of the pros who might be getting interviewed. I like to imagine that the golf visor graciously donated by the Highlands and Islands Tourism Authority gets worn by some yob spray painting obscene graffiti on an Edinburgh overpass, and that I've done my part to help the vagrants dress for success.

I looked around the press room and saw the usual Monday afternoon collection of British reporters, a few TV guys and the omnipresent swarm of Asian-based media. Having observed the way the Japanese and South Korea press cover a golf tournament *en masse*, it's a wonder there is anyone left back home in their country to read the reports from the multitude of reporters and cameramen. I've come to the conclusion that each man or woman reporter is responsible for preparing one sentence each, per day. If they all fulfill their quota, then the papers back in Osaka will have sixty or seventy graphs to choose from.

Other than a couple of the London newspaper beat writers, both of whom seemed to be heavily engaged in a close analysis of the photo of the winsome and topless Page 3 girl on their laptops, I didn't see anyone else I recognized. The usual major tournament press crowd would be filtering in tonight and tomorrow morning, and by tomorrow afternoon the joint would be jumping.

Someone clapped me on the shoulder. I turned to see Mike Morton, until recently the top editor for *The Golfer*, an ad-filled golf magazine cranked out by one of the publishing behemoths in New York. He was a short guy, somewhere in his fifties, but looked to be in good shape, and he had always had an air of intensity about him, as if he was wound on the tight side. The previous year, Morton had announced he was retiring, after 20 years, and moving to St. Andrews to research some books he wanted to write and generally enjoy a slower pace of life. It was an announcement that had caused me to have more than a few jealous pangs, since up and moving to the United Kingdom had long been one of my pet fantasies, if you don't include the ones featuring Taylor Swift. I had run into Morton now and then over the years, sometimes at a major event like this week, sometimes when I went to the PGA Show in Orlando, the annual trade show of the golf industry and an event where someone like Mike Morton would be expected to attend and schmooze with all the ball and club makers who bought ads in his magazine and supported him in the lifestyle to which he had, I am sure, become accustomed. I wouldn't say Morton was a good friend of mine, but rather a friendly acquaintance. He knew what I did, I knew what he did; there was always a veneer of professional respect between us.

"Welcome to the Auld Grey Toon, Hacker," he said now, as we shook hands. He handed me a business card. "I'm telling all the guys…if you need any good background on the town, its history or anything to do with golf in these parts, please give me a call. I'm glad to help provide anything you need while you're here."

"Oh, great," I said, thinking *I've been coming here longer than you have* but not saying it out loud. "I'll be sure and do that. How do you like living over here?"

"A dream come true, Hack," he said, "Dream come true. I mean, the weather can be a little trying. The winter took some getting used to. But other than that, it's like living in heaven."

"I'll bet," I said. "How's the writing going?"

He shrugged. "I'm hoping to start teaching a course in creative journalism at the University this fall," he said. "I'm doing some research now on a couple of golf history books, so I seem to be spending all my time in the library there anyway. I'd be killing two birds with one stone."

"Good idea," I said. "Do they give professors the same discount as the students on the Old Course greens fees?" University students pay a fraction of the usual cost of greens fees on the Old Course and the other courses in town. Were I about to become a college student again, that alone would make me consider applying.

"Ha-ha," he said, chuckling. Although I noticed his eyebrows crunched together like he was really frowning. "They told me I had to be a resident here at least for a year for that. But luckily, I know a ton of good people in town here, so I don't have trouble getting out to play whenever I want. St. Andrews is really a pretty small place, so it's not hard getting to know the right people."

"Sounds heavenly," I said.

Morton moved off to spread his good cheer with someone else. I waved goodbye to Bernard and headed back to the apartment, figuring a cocktail, a nice dinner and an early evening would be just about perfect. I strolled past Dunvegan's, the pub at the corner of North Street and Golf Place, and saw that it was cheek-to-jowl crowded. The Open comes back to St. Andrews every five years or so and I'd bet that the proprietor of the Dunvegan makes enough money in the seven days of tournament week to pay his bills for at least a year.

I knew a shortcut that took me across one of the university's pretty green quads between the main streets of the town. It always seems like walking into the pages of *Goodbye, Mr. Chips* with the grey stone Gothic buildings with their heavily mullioned windows framing another perfectly manicured green swath of British lawn, ringed by neat walks. Stone benches sit here and there, suitable for quiet rumination about complex mathematical formulas or the proper declension of Greek verbs.

But I was surprised to see a rowdy gathering in one corner of this quad. It looked like one of the student protests I had grown up with back in those long-ago days when I went to college. Curious, I wandered over where a motley crew of people was gathered, holding up hand-made signs and banners and chanting something I couldn't quite pick up. As I grew closer, I could read the signs.

ELIMINATE GOLF, one sign read. FREE THE PEOPLE FROM THE ROYAL AND ANCIENT YOKE was inscribed on another. BALLS TO THE WALL! was illustrated with a roughly drawn picture of a golf ball wearing a blindfold, positioned against an execution wall. Che himself would have been proud.

A tall, distinguished-looking man, dressed in neatly pressed jeans and a colorful sweater, mounted a wooden box and prepared to speak. He looked to be in his early 50s, with long blondish hair swept back dramatically, an aquiline nose, ruddy cheeks and lots of teeth. He held his hand up and snapped his fingers.

"People, people," he said loudly, trying to get the milling crowd of young people to pay attention. "Attention, please!" Slowly, the crowd fell silent. "Thank you all for coming. In a minute, we're going to parade down Market Street and over towards the golf course. The first thing you should know is that we do not have a permit for this action, and it is very likely that we will be confronted by the Fife Council police. We may even be arrested. In fact, it is very likely that we will be. But we are prepared to lose our freedom, however temporarily, for our cause. The cause of ending the slavery of this town and its incestuous connection to the game of golf."

"Hurrarrr!" The cheers from the gaggle of onlookers was reedy and less-than-enthusiastic.

"For too long, this town and its people have been held prisoner by the game of golf and the ridiculous waste of precious resources it represents," the speaker continued. "It is time to take back our town, to take back Scotland from this hateful so-called sport, the plaything of the imperial, capitalistic cabal that runs this country. We do not want golf, we do not want golfers, we do not want their silly clothes, we do not want their chemical pesticides and fertilizers damaging our planet, we do not want their drunkenness, we do not want their control of the people's land. What we want is to eliminate the game of golf from our historic land. Eliminate Golf!" he shouted. "E-Go!"

There were a few shouts of approval and whistles at this polemic. Taking advantage of the rush of emotion, the speaker shouted "Onward!" and, stepping down from his podium, striding out through the entrance of the quad and onto Market Street. Most of the kids standing around took up their signs and followed. They began a steady chanting: "Hey Hey, Ho Ho, the Game of Golf Has Got to Go!"

I managed to keep from laughing out loud. But a thought occurred to me and I walked up to one of the stragglers. He was about eighteen, with long rings of curly black hair, an intricate series of piercings in one of his ears and a look on his face of blissed-out stupefaction.

"Dude," I said, nodding at him. "How come there are students around here? I thought it was summer break."

He looked at me for a moment, until I came into better focus. Then he grinned, revealing some impressively brown teeth.

"Nae," he said. "I'm no student in this place. I'm from Cupar." I knew that was a smallish city not far away. "Yonder laddie came over this morning and asked if some of the lads would like to make a bit o'coin. Said we just had to march down the street with some signs. Be payin' 10 quid."

"Protest for hire?" I said, winking at him.

"Aye," he said, shaking his head. "But he dinna say anything about getting arrested. If I get arrested again, I may lose the dole, y'know?"

"Yeah," I said, nodding wisely. "You don't want that."

"Nae, nae," he said, grinning at me. "Especially over the gawf." He looked around to make sure no one was listening. "Don' tell nobody, but I like to play th'gawf," he said. "Me and the lads play a lot."

"Your secret's safe with me," I said, smiling at him.

"Right on, my man," the kid said. We knocked knuckles and he left.

Chapter Nine

I DROVE MARY Jane and our two roomies outside of town heading south. About ten miles down the coastal road, which swept through the rolling, well-tended farmer's fields on both sides, we came to a wide place in the road known as the village of Kingsbarns. A little further on, I knew, was the entrance to the Kingsbarns Links, a terrific daily-fee golf course built by Americans just a decade or so ago on the site of an old nine-hole course closed down and forgotten during World War II.

I pulled into the yard of an old coaching inn-turned restaurant and pub, a place I liked to visit whenever I was in the Kingdom of Fife. We crowded into the narrow pub in the front room, ordered up some local ales and waited for our table.

"I saw the weirdest thing today walking back from the golf course," I said. I told them about my brush with the Eliminate Golf group.

Mario was nodding. "I heard about them," he said. "Bernard told me that the R&A was concerned about some kind of demonstration breaking out during the tournament. They've apparently asked for extra security from the local coppers."

"Somebody is getting violent about...*golf*?" Mary Jane couldn't keep the incredulity out of her voice. "Good Lord, with all the issues one could choose in today's world to hurt someone over, I'm afraid golf doesn't make the Top Ten list."

"Top Thousand," Brad said, sipping his beer.

Mario shrugged. "These days, it doesn't seem to matter," he said. "Get a cause, cause a ruckus, break some windows, get on TV. The talking heads talk about you, at least for a night, and you're a star. Sell the book rights, make the rounds of all the talk shows, maybe some idiot in Hollywood wants to make a movie of your life story. Beats actually doing something for a living."

I told them about the less-than-enthusiastic participant I'd chatted with who'd admitted to being paid to protest. "The whole thing seems a little strange to me," I said. "I mean, OK, I get it. You're against the game of golf for some reason, the best place to stage a demonstration is in St. Andrews during the Open. I wonder what this professor guy's deal is. What is he really after? What's the point?"

"Publish or perish?" Brad deadpanned. We all laughed.

"Did either of you guys run into Mike Morton today at the press tent?" I asked.

Mario and Brad looked at each other and chuckled.

"Oh, yeah," Brad said. "He's trying to sell tickets for a bus tour of the East Neuk or something."

"What?"

Mario swallowed the last of his pint and put the glass down on the highly polished bar. "I've heard that he's hard up for money," he said. "I guess the great idea of coming to Scotland to live the good life hasn't been so good after all."

"How could that be?" I wondered. "He was the editor of that magazine of his for a long time. He must have been making pretty good coin."

"Have you checked out the cost of living in Manhattan lately, Hacker?" Mario smiled at me. "It's getting to be pretty hard to make it on an editor's salary, even if you are Mike "Salty" Morton. Besides that, there are the rumors…"

"Boys, boys," Mary Jane said. "You really shouldn't gossip about people. Remember, what goes around, comes around." She fixed Mario with a steady gaze, locking her baby blues on him. "Now, dish!"

Mario laughed. "Yeah, well, the word on the street was that he got canned, not that he retired gracefully," he said. "And apparently, it was because he was fudging around with the budgets at the magazine and got his hand caught in the cookie jar. They let him leave quietly, because they didn't want to admit they had trusted him all those years, but he was apparently spending like a drunk sailor and the accounting was not quite kosher, as they say."

"My, my," I said. "I don't think the cost of living here in Scotland is quite as steep as it is in New York, but it's not that far behind."

"I know seven places in South Beach where I can buy beer cheaper than it is here," Brad said. "And it's colder, too."

They told us our table was ready so we moved into the dining room, to a table overlooking a pretty courtyard in the back. It had neatly trimmed grass, pebbly walkways and some large terra cotta pots planted with tall ferny things blowing back and forth in the breeze. The courtyard was bounded by a low stone wall and beyond the wall it was dark with thick woods. A pretty young girl with a white apron strapped around her middle passed us menus and asked if we'd like another beer. We all refused—beer, as Brad had just reminded us, is not cheap in Scotland, and we were all mindful of our expense account limits. I winced a little as I reviewed the *carte d'jour* as prices had gone up quite a bit since the last time the Open had been in town. Three of us ordered burgers while Mary Jane went for the fish and chips. I figured we could just make do with pasta-and-sauce for the next couple of nights and keep the budget under control.

We swapped some tidbits as we ate, discussing the latest Tour gossip. So-and-so had changed swing coaches, this guy's marriage was disintegrating, that guy was nursing a sore back. It was the usual shoptalk—probably fascinating to an average golf fan, but just the mundane and ordinary to those of us who deal with this stuff every week. I noticed, however, that Mary Jane, who usually drinks up the gossip I bring home, was somewhat distracted. She kept glancing out the windows into the courtyard. I was sitting with my back to the windows, and when there was a break in the conversation, I smiled at her.

"Is there something going on back there?" I asked.

She blushed a little. "I'm probably crazy, but I keep seeing this little man in a dirty parka ducking in and out of the bushes. And he looks like he wants to get your attention."

I turned and looked. There was indeed a little man in a dirty overcoat standing at the side of the yard, next to the parking area. I recognized him at once: it was Johnny Swift. He was a local caddie I've known for years. He saw me looking at him, and made a c'mon wave with one hand. I turned back to the table, told them I knew the guy, and excused myself.

Outside, I shook Swiftie's hand and let him drag me further back into the garden, deeper behind the house and away from the parking lot and the main road. He kept glancing nervously in that direction.

"Good to see you, Swifts," I told him. "What's it been, four, five years?"

"At least that, mate, at least," he said, a smile playing at the corners of his lips dispelling, for a moment, the worried look that creased his forehead.

It had been far longer ago than that when I first met Swiftie at the bar of the Central Pub, probably my favorite drinking hole in the Auld Grey Toon. I know most Americans like Dunvegan's, where Tip Anderson, who famously caddied for Arnold Palmer in his prime, and some of the older caddies used to hang out hoping to trade endless stories about golf and golfers for a few free pints courtesy of besotted American golf tourists. Or the Jigger Inn, a tiny whitewashed cottage with a steep slate roof near the 17th green of the Old Course, famous for being the pub where an elderly and apparently inebriated Old Tom Morris fell down the steps into the basement, cracked his head and died. But the Central always seemed more authentic to me, with its wooden booths and benches and a greater mix of locals ranging from university professors to farmers stopping in for a quick pint after delivering their wares to the local markets. I had been standing at the Central bar, foot resting on the brass rail, admiring the rich color and taste of the local ale, when Swifty had tapped me on the shoulder. "Scuse'm guv," he had said. "Wunnerin' if ye might be in need o' a caddie t'morrow?" He stood just a bit over five feet and was wearing a dirty blue parka with a hood flopping down the back. His jet-black hair was greasy and tangled, his face wore a three-day old beard and, although he looked to be a few years younger than me, his eyes were old and peered out at me with something of the blank emptiness of despair.

I shouldn't have looked into those eyes. But I did.

"You know," I said, "I was just thinking it would be cool to have a caddie to play the Old Course tomorrow. How about joining me for a beer and we can talk about it?"

He looked at me gratefully, and shook his head somewhat sadly.

"Cheers, guv," he said, "But I canna do th'drink nae more. But Johnnie wouldna min' if he had a cup o' their nice soup and a wee bit o' bread for his supper."

I could suddenly see the signs of hunger on the man's face, and quickly ordered him some soup, and a bowl for myself. He told me his name, said he grew up in town and had been scuffling for caddie work in various places in Scotland.

"I was at Turnberry for a while," he said. "But then this new corporation came in and changed ever'thin'," he said sadly, shaking his head. "So I came back t'here."

"Don't you have to be licensed or something?" I asked.

"Oh, aye," he said, nodding as the hot soup and warm fresh bread arrived, his eyes lighting up. "I'm still just an apprentice. But in a few more years, I should move up to full caddie."

Once he had eaten, he relaxed a bit and told a

few jokes, then began asking me about where I was from, what I did and the usual scouting out of my financial prospects. He managed to sound enthusiastic, although his fallen expression gave him away, when he found out I was not one of the captains of American industry but just a hard-working journo likely not to have a pocket wad of rolled bills to dispense.

Despite that, he agreed to carry my bag early the next morning, after we agreed on a good price, and we met shortly after 8 a.m. on the first tee of the Old Course.

I would not have been surprised if Johnny had never shown up. Despite his protestations of sobriety, the drink is a big problem in the U.K. and Swiftie had the look of one deeply trapped in the clutches of alcoholism. But there he was in the gray light of morning, hopping from one foot to the other to try and get his blood flowing. He smiled when he saw me. After all, I was a payday for him.

"What time's yer game?" he asked me.

"Don't have one," I told him. His face fell as his imagined payday disappeared. I chuckled and put a hand on his shoulder. "Don't worry," I said, "We'll get a game. I'm a single and I've never had to wait more than half an hour."

Tee times at the Old Course have always been a bit tricky to get, given the worldwide demand for the chance to play a round on golf's Holy of Holies. But I learned a long time ago that the best way to circumvent the normal complicated tee time procedures was to show up as a single golfer and ask the starter to work me in. Everyone else, of course, has to subject themselves to the nail-biting tension of The Ballot system of tee time allocation, or pay through the nose to their tour group or hope their hotel can pull a few strings.

But a wise old gent long ago told me the only surefire way to get to play the course any day and any time I wanted was to show up alone. And it has never failed. Because there is always a dropout in those groups who are booked to play. Someone who drank too much lager the night before, or had to leave town early for business, or got lost on the way, or decided not to play in rain or wind, or any of a dozen other possible excuses. So sooner or later, a group will present themselves to the starter missing a player. And the starter, who is under orders to send out as many paying customers as possible, will simply plug in a singleton standing there ready to go.

This surefire ploy worked again. I had hit a few putts on the tiny practice green near the first tee when the starter called my name. A foursome of Glasgow blokes had turned into a threesome, as one of the lads had been called away to attend the birth of his child, perhaps the only excuse permissible to give up a hallowed tee time at St. Andrews. So Johnny and I had our game.

We met our playing partners—they were all high-tech industry workers from Silicon Glen, the area west of Glasgow city that had become Scotland's answer to the San Jose area—and set off down the first fairway. I had hit a nice ball down the yawning expanse of the first hole, a fairway shared with the incoming 18th, and had just 130 yards left into the green. Johnny, who hadn't received enough information about my game from the one swing, held out my bag to let me choose a club. I reached for the nine-iron.

He frowned a bit. "Might be th'eight, it might,"

he said.

I thought about it, but without feeling any noticeable wind in the early morning, I believed the nine was the right club. He didn't object. I hit a nice shot and watched as the ball flew up into the air, hung there for a while and then dropped like a stone. Into the depths of the Swilcan Burn, that narrow little water hazard which snakes around in front of the green. I cursed.

Johnny shook his head. "My fault," he said quickly. "I shoulda insisted on the eight. There's somethin' about this hole, it always calls for one more club than y'think."

After that, we both relaxed and had a good time. He was an excellent caddie who clubbed me correctly from that point on. And he had lots of great stories that had us all in stitches. He even helped my new friends read their putts and at the end, they all threw a few bills his way.

That night, Johnny offered to take me out "on the toon," an offer I couldn't refuse. We hit all of the pubs in St. Andrews and then he took me to a dance at some community center in Anstruther, a few miles down the coast. It felt like junior high school all over again, with desperate girls lined up along one wall of the hall and desperate boys on the other; a large disco ball sending shards of light across the faces of desperation on both sides. After that, we hit a late-night Indian take-out place for a bit of curry. I got back to my hotel at roughly the same time the sun began to rise.

But every time I returned to St. Andrews after that trip, I tried to find Johnny. If he wasn't on the roster of the caddie master, I could usually find him at one of the pubs, fighting his constant rearguard action against booze. I'd make sure he had a good meal, would take him out on the course if I could, and once, memorably, hooked him up with a young American pro who was trying to qualify for the Open at Lundin Links, just down the coast. They missed by two shots, but Johnny was paid two hundred pounds and was very pleased.

He did not look pleased now, as he kept glancing nervously around, and flinching every time a car drove down the main road.

"What's up, Swifts?" I finally asked.

"Och," he said. "I'm a bit on the lam."

I sighed. "Who's after you now?" I asked. "Cops again?"

He shook his head. "Nae. I canna be sure, but I think it's the bloody Russkis want me dead."

I laughed. Inappropriate perhaps, but who wouldn't? Johnny Swift was the antithesis of the international danger man, he couldn't hurt a fly if he tried and his biggest problem was staying away from the bottle. At which he too frequently failed. So the idea of anyone being after Johnny was pretty funny, much less the idea that some secret agent taking orders from the highest part of the Kremlin wanted to eliminate the poor sod with extreme prejudice. That was frankly hilarious.

Johnny must have agreed, because he flashed me that lopsided grin of his, showing a few of his browning back teeth. "Yah," he said. "Sounds bloody ridiculous, yeah?" He fumbled in the pocket of his dirty blue parka and came out with a cigarette and a plastic lighter. His hands shook a little as he went to light it. He sucked in a lungful and blew it out again with a deep sigh.

"I dunno who i'tis," he said. "I may have seen somethin' I'm not to have seen. But I swear, I didna see a damn thing! Nae a'thing!"

"Okay," I said, patting him on the shoulder. "Calm down. Start at the beginning. Tell me what happened."

He took in another large lungful of smoke and leaned forward as if to whisper something to me. But just as he did, we heard an engine whine in an angry downshift and tires squeal as a dark sedan swept from the main road into the parking lot off to our left, braking heavily and scattering the pebbles from the lot's surface in all directions as the car crunched to a stop. I turned my head to watch as three of the car's four doors flew open and three dark-suited men dressed in tight-fitting dark-blue suits jumped out. I turned back to look at Johnny...and he wasn't there. He had disappeared without a trace.

One of the blue-suited stiffs walked up to me. He was about six feet, tough-guy heavy with no neck, a cueball-bald head and a malicious mustache-and-goatee combo that tried to make him look tough. It worked. He looked tough.

"Where is Swift?" he said to me in a heavily accented voice. It sounded Slavic, maybe Nordic. Hard to tell.

"Who wants to know?" I said. He looked at me sideways for a second, then brushed past me—not trying too hard to avoid giving me a little push with his shoulder—and headed for the dark woods behind the garden. He leapt effortlessly over the wall and plunged into the darkness of the thick woods beyond. The other two heavies had also disappeared, circling around to the right and left to try and head Johnnie off at the pass. If there was a pass back there.

I thought about going after Johnny to see if I

could help, but I knew that he would be as good as gone. He knew this countryside like the back of his hand, and if there was a place he could hide, he would know where it was and how to get there fast. I would just be blundering around in the woods and presenting a good target for some pissed-off heavies with bald heads, no necks and frightening facial hair. I decided to go back inside and finish my dinner.

I returned to the table, sat down, picked up my napkin and placed it back on my lap. My friends stared at me with wonder.

"What the hell was that all about?" Mario asked.

I shrugged and picked up my fork.

"Guy works here in the kitchen," I said, trying to keep my voice even. "He's been a caddie in town for ages. I've known him for years. He saw me eating dinner and wanted to say hello."

"Who were those guys in the suits?" Brad asked.

I shrugged. "Don't know," I said. "They didn't say."

"It looked like they were after your caddie friend," Mario said. "The way he took off and all."

"Really?" I said. I took a bite of my burger. It was cold. The guys got the hint and went back to eating.

I hadn't been brave enough to glance over at Mary Jane. Now I did. Wish I hadn't. She was sitting there with her arms crossed in front, hand on opposite shoulder. And on her face? Pursed lips. Kneaded brow. Dark coloring high on the cheekbones. Not a happy camper. At all.

Chapter Ten

I DECIDED TO spend the next morning at the tournament press facility. The temperature at the apartment was decidedly chilly after the events of the previous night, and not from the weather or the central heating. I hadn't heard a peep from our roomies, so I didn't know if they were long gone or sound asleep. After a series of one-word responses to some of my questions, I wrote down the name of a pub with some walking directions and a map and told Mary Jane to meet me for a late lunch there around one. She made a sound that didn't sound like "Go to hell," so I took that as about as good a sign as I was likely to get and left.

Down at the press tent, I sat for a while at the narrow desk space that had been deigned to be "mine" for the week and scanned some of the British papers. I love how in the U.K. you buy a paper *because* of its political leanings and bias rather than go through the fiction of pretending that there is none, as we do on our side of the pond. The left reads the *Guardian* and the *Indepen-*

dent and the right reads the *Times* and the *Telegraph*; and the vast majority of the people who don't, really, give a damn one way or the other, read one of the much more exciting tabloids, ogle the topless Page 3 girls, scan the show business gossip and flip to the sports. And oh, how they cover sports in the U.K. Again, they don't worry about maintaining the line between factual reporting and reporting with a predetermined opinion. If a writer thinks Nick Faldo played lousy golf, he writes "Nick Faldo played like rubbish today," and nobody, except maybe for Nick Faldo, thinks anything of it. In the U.S., we either have to quote somebody saying Nick Faldo played like rubbish, back the claim up with rubbish-like statistics or have the editor slap a "News Analysis" deck on the piece to get away with something like that. My Brit friends are much freer in many ways than we are in the home of Freedom of the Press.

So, after skipping lightly over the news from the county cricket league, the European track championships and something to do with Formula 1 motor racing, I got down to the juicy bits on golf. Colin Montgomerie was said to be whining about something again—the British press for some reason has always disliked Monty, and he gives it back to them without hesitation—Sergio was being romantically linked to some hot Belgian model, and there was a brewing minor scandal over sponsorship kickbacks at some tournament in France. Gee, go figure.

Once I felt caught up on the news, I decided to wander over to the practice range and see if I could find any of the small contingent of players from New England. As in everything else, all news is local, and that blithering idiot known as my executive editor would expect some kind of news notes or a sidebar piece on the "local" players in the tournament. It would be a small piece: in the field this year were two aging journeymen players from Rhode Island, a couple of Connecticut natives who now lived in Orlando and one odd duck from upstate Vermont. At least he could be counted on to answer one of my questions with an "Ayy-yup!"

After the brief walk over to the visitors' clubhouse, a much needed facility which the Links Trust had erected two decades ago down the beach a ways and overlooking the start and finish of the New Course (opened in 1895, which hardly made it new, unless compared with the Old, which dates from the beginning of the Paleolithic Era), I spent a happy couple of hours on the range, chatting with various players, caddies, rules officials, agents and hangers-on. You can pick up all the gossip you want on the practice range, especially during a major tournament, when all the corporate bigwigs and sponsors are in town and like to see and be seen. And talk. Of course, one must always take information gleaned on the range with more than a grain of salt—it is mostly gossip, after all—but there is always some little nugget of information that can be turned into a sidebar or even a featurette. If there is any difference between the two.

I did get fifteen minutes with Bertie Wolf, native son of Enosburg Falls in the Northeast Kingdom of Vermont, who gave me his wide-eyed views of playing in his first British Open. Even though he has lived in Arizona for more than ten years now—you can't live in Vermont and shape your game for the pro tour in a place where summer lasts for maybe a week—he still dropped his r's, broadened his a's, and was full of the euphemisms and colorful analogies of a down-home dairyman. Good copy, as we like to say.

I glanced at my watch and saw that it was almost one, so I headed back into town to the White Swan, which from the outside looked like something of a dive. It was located well away from the main streets of town, accessed down a side alley and at the bottom of a dark set of stairs. But inside, it was neat, clean and cozy and managed by an old friend of mine, Mrs. Colgate. When you go back to a town many times over the years, you learn where the good places are, and the Swan was a place I never missed in St. Andrews. Mrs. Colgate made the best meat pies in Scotland.

When I walked down the stairs and inside, I saw Mary Jane in a booth in the back, sitting with someone whose back was to me. I walked over, and Sir Hamish turned to follow Mary Jane's smile across the room.

"Hacker, dear boy!" he exclaimed, jumping up to pump my hand. "I have been enjoying a lovely chat with your lady! Quite a coincidence running into her here, of all places!"

I slid into the booth next to Mary Jane and gave her a kiss. She kissed me back, which I took as a sign that I might be forgiven again.

"Best lunch in town," I said. "One of Mrs. Colgate's meat pies, some chips and a lager."

"Oh, I quite agree," Sir Hamish nodded enthusiastically. "Agatha Colgate is one of the best cooks in all of Fife. Lovely lady…known her since she was a girl."

"Is there anybody in Scotland you don't know?" I wondered.

Sir Hamish laughed. "Oh, there may be a few," he said, "But give me time. I'm working on it!"

We placed our orders and I passed on what gossip I had picked up that morning on the range. Our lunches arrived and I dug in.

"Have you learned anything more about the Kinkaid murder?" Sir Hamish asked after we had all eaten in silence for a while.

I glanced nervously at Mary Jane and shook my head. "Nope," I said. "I'm just a golf writer this week. Except for the fact that the victim worked for the Links Trust, there's nothing for me to write about. Only mystery I'm interested in is when Tiger will get his A-game back and why Mickelson throws up on his shoes every time he plays over here."

"Pity," Sir Hamish said, a bit of a twinkle in his eye. "I may have stumbled upon an interesting factoid or two. But if you're not interested…"

I didn't respond. Took another bite of my meat pie. Studied a French fry before popping it into my mouth. Then I took a swig of lager. Mary Jane dug an elbow into my side. "Oh, for Christ's sake," she said, "Go ahead and ask. If you don't your head will probably explode or something and then where will I be?"

"In the White Swan amid a bloody mess, with some explanations to the bobbies in order, I should think," Sir Hamish said, and we all laughed.

"OK," I said. "Whaddya got?"

"I had an interesting conversation yesterday with the Fife Sheriff," Sir Hamish said. "Here in Scotland, the Sheriff is roughly equivalent to a state judge back in your country. They hear both civil and criminal cases and they conduct all the inquiries into fatal accidents and sudden deaths."

"And this Sheriff is an old friend of yours," I said.

"Quite," Sir Hamish said, nodding. "He's an old classmate of mine at Cambridge. He's also a good customer for some of our very finest whiskeys, but that's beside the point. He told me that his office had held a preliminary hearing on the death of Colin Kinkaid, with testimony from the Fife coroner and the police."

He stopped and drank a little ale. Sir Hamish was good at the dramatic pauses.

"Death was laid to a fracture of the fourth and fifth cervical vertebrae," he said.

"A broken neck," I said, nodding. "Was that the result of the fall down into the Bottle Dungeon?"

Sir Hamish shook his head. "No, no," he said. "He was murdered. The evidence shows that someone twisted his head abruptly, death resulting. Quite brutal, actually. The bruises noted from the fall into the dungeon were all post mortem. But they did find something else that was interesting."

He paused again. This time it was Mary Jane who motioned impatiently with her hand for him to spill the damn beans.

"The police and the coroner found some unusual material in the cuffs of his trousers and on the back of his jacket," he said.

"What kind of material?" I asked.

He waved his hand. "Oh, some seeds and burrs and stuff one would pick up walking through fields and forests. Certainly not something one would expect to find on a body tossed down into the Bottle Dungeon: that is all rock and moisture. And, knowing that Kinkaid was pretty much an office worker, the coroner thought that somewhat unusual, so he took the samples and analyzed them."

"And?" I prodded.

"And he concluded that Colin Kinkaid had been walking in the marshes of the Eden Estuary just before he was murdered. There were sedges, bitterroot and other plant life native to the riverbank caught in the folds of his clothing."

"Is that unusual?" Mary Jane wanted to know.

Sir Hamish shook his head. "Not necessarily," he said. "Most golfers playing the Old Course never even notice the river. One has to climb up to the top of the bank behind the eleventh green or the eighth tee to get a good view of it, and from there, all that can be seen is a rather dreary view of mudbanks, tides going in and out and perhaps a brave duck or two paddling around. But further upstream, the River Eden is quite lovely. They say the birding is quite good during certain times of year, and anglers crowd the beats for brown trout and salmon."

"Is it hard to get to?" I asked. "Did Kinkaid have to bushwhack across the fields to get to the river?"

"Not at all," Sir Hamish said. "There are maintained pathways at several places along the riverbank. The RAF base at Leuchars, just across the water, has walking paths into the marshes. And there are now several other access points and pathways all the way upriver to Guardbridge. Kinkaid could have been walking on almost any of them when he was accosted and murdered."

"They can't pin the location down any closer?" I asked.

Sir Hamish shook his head. "Afraid not," he said. "The material they found on his clothing was generic in nature. It could have come from anywhere on the river. For that matter, it could have come from almost any other riverbank here in Scotland."

"Well," I said. "I guess it's a clue. Not a great clue, but …"

"At least they won't be able to say that Hacker hasn't got a clue," Mary Jane said dryly. We laughed. We finished our lunch and I glanced at my watch. I needed to go back and crank out a notes column to send back to Boston. Mary Jane told me that our two hard-working roommates had gone over to Carnoustie to play, the lazy bastards.

"I say," Sir Hamish said as we were leaving, "Do you two have dinner plans this evening?"

"If you can call tinned spaghetti a 'dinner plan'" Mary Jane said with a laugh.

"Good," he said. "Come and join me at Johnny Cheape's tonight. You'll enjoy meeting him. He's something of an odd bird, but he's basically harmless. There will probably be a few other eccentrics there as well."

"What do I wear?" Mary Jane asked. "I didn't bring much in the way of fancy clothes."

"Oh, come as you are," he said. "Nobody dresses for dinner anymore. Too bad, really. I always thought it a nice touch. But the world changes, doesn't it?"

Chapter Eleven

SIR HAMISH GAVE me directions to Wormwood, the centuries-old seat of the Cheape family, which was out in the countryside a few miles from St. Andrews. Once beyond the central area of the old town, which is not that large, one quickly is reminded that most of Fifeshire is agricultural and remains basically unchanged over the last several hundred years. In the long, lingering twilight of a Scottish summer, we followed a two-lane B-road bordered by hedgerows past miles of working farms, took the cutoff as directed and, after a dip down into a valley created by a fast-flowing stream heading to the North Sea, came to the estate's entrance.

After rumbling across the cattle gate, we followed the drive as it split in two to create a circular path up a rocky hill topped with broad, leafy trees. I would have bet my last farthing that TV golf announcer David Feherty would have been able to identify the genus of each tree—he seems to have studied botany in his distant past; but to me, they were just leafy and green things. As we approached the crest of the hill, Mary Jane pointed off to the right at a herd of red deer grazing on the manicured grass at the edge of the dark forest beyond.

Then she gasped as the Vauxhall chugged over the crest of the hill. Because I'm a trained journalist, I didn't gasp, but Emily Bronte might have fainted dead away. Laid out before us was a broad plain: the drive ran down the middle, with wide fields on both sides encased in a beautiful split-rail fence. In the pasture to the left was a herd of Highland cattle, with the heavy, curved horns and the shaggy, red-tinged hair that make them appear almost prehistoric. They were chomping away placidly at the moist green grass. The field on the right of the drive was occupied by a half dozen noble looking thoroughbred horses. The older ones wore woolen blankets of a dark green color and bent their heads on long, graceful necks to nibble quietly on the lovely green grass, while two or three young colts gamboled in the twilight, playing a game of horse tag.

And beyond this placid and rural vista, sitting atop an escarpment of stone, was Wormwood. The three-story house was built of gray granite with a slate roof, with two gracefully curving arms off each side of the main façade. Warm golden light spilled out of its many windows and pooled on the graveled area in front. There was a large circular fountain in the middle of the drive in front of the house which was gushing water at the feet of a naked marble nymph.

"I don't think I'm dressed right for this place," Mary Jane said. I thought she looked lovely in her pretty skirt and sweater.

"Hey, Hamish said it was informal." I said. Then I looked down at my khakis and golf shirt dressed up by my well-worn blue blazer. Maybe she was right: we both seemed a bit underdressed to meet with the aristocracy.

"Oh, well," I said. "They're probably expecting your basic American rubes, so we might as well look the part."

I pulled the car up next to the three or four others already parked off to the side, and we approached the front door on foot, skirting around the gushing statue. A butler materialized at the entrance, greeted us and showed us in with a minimum of bowing, scraping and forelock tugging. The entrance hallway featured a high, arched ceiling, heavy mahogany paneling and a broad marble stair climbing to a landing beneath a set of arched stained glass windows.

"His Lordship and guests are having drinks in the library," Jeeves informed us, and led us through two long sitting rooms filled with groupings of antique chairs, desks, tables and sofas and walls covered with ornately framed oil portraits of what looked like every Cheape who had ever lived. Finally, we arrived at the library, where the butler bowed us in and disappeared.

The library was a large, rectangular room with 20-foot ceilings. The walls were covered with shelf after shelf of leather-bound volumes. A large stone hearth, in which a cheerful wood fire was burning, took up one end of the room while the opposite wall was made up mostly of arched windows with elaborate leaded mullions, offering wonderful views of the pasture with the Highland cattle and, in the distance, a rocky crag rising high into the pink Scottish twilight. It was a view that would have gotten Turner all hepped up and calling for a canvas and some brushes. In front of the windows was an immense, leather-topped desk, on which sat a large silver tray filled with crystal decanters of every sort of alcoholic beverage.

There were perhaps a dozen people in the room, some sitting on the red leather loveseats near the fire, others standing around chatting, drinks in hand. None of the ladies was dressed in ball gown and tiara, and I felt Mary Jane relax next to me. Sir Hamish saw us and, grabbing a tall, sandy-haired man by the arm, came over to greet us.

"Hello, good people," he said. "Wonderful you could come! Allow me to introduce our host, the Marquess Cheape of Wormwood. Lord Cheape, this is Mr. Hacker and his lovely lady, Miss Mary Jane Cappalletti."

"You are very welcome," Lord Cheape said graciously, shaking my hand. "But please, call me Johnny. I don't go in much for all that lordship business." I put his age at about 50. He had sandy blond hair flecked with gray bits, a nicely tanned face with eyes that crinkled at the corners and was wearing neatly pressed black linen trousers and a blue-and-white striped oxford shirt, open at the neck. He was short, about five-seven, narrow waisted and seemed to exude a sense of gracefulness. I remembered that Sir Hamish had told me that Cheape had once been a semi-professional race-car driver. His grip was firm and his bright blue eyes sparkled. "Did you have any trouble finding the place? I'm afraid that it can be quite confusing once you get off the beaten track a bit."

"Not at all," I said. "The directions were excellent."

Lord Cheape turned to Mary Jane, took her hand and gave her a European-style air-kiss, one on each side of her cheeks.

"Thank you so much for having us," Mary Jane said. "What a lovely home! You must show me around before we leave!"

Lord Cheape smiled a toothy grimace and inclined his head. "Delighted," he said. "Now, what can we get you two to drink? Yuri?"

He looked around as he called out, and a tall, heavyset man with a huge, glistening bald head and dressed all in black—slacks, blazer and open-necked dress shirt, offset by a single strand of braided gold draped around his neck—came forward. I ordered a gin and tonic and Mary Jane asked for a glass of white wine, and Yuri busied himself making the drinks while we went through the usual awkward ritual of telling Lord Cheape where we were from and what we did for a living.

"Ah yes," Lord Cheape said to me. "Cavendish said you were a journalist here to cover the tournament. It should be a cracking good show, eh?"

"I hope so," I said. "The Old Course needs a little help from the weather to keep these guys honest."

"So true, so true," he nodded. "With today's technology and level of athleticism, I'm afraid the old lady is simply no match unless the wind gets up a bit. But fear not…it usually does!"

Yuri came over with our drinks. As I was taking mine, I thought I heard Lord Cheape say to him "spasiba." Yuri replied: "puzhalsta." Utilizing my highly honed sense of investigation, I realized that the huge bald man was a Russian.

"I understand that your family owns the land on which the Old Course is laid out," I said.

"Yes," he nodded. "One of my forebears purchased the land from the town of St. Andrews in 1782. He was the captain of the R&A at the time, and the town sold it to him because it was in dire financial straits. He is said to have saved the course by ejecting dozens of rabbit farmers who had pretty much let their animals roam free across the links, with disastrous results to the turf. By 1821, the land had been fully reclaimed as a golf course, and so it has been ever since."

"Rabbits?" Mary Jane said, eyebrows raised.

"Yes," Lord Cheape nodded. "They were raised both for their fur and their meat."

"Isn't there a bunker on the course named 'Cheape's'?" I asked.

"Very good, sir" he said nodding, with a brief smile. "It lies between the second and 17th fairways. My family also retained the rights, for many decades, to harvest sea shells from the links. Beneath the links, actually. There are great deposits of shells under the ground, left behind by a receding sea over the centuries. This material was used to pave many of the first roads in these parts, as well in the construction of many buildings in the town. I believe the last time we exercised that right was in the 1990s. Took 'em out from beneath the Eden course, if I recall. Of course, the people of the town have always had the rights to use the links land for purposes other than golf, such as exercise, dog-walking, and drying their fishing nets, although I don't believe anyone has done any net drying for many, many years now."

"And I assume you are yourself a member of the Royal & Ancient?" I asked.

Lord Cheape glanced at me with a smile. "Oh, I suppose I am," he said. "But golf is not exactly my game. I am frightfully busy with my overseas interests these days."

I caught a warning glance from Sir Hamish and decided to drop my questions. Mary Jane also caught the glance and picked up the conversational chain.

"Are you married Lord, er, Johnny?" she asked.

He smiled at her. "Not at present," he said. "I have done my duty and created an heir and a spare, but they live in London with their mother and don't seem to care for Scotland all that much."

"Well," Mary Jane said, "It's certainly a lovely house. Are these pictures all of your relatives?"

Lord Cheape took her arm and walked her over to one of the hallway walls filled with portraits, pointing to and describing the history of his various ancestors. Based on the paintings, the Cheapes seemed to prefer high starched collars, gilded swords and hunting dogs the size of small ponies. I thought I could detect a familial trait towards cross-eyedness, but decided not to make mention of it. It could, after all, have been the result of the uncomfortable starched collars. I turned to Sir Hamish.

"Dangerous ground," he whispered to me. "Johnny and the R&A have been at each other for decades now. He doesn't think they respect his ownership rights and they tend to see him as an obstacle to progress and something of an anachronism."

"I guess respect for the landed gentry only extends up to the point where money is being made," I said.

"Quite so, Hacker, quite so," Hamish nodded.

"Drink, gentlemens?" I jumped a little as Yuri, who had suddenly materialized next to my elbow, spoke. I handed him my glass which had somehow gone empty.

"Thank you, Yuri, I think I will have another G&T," I said. "You are from Russia?"

He looked at me expressionlessly as he took my glass with his thick fingers and placed it carefully on a silver tray, his small black eyes peering out at me flatly. "Da," he said finally, with a slight nod. He turned on his heel and glided over to the table where the bottles were waiting. Not a big talker, our Yuri, I thought.

Sir Hamish and I drifted over to the hearth where the other guests had gathered. He introduced me to all of them, and I knew I'd never remember any of their names. One of the men was a horse breeder from Abu Dhabi, another a banker from Zurich. Finally, he came to a tall, distinguished gentleman standing, wine glass in hand, next to the stone hearth. I recognized him immediately.

"This is Dr. Cecil Knox, a professor at the university," Sir Hamish said with the barest bit of twinkle in his eyes. "I thought you two might enjoy meeting each other."

Knox's handshake was firm, and his sharp black eyes blinked several times.

"Oh yes," I said, "You're the anti-golf guy! I saw you at the rally in the quadrangle yesterday. Did you manage to get arrested?"

Knox's head jerked back and his shoulders stiffened. "Unfortunately, the local authorities did not permit us to march as we had wanted," he said, frowning at either my impertinence or the memory of his failed protest. "We were herded like sheep into a park and not permitted to leave. I have registered my complaint with the council." He looked at Sir Hamish and me, trying to see if we were sympathetic. I think he decided we were not. "And I suppose you are a golfer, like Sir Hamish here?"

"Well, yes," I said, "I am. I'm a journalist who covers the game for my newspaper back in Boston. I would love to talk to you about your organization and what it hopes to achieve."

I sensed Mary Jane come up beside me, and I introduced her to the professor, who bowed politely amid one or two more twitches.

"We believe that golf is an utter waste of time and resources," the man began in a deep baritone voice that I could tell had attained its timbre through years of college-hall lecturing. "Furthermore, it despoils the environment, destroying important habitat and deters the use of natural resources from the common good. In short, it is quite an abominable activity."

I was going to congratulate him on his expert use of alliteration—he managed to use the verbs 'despoil,' 'destroy' and 'deter' in one well-wrought sentence—but decided he might not appreciate my native American wit. "But golf seems to be a very popular form of recreation," I said instead. "Especially among people from every economic stratum here in Scotland."

"The people," Knox sniffed, "Often are not aware of the consequences of their activities, nor the deep-seated influence of the overweening patriarchal construct, and therefore need to be educated. We have begun a campaign to let people know exactly how destructive the game is here in their native land."

"But golf is fun!" Mary Jane piped up. "How can you be against people having fun?"

Knox blinked twice and fixed her with a look of pure disdain. "Fun, madam?" he said. "When the very existence of the planet hangs in the balance, you wish to talk about 'fun'? I consider that both irrelevant and irresponsible." He loved his alliteration, our professor.

"So to save the planet, you propose turning every golf course into what?" I asked. "Agriculture? One reason golf cropped up on these coastal links, like the ones here in St. Andrews, is that such land is largely unsuitable for anything else."

"That may be true for crop-based schemes," Knox said, blinking rapidly, "But livestock can and do thrive on the seaside grasses. And some experiments have shown that plant material that could be used for bio-fuels would grow well in these micro-environments. Eliminate Golf has conducted studies that show a transformation of coastal land now being used for golf—we're talking thousands of square hectares—could contribute billions of dollars of new, environmentally friendly enterprises, as well as creating much more space for such development as low-income housing and other much needed infrastructure. Why, just imagine a series of wind turbines right here on the Eden estuary! A field of solar panels! We could probably generate enough electricity to provide all the power needed in all of Fifeshire!"

"And the long history of the game here in St Andrews, not to mention the hundreds of millions of dollars in golf-based tourism jobs in this area? That means nothing?" I pressed.

He shook his head. "History is a modern construct," he said. "It is not something writ in stone, but is fluid and ever-changing. We believe that golf, once eliminated, will quickly be forgotten as the newer and higher use of the resources become evident and more widely accepted."

"'A modern construct?'" I said. "Isn't that academic-speak for something you don't really have a counter-argument for? I mean ..."

I felt Mary Jane's hand on my back as a gentle warning sign. But the butler came in and announced dinner, so my conversation with the professor stopped thankfully short of fisticuffs.

Sir Hamish grabbed my other elbow. "Good show, old chap," he said. "I don't think the good professor has been challenged like that in a long time. His fellow faculty I think tend to either agree with him totally or think him totally mad. Either way, he usually gets no debate."

I shrugged. I was used to conversing with fatuous college professors spouting utter nonsense. Boston has more of them than Augusta National has fast putts.

We followed our host into the adjoining dining room, where a long elegantly set table occupied yet another heavily paneled room bedecked with hunting portraits. I couldn't decide if the paintings were celebrating the aristocratic hunters, dressed to the nines in their shiny black boots, bright red jackets and plumed hats, or the horses and dogs. The dogs looked good, in any case. Better, in most cases, than the bleeding harts riddled with arrows.

Mary Jane and I put Sir Hamish between us as we sat on one side of the huge table, which was covered in white linen and silver candelabras. There was a regal woman dressed in a gold dress to my right. I introduced myself, and she smiled. "You're the journalist, aren't you?" she asked with a smile. I agreed with her. "How terribly interesting," she said. Then she turned back to her companion on the other side and ignored me for the rest of the dinner.

The first course was oxtail soup, a rich dark steamy broth, served with hot, freshly baked rolls. I asked Sir Hamish, *sotto voce*, about Johnny Cheape and his Russian retainer, Yuri.

He shrugged. "I believe Johnny has been doing

quite a bit of business in the new Russia," he said. "Perhaps Yuri is part of some arrangement."

"Lot of you aristos hiring servants from the former Soviet Union?" I asked, tongue in cheek.

He laughed. "I suppose one can get them cheaply," he said. "Perhaps I should look into it."

"So, Mister Hacker," our host's voice boomed out into the room from his place at the head of the table. "I see that you have met our good professor Knox. I take it you disagree with his organization's goals?" Johnny Cheape's lips were drawn into a tight little smile, his head cocked to one side. The room fell silent and everyone at table turned to look at me.

I smiled back at him. "Indeed I do," I said. "But I certainly respect his beliefs and his right to espouse them, however crackpot they may be. But I am curious why Lord Cheape of Wormwood, whose family has such a long and storied connection with golf in this town, would have this heretic to his home for dinner."

My comment hung in the air for a silent and uncomfortable moment. Then the lady to my right giggled, which broke the silence and permitted everyone else to exhale with a titter or a groan. Cheape's lips tightened further and his face grew a shade redder, but he eventually laughed along with everyone else.

"Quite right, Mr. Hacker, quite right," he chuckled. "I suppose in the old days we would take the good professor here out and have him burned at the stake. But I approve of new ideas and debate, like you, even some with which I may not agree. But I hasten to add that I find a great deal of Professor Knox's theories to be quite interesting."

"So you would approve of transforming the Old Course into a wind farm?" I asked.

Cheape laughed, and waved his hand as if brushing off a fly. "Oh, I don't think that's a relevant question for this generation or perhaps for several generations to come," he said. "But we cannot know what will happen in fifty or a hundred years' time. There may indeed come a day when the many of the things we now take for granted are no longer acceptable. There may come a day when golf has run its course and we must begin to marshal our resources for the survival of the planet instead of for recreation."

Lord Cheape looked around the room. I glanced across the table at Professor Knox and saw him nodding earnestly in agreement.

"I think it is reasonable to assume that what we celebrate as sport in this culture at this point in history may one day evolve into something else, or simply disappear," Cheape said. "For example, two thousand years ago this week we might have gathered together to watch a gladiator's combat to the death in the Roman arena, instead of the Open Championship. Five hundred years ago the people in these parts would have attended the burning of a witch or the hanging of a thief for the public recreation of it. It was probably just as inconceivable to the ancients then that their form of recreation and sport would one day completely disappear and be replaced by other forms. But so it has. So I don't think the professor is as, how did you say…oh, yes … as *crackpot* as you might think."

There was a murmur of approval at Cheape's little speech. I wanted to leap upon the man and stab him repeatedly with my salad fork, but I knew that others would look upon that with some displeasure. Not a good construct as the wild-haired, fidgeting professor would say.

The rest of the dinner proceeded without incident, and afterwards we all returned to the library for coffee and brandies. The conversation ran more towards modern-day politics and economics, but just about every man at the dinner eventually made his way over to me, shook my hand and whispered that he much enjoyed the game of golf, was looking forward to the weekend tournament and had I ever met Tiger Woods? Before the night was over, I told my Tiger stories about six times over.

Yuri was busy pouring brandies and whiskeys to the guests. I noticed Mary Jane staring at him while he worked.

"What?" I said to her with a whisper. "You're not thinking that I should go bald are you?"

She smiled and shook her head, but her eyes never stopped watching Yuri as he circulated through the room.

"I've seen him before, somewhere," she said.

"Ah yes," I said. "Must have been that party in Vladivostok. Summer of '03. Everyone was there…Vlad, Boris, Natasha…"

"Shut up, you fool," she hissed. "I think he was driving the car the other night when you were talking to your caddie friend."

I turned and took another look at Yuri's glistening bald head reflecting the overhead chandelier lights in the library.

"I dunno," I said. "I didn't get a good look at anyone other than the guy who went chasing after Swiftie. Never really saw the guy in the car."

Mary Jane shook her head. "I can't be sure it was him, either," she said. "But it could be. And he's been checking you out pretty closely all night."

I shrugged. Swift had said the "Russkis" were after him. Yuri was a Russki. The other guys in the car that night had accents that could be Russki. Might be a clue. But a clue to what? I had no idea.

We made our good-byes at a reasonable hour and Sir Hamish, who was staying at the Cheape mansion, walked us out to our car. We thanked him for the invitation to an interesting dinner.

"Yes, Johnny enjoys having people from different backgrounds to his house," Sir Hamish said, looking back at the great edifice that rose above us. "He likes to pretend its one of those great salons of old."

"I wonder where Professor Knox gets the money for all his anti-golf research," I said. "Perhaps Lord Cheape is a financial backer."

"Johnny?" Sir Hamish was nonplussed. "I'd be surprised if he had much extra to throw around on such crackpot ideas. Unless his business is suddenly doing well. No," he shook his head, "It's more likely that he just had him over to listen to his nonsense and pretend to be interested in his ideas. Next week the guest list might include a steeplechaser, a London banker and a Romanian gypsy.

Mary Jane kissed him goodnight and we made our way back to town. When we got back to our apartment, the television was on and our two roomies were sound asleep in their chairs, mouths open, empty beer cans on the cocktail table, snoring in time to the music coming through the telly. We made enough noise picking up and turning things off to wake them and we all went to bed.

Chapter Twelve

Johnny Swift came to see me bright and early the next morning. Well, in truth, I was still sound asleep at about eight when Mary Jane woke me up with a gentle shake.

"You have company," she said.

"Wha-?" I had been dreaming of playing the Old Course, and was looking at a ten-footer for birdie on the Road Hole after two almost perfect shots. The kind of shots you hit only in your dreams and never while awake and flailing.

"John Swift is here."

I cursed softly to myself—I mean, how many times in a lifetime does one have the opportunity to birdie the 17th at St. Andrews, even if only in a dream?—and threw on some clothes.

Swiftie was sitting in our living room, nursing a steaming cup of coffee and looking pleased with himself. He was still wearing the same dirty blue parka and jeans he had on the other night. His hair was a ridiculous greasy nest in a reddish tangle.

"How in the world did you know where I'm staying?" was my first question.

He smiled enigmatically and placed a finger next to his nose. "There's a lot Johnny Swift knows," he said.

Mary Jane brought me a cup of coffee which I accepted with gratitude. "You should ask him how he managed to break in while we were sleeping," she said. "He was here in the living room when I got up about a half hour ago."

"Breaking and entering?" I was aghast. "John, how could you?"

Swiftie grinned at me. "How could I?" he said. "Hacker, me boy, I learned all about breaking in when I was in the stir. Lotsa experts on the subject there. I just paid me attention."

"But why?" I asked.

He took a sip of his coffee and closed his eyes for a moment in appreciation. I imagined it had been a while since he had had something warm to drink.

"Needed a safe place," he said. "Net's closing in on John Swift. They knows me usual hidey holes. Couldna bring trouble to me friends, now, could I?"

"But you can bring trouble to me?" I said. "Thanks a bunch."

"Nae, nae," he said, smiling again. "They dunna ken that I know ya. Was careful not to be followed. Johnny Swift would nae put his friends in danger."

"Who is 'they?'" I asked. "What's going on?"

"I tole ya…it's the Russkis," he said, shaking his head. "Right vicious lot, they are. They'd like to bash Johnny's head in and go have a cuppa."

I was still confused. My coffee hadn't kicked in yet. Mary Jane came to the rescue.

"Those men the other night at the restaurant," she said. "They seemed to be chasing you. Were they the Russians?"

"Aye, lass," Johnny said, nodding vigorously. "Them's the bloody Russkis want to see Johnny Swift in the grave. Been hot on my trail for coupla weeks now."

"Why?" I said. "What have you done that some steroidal goons want you dead?"

"Ach," Swiftie said, shaking his head sadly, "'Tis a long story, that. Perhaps if your lovely lady can pour me a wee bit more of your excellent coffee, I can find the strength to tell me sorry tale."

Mary Jane brought the pot over and filled his cup. Then she filled mine. I heard a brief stirring from the other bedroom, then a steady chorus of ragged snores resumed. I nodded at Johnny to begin.

"'Bout two months ago, I was called in to see that Kinkaid feller," he said, settling back into his chair. "Y'know...the one from the Links Trust that was later killed? He was the man ya had to see if there was any complaints from the customers over the caddying bit, y'see?"

"Someone complained about you after a round and you had to go see the boss," I said.

"Right you are, Hacker, right you are!" he continued. "It wasn't nuthin' serious-like. I'd had me a double bag, man and his lady. I think they was from the States, though it might have been Canada. Can be hard to tell sometimes. Anyway, he was a right insufferable bastard, thinkin' he knew everythin' about everythin'. Get those types all the time. Ya learn to put up with it, smile a lot, agree with everythin' he says, make him feel like a big deal, which is what he thinks he is anyways. Sometimes you can gie him the wrong club, or read his putt wrong or not look too hard for his bloody lost ball…things like that there. Makes ya feel a wee bit better."

He paused and took another sip of coffee.

"This wanker, though, he started right in on Johnny, he did, tellin' me what to do and where to stand and how to keep the bloody clubs from clinking too much when I walked. Like I'd never carried the clubs before in me entire life! Hah! Well, once he saw that I wasn't a goin' to talk back, just smilin' and noddin' and sayin' nuthin' … he turned on his lady. Started in tellin' her do this, don't do that…everthin' about her was wrong. Mighty unpleasant, he was, and it started to get to her after a while. She was near to cryin' and ya hate to see that."

"I hope you punched him in the nose," Mary Jane said. "He sounds absolutely horrid." She had been making toast in the small kitchen, and brought us a plate of buttered, jellied slices. Swiftie downed two in a flash.

"Nae, lass," Johnnie chuckled. "Wanted to, believe me. But strikin' a customer's somethin' that'll get ya the sack quick as a whistle. Nae…I just suggested that she might do a wee bit better if he let her golf her ball and concentrate on his own. Well, he didna take kindly to my suggestion, but went all dark and red inside. Started cursin' John Swift and tellin' me he'd have me canned and that it'd be a cold day in Hell afore I was caddyin' again on this course. I think he musta forgot he wasn't at his fancy smancy American course any more. But sure as sunset, he stalked off when we was done and complained to the caddiemaster, who sent a note doon to th'office and I had to go see Kinkaid and explain meself. Never gave me a tip, neither. Just a bloody wanker. Ya get those sometimes. World is filled with 'em."

He stopped and ate another piece of toast.

"So's I goes to see Kinkaid few days later and I'm sittin' in his fancy office over at the Trust and I'm tellin' him the story. He's noddin' and smilin' and writin' things down in his notebook. I'm figurin' he'll be tellin' me to go and sin no more like he's always done afore. Kinkaid was kind of a funny fellow."

"How do you mean, funny?" I asked.

"Well, he was a bit of a toff, truth be told," Johnny said, stroking his fuzzy chin. "Most of the lads been called down like me from time to time…it's like an occupational hazard innit? …and he was always fair to most. I mean, ya show up for work with a snoot full, or you be cursin' out loud or such and he'd drop the hammer on ya sure enough. I mean, rules is rules, yeah? You break one, you pay the piper. But Kincaid'd hear your side and most of the time, he'd just send ya away with a warning and tell ya not to let it happen again."

"What's a toff?" Mary Jane asked.

"Like someone thinks he's a better sort of person than you," Johnny said, nodding at Mary Jane. "Has some airs, ya know? Prolly went to university and such. Looks down his nose at us poor bastards what gotta actually work for a livin', ya know? He was a fair man, Kinkaid was, but you always had the feelin' he was like talkin' down at ya, y'know? Like he thinks his shite don't stink but he knows that yours does. Regular toff, he was. May he rest in peace, of course."

"Of course," I said. "So what happened that day? When you went to see the toff."

"Oh, aye," Johnny said, shaking his head. "I do tend to wander off the path a bit, don't I? Well, like I was sayin', I'm sittin' there in Kinkaid's fancy office tellin' him about the chappie and his woman, and sudden like the door busts open and these Russkis burst in."

"How'd you know they were Russian?" I asked.

"Well, at the time, I didn't," he said. "So Kinkaid stands up and goes all white an' all and yells at them to get the hell out of his office."

"How many were there?" Mary Jane asked.

"Two of 'em," Johnny answered, looking at her. "Big blokes they were, dressed all in black. One of 'em was bald as a baby."

"What happened then?" I asked.

"Well, Kinkaid looks at me and says something to them that I didn't quite hear. And one of the blokes turns to me and gives me the thumb—" he motioned with his own hand—"Tells me to git on outta there. Well, I musta smarted off to him or sumpthin' 'cause the next thing I know I'm slammed up agin the wall and then tossed right oot the door! By the very scruff of me neck!"

Johnny looked at Mary Jane and I in turn, his face serious with an expression that said 'can you believe that?!?'

"An' I look at Kinkaid's secretary and she looks at me and I goes 'Can you bloody believe that?' and she goes 'I'm callin' security or the constables' or somethin' and I goes 'I'm bloody outta here!' and I skedaddle." He looked at me. "I try to stay as far away from the constables as is possible," he said.

"But how did you know the two guys were Russian?" Mary Jane asked. "Did they speak in Russian?"

"Nae, lass, nae," Johnny said. "It was the next night, or the one after, me head's not rememberin' so well, when I was down to Dunvegan's with a nice bunch o' blokes who were standin' me a drink—just a cola, not any of th'drink…I don' do the drink. And Jackie, who tends the pub there, leaned over and told me that two Russian gents had been in earlier askin' 'bout me. 'What fer?' I wanted t'know and he says 'I dunno lad.' Just that they was lookin' for Johnny Swift and they was big Russian fellers, one of 'em bald as a cue ball. When I heard that, I knew somethin' was up and I went to ground. Nobody can hide in this toon better than Johnny Swift, and I'd like to meet the man who thinks he can find me when I don't want to be found."

Mary Jane and I exchanged glances.

"Now John," I said. "First of all, just because some Russkis want to see you doesn't mean you're in trouble. Maybe they just want to hire you as their caddie. There's gotta be a good reason for all this. I don't see why you're on the run."

"Oh you don't don't ya?" he replied hotly. "Well it wasn't but another week or two later that Colin Kinkaid turned up dead as a mackerel, tossed down into the Bottle Dungeon. And I for one do not intend to wait around and suffer the same fate as that poor bugger."

He shook his head sadly. Then a thought occurred to him, and Mary Jane and I could almost see the light bulb go on above his tangled head of hair.

"I jest remembered somethin', Hacker," he said, snapping his fingers. "When I came flyin' out the door of Kincaid's office, there was another bloke waiting to go in and see the man. I'd forgotten all about him until just this minute. You might know the lad, he's one of yours."

"An American?" I asked.

"Aye, he's that Yank what's come to the toon to live like a Scot," Johnny said. "Dunno his name, but he said he wants to write a book like."

"Morton?" I asked. "Mike Morton?"

"Aye," he said, nodding. "That's' the one. Seen him around toon now and agin. People say he's been havin' a time of it."

"How so?"

"Well," he said, "The word is he's a wee bit hard up against it, currency ways. When he first came over last winter, he was stayin' in one of those fancy places in Hamilton Hall. Y'know the place, right? Used to be a dorm for the students and then some Yank with millions came over and is tryin' to fix the place up all luxury and such…sell the flats for millions."

I knew what he was talking about. The five-story red-brick building with its distinctive turrets sat on Golf Place just behind the 18th green of the Old Course. Some developer had purchased the property and sank millions into stripping it bare inside and building it out as fancy condos for visiting golfers. I hadn't heard how sales had gone, but found it hard to believe that anyone would buy a vacation home in this Auld Grey Toon known for its cold fog and sideways rain, even if they were golf aficionados. Especially a vacation home costing three or four million dollars. Then again, the ways of rich people are mostly a mystery to me.

"He's not living there now?" I asked Johnny.

"Nae, nae," he said, shaking his head sadly. "Heard that he was supposed to bring in some rich people as customers, but never did. So they gave him the boot. He's livin' now in a small flat by the canal. And lookin' for another job. Maybe that's why he was waiting outside Kincaid's office that day. I dunno."

I stood up. "Okay, that's interesting and all, but it doesn't get back to why these Russian fellows are supposedly chasing you all over town," I said. "Maybe we should go find them and just ask what the hell they want."

I had some other good advice to give him, but just at that moment we heard a loud bang from the hallway behind us followed by a loud profanity. Moments later, Mario staggered out into the lounge, sleep disheveled, rubbing his knee and limping slightly. "I've run into that dresser three mornings in a row, for Chrissakes. You'd think I'd remember it was there, but noooo..."

His voice tailed off. Mary Jane and I had turned back from his noisy entrance and were now staring at the chair where Johnny Swift had been sitting. It was empty. He had skedaddled. Again.

Chapter Thirteen

WEDNESDAY AT A major is always one of the busiest days of the week, for the media, anyway. While some of the players like to play a full practice round in a final dress rehearsal, others opt just for a quick nine, mainly to see if the weather has changed the way the course is playing. Others don't go out on the course at all, but just spend an hour or two on the range and the putting green. It can be a challenge finding someone to chase around for a last-minute quote.

But we usually don't have to do much chasing. As at the other major tournaments, the Royal & Ancient parades player after player into the media room to tell the press how they feel, how they see the tournament unfolding, how the course is playing … all the mindless chatter that means less than nothing, but which the press will play up in the next day's papers as big news.

Colin Montgomerie, as senior Scot in the field, did his thirty minute appearance in the press tent, and was as forthcoming and gracious as he usually is. He explained patiently, not for the first time, that not having won a major championship in his career was certainly a disappointment, but hardly the end of the world; and that his overall record as a professional golfer was one that he was proud to own. "Winning majors is hard," he said with a wry grin. "If it was easy, I would have done it years ago!" Perhaps his fate is to be the best player never to win a major; but even that, in a warped way, could be counted as something of an accomplishment.

The parade of players continued through the early afternoon. We heard from Sergio Garcia, Rory McIlroy, Adam Scott, Francesco Molinari, Louis Oosthuizen. The idea that golf is truly an international game was never more evident than at The Open.

I had finally had enough of listening to their platitudes, none of which were going to write my pre-game column that was due in a few hours. I decided to walk over to the range and see what was going on there. At St. Andrews, the practice range is set up on the other side of the visitor's clubhouse, a few hundred yards from the first tee, over where the road curves around the West Sands.

But as I came out of the media tent, I noticed a crowd gathered around the first tee, and wandered over to see what was going on. Padraig Harrington, the great Irish star, had just hit his tee shot on the first hole, and there was raucous applause and cheers from the gallery, most of whom seemed to be comprised of his countrymen. Harrington grinned his lopsided Irish grin and knocked knuckles with another player who stepped forward to play.

This player was much younger than the veteran Harrington. His red-tinged hair was longish down the back and his ruddy cheeks had that downy look of youth.

He gave Padraig a wide, toothy grin and said something we couldn't hear, but it made Harrington laugh. Then his face got serious, his eyes narrowed and after teeing his ball, he stood behind it and stared with concentration down the fairway.

"C'mon, Conor lad," someone shouted from the crowd. "Show 'im what y' got!" Others immediately hushed the man, but the golfer, who I now knew was the young up-and-coming player Conor Kelly, never wavered. He waggled his club, took up his stance, cast one final glance down the target line and then made a long and graceful swing, his body recoiling in the classic reverse-C shape that young golfers can get away with before their backs become too old and stiff.

Kelly's supporters in the crowd reacted with pleasure, barking out their cheers. Harrington came over and patted his younger countryman on the back and they set off side-by-side down the fairway, their caddies trailing in their wake, hefting their large bags filled with rattling clubs, and the fans cheering as they went.

I decided to follow them for a few holes and watch the fun. I had never seen Conor Kelly play in person, but had heard his name tossed around as a future star. And with the large Irish community back home in Boston, it occurred to me that a piece on this up-and-coming young golfer might go down well.

There have been enough words written about the Old Course at St. Andrews to fill the Encyclopedia Britannica and then some, and I don't think the lot of them come close to describing what that golf course is like. When you try to strip away the mystique and history of the place, you end up with what sounds pretty boring: a course which they really have to strain to stretch out to 7,000 yards, one that is basically flat and featureless, with its huge greens its most unusual feature. Of mild interest are the wide double fairways and double greens on all but four holes. Sure, there are bunkers all over the place, including many that you can't see, but most of them are concentrated down the left side, both going out and coming home, so a golfer who can hit a reasonably straight tee ball, control his distance with his irons and sink a few putts should be able to get round the place without too much trouble. Especially those who are good enough to embroider their names on the sides of their golf bags.

But that's just the first trap the golf course lays for the unwary golfer who steps out on it. Doesn't look like much, but it always plays much harder than it looks. Always. Yes, it looks flat and featureless, but it isn't. The ground is actually as varied and uneven as the surface of the North Sea on the far side of the dunes. These infinitesimal humps and hollows can toss a golf ball one way or another, often right into the welcoming pit of a deep, sod-faced bunker. And even if the ball stays on the turf, rare is the lie that is flat: the ball is always a bit above the feet, or below them, or the lie is uphill or down, sometimes by a lot, but often by just a little. That total lack of consistency has the effect of making every shot…*every shot*…a challenge that requires thought, recognition, and adjustment.

The putting greens are just as tricky as the fairways. Never mind the occasionally massive 100-foot putt that a golfer will face on those huge double greens, or some of those steep sweeping upslopes of six or seven feet a putt must sometimes climb before sweeping back downhill towards the hole…it is the five-footers to save par, or worse, putts that look flat but aren't, that will drive most golfers completely around the bend. And not even the caddies who've walked the ground for sixty years can always find the right line on those greens.

Now, add in the vagaries of the weather; the constant breezes, winds and gales that can whip in off the sea and then change with the tide to blow entirely the other direction in a second's time. It is a very real possibility that one can tee off in bright sunshine, encounter rain, sleet, hail and wind along the way, and finish again in the same bright sun. The temperature changes from hole to hole, especially, for some unknown reason, around the Loop holes at the far end of the course, where the sudden damp cold will take a crucial five yards of distance off a shot and drop your ball into the soft sand of a waiting bunker. I'd like some of those so-called climate scientists to stop making up their temperature data and spend a year or two on this one square mile of ground tucked between the Eden Estuary and the North Sea and try to explain to us exactly what the hell is going on.

Take all those factors and then add in the history of this place where golf has been played for more than 600 years; a course upon which every great golf champion has walked; where if one's hands do not get sweaty and one's mouth does not get dry, then one must wonder if they are really human and alive. Or really a golfer. Given all that, it's not too hard to understand how the young Bobby Jones, as genial and even-tempered a golfer as ever lived, could have been driven, during the first tournament he ever played on the Old Course, to tear up his scorecard in frustration on the short eleventh hole and walk off. It's such an easy, open, flat, outwardly expressionless and dull seeming golf course, he must have thought, and *I can't lick this thing*! He eventually learned how to lick it. Or at least how to read its many moods and wrestle it into occasional submission.

The first hole, on which Padraig Harrington and Conor Kelly now walked, is the perfect example of the mystery that the Old Course represents. It's a simple par-four opener, just 370 or so yards; for the pros and even for most amateurs, a simple drive and a wedge. The fairway, shared with the incoming 18th, is huge, wider than the landing deck on an aircraft carrier. Granny Clark's Wynd, the paved public roadway that leads from the town out to the beach, bisects the fairway and the only hazard on the hole is the narrow Swilcan Burn, the stoned-in creek which snakes underneath the small, Roman-built arched-stone bridge on the 18th-hole side of the fairway and curls temptingly around the front edge of the first green. But there is something about that muddy little burn, the perspective it presents to those playing the hole, or, as I believe, some unknown metaphysical force that plays tricks with the distance, or the eye, or the mind, and sucks many a ball into is murky, slimy depths.

In any case, both Irishmen safely crossed the burn and reached the green with their soft wedge approaches and both made pars.

The second hole begins the long straight march out to the River Eden. The tee is set a slight angle to the fairway, but only the single gaping maw of Cheape's bunker worries the big hitters who can usually bomb the ball down the left side. Harrington played a safe three-wood into the fairway, but Kelly, who like most young players these days boasted prodigious length, uncorked his usual huge drive and, when he arrived down the fairway after it, found he had rolled into the front of the dreaded Cheape's. Harrington made an easy four,

Kelly came up short and had to chip over the ridge that protects the front of the green and made a predicable five. The old man was one-up.

Holes three and four are also par fours, the first a short one, the second a bit longer. Both players made routine pars on both boles. On the long fifth, Kelly slashed his drive miles down the fairway, hit a controlled three-iron into the green and sank a lovely forty-footer for an eagle. All square. The crowd following the two hooted their approval.

On six, called "Heathery," Harrington again opted for a safer three-wood on the blind tee shot over the gorse-covered hill, while Kelly's cannoned driver went left and he again found a bunker and made bogey. On the seventh, it was Harrington's turn in the sand, as his approach shot wasn't struck with his usual precision and it dropped against the sod-faced wall of the humongous Shell bunker, a battleship-sized bastard. He tried to chop the ball out straight at the hole, but it thudded into the sod halfway up the face and dropped back down. He grinned, aimed away from the hole to give himself a better angle and got safely out. But he lost the hole.

The wind had freshened as they reached the eighth tee, and both players had to hit five-irons into its teeth on the short par three. The green on this hole tilts away from the tee, and both balls hit the hard green and bounced over the back. But both Irishmen chipped up close and made their pars.

I decided to wait for the match to make the Loop. Nine and ten are side-by-side flat and shortish par-fours and depending on the wind speed and direction, either green can be reached from the tee with a good, solid smack. Of course, as with every other hole on this hellish golf course, a shot slightly off-line or mis-hit can easily carom off into the waiting arms of a bunker, and what had appeared to be a relatively simple hole suddenly becomes a fight to the death for par. While the two golfers and the good-sized crowd continued on, I walked over to the eleventh/seventh green, one of the more severely sloping on the course, protected by a very nasty pot bunker called Strath in the front, and another deep one called Hill to the left. At the ridge behind the par-three green, you finally get a view of the muddy flats where the River Eden spills into the sea. Across the water to the north are the runways of RAF Leuchars, from which fighter jets are often roaring off on patrol. The hole is called High, probably because of the views from this ridge in the back.

I could see the two Irish golfers and the crowd following them as they moved away down the ninth. I turned instead and admired the view to the north, where the purple Grampians begin to rise in Aberdeenshire, away beyond the River Tay, and then turned to study some of the die-hard fans who had come out this afternoon to watch the golfers passing through. A number had gathered around the ropes of the eleventh green—it's always a fun hole for spectators: birdies are rare, pars are hard-won and there's always a good chance someone will shoot a nasty five or six.

I noticed someone else waiting at the high back edge of the green near me. He looked familiar for some reason, and I did a double-take. Conrad Gold was standing there, looking down the flat plain of the ninth and tenth fairways through an expensive-looking pair of binoculars. He was wearing a sleeveless down jacket over a navy blue sweater and a pair of grey flannel trousers, and a woolen Scottish cap protected his famously hairless head. His grounds pass, the ticket that everyone at a golf tournament wears, was tied to his belt and fluttering in the steady breeze.

I walked over, introduced myself and told him I had been one of the American invitees at his grand opening extravaganza some years before.

"Ah," he said, nodding and sticking out a hand for me to shake. "Yes, that was quite the thing, was it not? Imagine you got a good story that day, eh? Imagine everyone had a good laugh at my expense."

"Actually," I said, "I always thought the Links Trust were the ones who made the mistake. What would it have hurt for them to budge a little?"

He looked at me sideways to see if I was being honest. "Off the record?" he said. I nodded. He continued. "The story that I had not cleared the match with the Trust was a total fabrication," he said. "I had personally arranged all the details and been assured that Mr. Woods and Mr. Garcia would be most welcome to play the course that afternoon."

"What happened?" I asked.

"It was that dreadful Kincaid fellow," he said. "He was the one person with whom I had made all the arrangements, and he was the one who announced that there would be no match that day."

"Why would he do that?"

Gold looked through his glasses at the far-off crowd, now gathered around the ninth green. "He had called me two days before the match was scheduled," he said. "Told me there would be a supplemental fee, payable to him. In cash."

"He held you up for money?" I was astounded. "That's incredible!"

Gold nodded. “Indeed,” he said. “Rather tawdry, no? I don’t remember how much he wanted. It wasn’t the amount that offended me, it was the principal of the thing. I mean, I’ve paid off many an official over the years to get one of my hotels built. It’s all part of the game, isn’t it? But this was different somehow. I mean, the Old Course is a public treasure. It’s owned by the bloody people, for goodness sake! So I told him where he could stuff it. Then I forgot about the whole thing. That was my big mistake. I should have reported him at once to Alistair Thorndyke, who at the time was the chairman of the Trust. But I was busy with a thousand last-minute details in preparation for the hotel opening, and that gave Kincaid time to cover his tracks and make it seem like he and I had never had the first conversation. By the time the day of the match arrived, Kincaid had been able to convince Thorndyke that I was trying to pull a fast one, and Alistair had no choice but to back his own man.”

“Good God,” I said. “Is that why the police thought you might have been the one to kill the man?”

“Oh, I’m sure,” the man agreed. “After the embarrassment of that debacle, it was well known that Kincaid and I were mortal enemies. I told him to his face that I would one day get even with him.”

“Did you?”

He smiled, a rueful smile. “Other than forbidding his execrable presence in my hotel, I’m afraid not,” he said. “I was not the one who killed him, although I certainly salute the man who did. Good day to you, sir.” He nodded at me pleasantly and walked off, losing himself quickly in the crowd of people beginning to gather around the green.

The friendly match between the Irishmen had now finished the tenth hole and they were walking over to the eleventh tee. But I had suddenly lost interest in the game. I began the long walk back following the seven holes that led straight back towards the town.

Chapter Fourteen

I WROTE UP a nice piece about Conor Kelly, the up-and-coming Irish boy wonder, sent it off to Boston through the Internet tubes and made it back to the apartment about six. Mary Jane and my two roommates were sitting around in the lounge, listlessly watching the BBC news on the telly. After a few minutes, I realized that British television news closely resembles American television news. It was filled mostly with stories about someone murdering someone else followed by a discussion of the days events dumbed down to the lowest possible intellectual denominator. Parliament, it seemed, was in an uproar because the Prime Minister had spoken rudely to some woman in the opposition party.

"Must be a slow news day," I said.

"Naw," Mario said, "It's pretty much like this every night."

"What do we have on tap for dinner?" I asked. I looked at Mary Jane, but she frowned.

"Don't look at me," she said. "I spent all day wandering through town. I even climbed St Rule's Tower. It's 188 steps. I'm beat and I'm not cooking." She wasn't whining, really, but all of us could tell she meant it.

"We could go to the U.S.G.A.'s shindig," Mario offered. "They usually have heavy hors d'oeuvres. Bet we could find enough to eat to tide us over."

"Where is it?" I said.

"That fancy hotel....Conrad Gold's Emporium for Very Rich People," Mario said.

"Cool," I said. "I just had an interesting chat out on the course with His Baldness, Sir Conrad The Great, Just Ask Me."

"Damn," Mary Jane said. "That means he's probably gonna get murdered. Let's go before that ruins the party and they take all the food away." My roommates chuckled.

"It's true, Hacker," Mario said, shaking his head. "Knowing you can be an occupational hazard."

I flipped them all a bird and went to change clothes.

For most of the world, the four major golf tournaments are interesting spectator events where the world's most accomplished golfers get together and see who the best is that week. But for the insiders of the game of golf, each major is like a business convention. Whether it's at Augusta National, the U.S. or British Opens or the PGA Championship, all the grandees of the game get together, swig down a few dozen bottles of champagne and single malt, smoke some expensive cigars, slap each other on the back, tell a few dirty jokes, rehearse the secret handshake, and otherwise do whatever it is golf administrators and rules mavens do. In fact, the Rules

Committees of the R&A and the USGA schedule their annual meetings during the Open Championship, so they can get together and discuss whether or not a golfer is entitled to relief if his ball lands in a wasp's nest being attacked by a hawk during a solar eclipse. To me, it has always sounded like a good excuse to have the company fly a bunch of dodderers over the pond so they can play some golf, drink a lot of whiskey and pretend to work. Most of the decisions on the rules they come up with only reinforces my belief.

Because these conventioneers get together four times a year, they don't need any of those "Hello My Name Is _____" sticky things on their lapels. They know each other very, very well. Many of them sit on each other's corporate boards. They play at each other's clubs. They probably boink each other's wives. Or husbands, as at least some of the American golf organizations are beginning to admit the female gender (and perhaps some of the other apparently endless varieties) to the inner circle. And one always wonders about the Brits in any case.

So the U.S. Golf Association was throwing its traditional Night Before reception at the Open Championship, and I knew there would be at least one blue-blazered old fart standing around who would be able to tell you that this was the hundred-and-somethingth consecutive time that the American organization had hosted its British and international counterparts for a little pre-game soiree, not counting the War years, of course, when we were more interested in blowing each other's heads off. The R&A sends its white-haired, pink-cheeked geriatrics over to the Masters and the U.S. Open, and there are regular rounds of parties for bigwigs all week long at the PGA.

Even though Mario Cassio was an Italian boy from the Bronx, as the golf writer for the New York *Daily News* he had more occasion than the rest of us to suck up to the blue-bloods from Golf House, the USGA headquarters located in nearby New Jersey, and thus had managed to snag an invite to their party. The four of us waited until a half-hour after the party began in order to allow the drinks to begin flowing before we crashed it. It usually doesn't take too long for the USGA guys to get in their cups and forget who they invited and who they didn't. Not that they care that much anyway: the organization is swimming in money, most of it old, East Coastal and heavily invested in tax-free municipals. We all piled into my car and I made the short drive to the outskirts of the city center, where Conrad Gold had purchased and renovated his elegant hotel. Like most of the grand houses in St. Andrews, it had originally been built by an 18th century merchant who had tried to out-do his neighbors in elegance and style. And, as with most of the other grand houses of that era, it had eventually become much too expensive to keep up as a single-family home, if not for the original builder, then certainly for the generations that came after him. Some of these grand old white elephants had been torn down, or burned; others had been taken over by the local council government as offices or hospitals or schools; still others had just rotted away, empty and unloved. *Sic transit gloria.*

Gold had been lucky enough to find one that was still in use and therefore somewhat cared for. It's last use had been as a private boys academy, but at least they had kept the roof in good order, so the interior, even though it had been converted into dormitory rooms and classrooms, was still dry, solid and rot-free.

The renovation of the school into the Gold Standard Resort at St. Andrews luxury hotel had been expensive, but without the house's good bones, it would have been impossible.

The Dundee merchant's exterior decorations, the elaborate stone carvings, arches and vaulted groins had all survived the rise and fall of the markets, comings and goings of wars, the passing of the decades and the lashing and stresses of the weather in the Kingdom of Fife and all that stonework gave the place a somewhat Gothic but still substantial appearance from the outside.

We pulled into the gravel car park, set off to one side of the main house in what appeared to have once been the stable area, around eight o'clock. In the long and lingering twilight of the Scottish summer, it was still quite bright outside, but the hotel's dramatic façade was illuminated with upsweeping floods which cast shadows that made all the windows look like eye sockets.

"Who wants to bet this place has some hunchback named Igor working in the basement?" asked Brad. As would any self-respecting movie fan, he pronounced it "Eye-Gore" in homage to Mel Brooks.

"I don't know about that," Mary Jane said. "But I'll bet Hacker's new best friend Sir Hamish Cavendish is here tonight. This looks like his kind of hangout."

"Oh, I say, Hacker, old chap," Mario said in his worst British accent, "Have we become friendly with the local aristocracy and all that? What ho. Jolly good. Tut, tut."

"Go ahead and make fun," I said. "But the man makes a whiskey that's to die for. Good to know people who can do that."

The concierge inside the elegantly appointed lobby pointed us to the courtyard in the back—he actually called it *the palazzo*—and we walked through the large, 15-foot French doors, across a terra-cotta floored porch and down the marble steps to a sunken formal garden. White marble balustrades surrounded the space, enveloped by the twin wings of the hotel building and pebbled walks bordered by low boxwood hedges bisected the gardens, which featured lovely sculpted marble fauns and satyrs, each dramatically floodlit from beneath. In the center of the garden a round fountain featured a large grimacing marble Neptune holding a pair of water-spouting fish in his arms. Neptune did not look happy holding his spitting fish, and I can't say that I blamed him.

A waiter dressed in starched white shirt and apron came by carrying a silver tray filled with flutes of champagne, and we all took one without the first feeling of guilt. Mario pointed off to one side where a white tent was filled with mingling guests sampling the buffet line. We nodded, and, so that we didn't look too obvious as freeloaders, Brad and Mario headed over to check it out while Mary Jane and I, champagne in hand, strolled with the other guests through the fragrant gardens under the pleasant evening sky. A harpist and a violinist were playing something Chopinesque from the back porch and the notes drifted across the soft evening air.

"So this is how the other half lives, huh?" Mary Jane said, sipping delicately from her crystal flute.

"I would say the other one percent," I said. "I don't think anywhere near half the people in the world live like this. Certainly nobody I know does."

"Do you feel guilty?" she asked. "Like we're trespassing at someone's party? I mean, what if this was someone's wedding, someone we didn't know? Would you still drink their champagne and eat their food?"

I thought about it for a minute. "No," I said, "I don't think I would. Because that would be much more of a blatant act of stealing. Knowingly drinking the wine of someone you don't know is like larceny."

"But we really don't know the person or persons who are paying for this wine," she said. She looked at me with a small smile, but I could see in her eyes that she was quite serious. "Why are we not stealing now?"

"Well, we know that the party is being thrown by the U.S. Golf Association," I said. "They are entertaining people from around the world of golf. Even though you and I were not, strictly speaking, *invited*, as a golf writer for a major metropolitan daily newspaper, I am part of the world of golf, as are Mario and Brad, who were invited. By covering golf and writing about it, we are promoting the sport, which is what the USGA wants us to do. The more people who play the game, the more the USGA stands to benefit, financially and otherwise. So you can easily make the case that my being here is in fact *compensation* for my many years of service promoting the game of golf to the readers of the Boston *Journal*. They owe me this drink, and the little munchies I am about to consume. So no, I do not feel guilty in the least."

"I see," she said.

"But you, on the other hand, are a freeloader of the first resort, and I'm afraid I'm going to have to turn you in to the hors d'oeurve police."

She laughed and bumped her hip against mine affectionately. "I don't suppose there's any way I can talk you out of that, is there?" she said, a sudden mischievous glint in her eye.

I bumped her back. "Well," I said, "Since I've already demonstrated how my moral compass exists on a sliding scale, I am sure we can work something out to our mutual satisfaction."

"Huh," she said. "That's what they all say. I think men's definition of mutual satisfaction is often on a sliding scale with the truth."

I was about to point out that she hadn't seemed to have had any complaints about satisfaction the last time, when I caught sight of a familiar figure across the garden. "You were right," I said, nodding. "There's Sir Hamish. Shall we?"

She followed my eyes, saw Sir Hamish and smiled. "Lead on, MacDuff," she said.

Chapter Fifteen

"DEAR BOY," SIR Hamish said when he saw us, "I had hoped to see you here tonight. And I'm so glad your lovely lady is with you. How are you, my dear? You look ravishing."

"I do declare I'm blushing," Mary Jane said in her best Scarlett O'Hara voice.

"And it makes you even lovelier," he said, kissing her hand. That made her blush for real.

Sir Hamish looked around the party. "I was just talking with someone I thought you should meet," he said. "Ah, there he is." He motioned to a man standing near one of the marble fauns in a corner of the garden. He was wearing a dark blue uniform with epaulets on his shoulders, brass buttons and a row of ribboned decoration on his chest and he held a brimmed hat under his arm, with a distinctive black-and-white checked band. We walked over. He was a shade under six feet tall and had close-cropped hair that was dark on top and silvery along the sides. His jaw was square and his eyes small and inquisitive, peering at us as we approached.

Sir Hamish made the introductions. "Hacker, this is Deputy Chief Constable Wallace," he said. "DCC Wallace, may I present Mr. Hacker, a journalist from the States. And this is his lovely lady, Mary Jane." We all shook hands. "DCC Wallace is in charge of the investigation into the murder of Colin Kincaid," Sir Hamish told me. "And Hacker here has a reputation as something of a sleuth in the States."

I smiled at the man. He didn't return it. "Wallace?" I said. "Your first name isn't William is it?"

That got a bit of a rise at the corner of his mouth. "No," he said, "Andrew. I don't believe I am related to the gentleman, except of course through some unknown ancestral connection. Terrible film, by the way. Historically, it was complete crap."

Mary Jane looked confused. "*Braveheart*," I told her. "Mel Gibson."

She got it. "Free-dom," she said, nodding.

I turned back to Wallace. "I assume you're a golfer, or you wouldn't be here," I said.

"Not a good one, I'm afraid," he said. "But I'm here officially as a representative of the constabulary. We do lay on some extra men for the Open. Security and all that. Part of the job these days."

"How is the Kincaid investigation going?" I asked. "I take it Conrad Gold is no longer a suspect. It would be a little awkward for you to attend a party here if you thought he was the killer."

Deputy Chief Constable Wallace didn't bat an eye. "Mister Gold was himself not in the country on the night that Kincaid was murdered," he said. "But he is also a man with considerable resources, and he has freely admitted that he had a history with the victim of the crime. The investigation is ongoing."

"And there are no suspects yet?"

He looked at me with the blank level gaze that police brass the world over have down so well. It gave nothing away, save a very slight impression of contempt towards the question, or perhaps for the questioner.

"I am not at liberty to say," he said.

I shrugged. DCC Wallace had gone into full clam mode, snapped shut and closed for the duration.

Mary Jane came to the rescue.

"Chief," she began, peering up at him with her full 1000-watt smile, "I was wondering. Is there a big problem here in Scotland with organized crime gangs from Russia? I've read somewhere that they are moving aggressively into many parts of Europe."

He looked into her pretty face and his blank gaze softened just a tad. He inclined his head toward her.

"Quite right, my dear," he said, nodding. "The bratva gangs have indeed moved into most major urban areas, both on the Continent and here in the U.K. They have taken over large segments of organized crime activities, including the heroin trade, gun smuggling and prostitution. They are ruthless, determined and have no respect for the sanctity of life or for the law. My colleagues in Edinburgh and Glasgow have had their hands full over the last five years or more. But no, m'dear, I have seen no indications of the presence of such activities here in Fifeshire. We are still mainly a rural county and our major crime problems tend to run to youth gangs in the housing estates, public drunkenness and a bit of cannabis use."

"So there's no reason to believe that Johnny Swift is being chased by some Russian gangs like he says," I said.

Wallace started, his high-ranking copper's reserve momentarily shattered.

"How do you know John Swift?" he asked, eyebrows knitted and worry creases etched across his forehead.

"I've known Swiftie for years," I told the man. "He's caddied for me many a time on the Old Course. And right now he's told me he's gone into hiding because he thinks some Russians are after him. He thinks it's somehow related to the Kincaid murder since he was one of the last ones to see Colin Kincaid alive."

I could tell Deputy Chief Constable Wallace was rocked.

Mary Jane piped in. "You'll have to forgive Hacker, Chief Wallace," she said. "He's supposed to be this mild-mannered golf writer for the Boston *Journal*, but he's always getting caught up in these murder cases. It's uncanny how it happens, really."

He looked at me with interest. "Indeed?" he said. "I've known constables that always seem to be the ones that are on duty when the messy cases are called in."

I nodded. "Yeah," I said, "The Boston cops call them the Blood Catchers. Not so hard to understand, really. They're just the ones assigned to patrol the housing projects and the places where bodies tend to pile up."

Wallace looked at me again.

"I used to cover the police beat until I switched over to sports and golf," I explained.

"Where one would not expect that many bodies to pile up," he said, this time with a slight smile.

"I know," I said. "Unless you count all those that Tiger has vanquished over the last ten years."

He nodded knowingly. "Quite so," he said. "Who was it who said that sports is like war but without the killing?"

"I believe it was Ted Turner," I said.

"The sailor?" Wallace was surprised.

"And the TV magnate," I said, nodding. "Known more for marrying Jane Fonda than for his philosophical wisdom."

"Indeed." The policeman paused, thinking. "We are aware that Mr. Swift had an appointment with Kincaid a few days before he was murdered," he said slowly, trying not to divulge any secrets but obviously wanting some information. "And we've been trying to locate the gentleman. He's a bit of a known tippler, but we believe he will surface soon. He's got to come up for air eventually."

"I'll tell him you said so," I said.

"You've seen him then?" The constable's voice was suddenly sharp. "We should want to know of any contact you have with the man."

I shrugged. "He dropped in suddenly the other morning," I said. "And then he dropped back out again. If I see him again I'd be happy to tell him you are looking for him. He might even welcome a bit of police protection. Though from what you say, he may be deluded in thinking some Russians are after him."

"We would be very interested in talking with him," Wallace said. "Very."

I nodded: message received. "By the way," I said, remembering something. "Did you find out what Mike Morton was seeing Colin Kincaid about?"

DCC Wallace was good, but I saw his eyebrows shoot up perceptibly at my question. "You are quite the sleuth, aren't you Mister Hacker?" he said. "Morton told us that he had an appointment to discuss an employment opportunity with Mr. Kincaid."

"Doing what?" I asked.

"Some kind of special writing project," Wallace said. "Morton said that Kincaid had been interested in sponsoring some kind of booklet or article about the history of the Links Trust, but had decided that the budget would not allow for it this fiscal year. He said Kincaid had agreed to put in for the funding for next year, and they had agreed to wait to proceed until the funds were available."

"Did they actually have the meeting?" I asked. "Because from what Swiftie told me, it sounded like the two big galoots wanted to take Kincaid out for a long ride somewhere, if you get my drift."

"Yes, well … no," Wallace stammered. "Morton said that Kincaid apologized and asked if he could come in the following week. And then he did leave with the two Russian gentlemen."

"Do you know where?" I asked. "Or who these guys were?"

"I cannot comment further," Wallace said. "The investigation continues."

"I understand," I said, understanding mainly that Wallace wasn't going to give me anything further. "I still would like to know why Kincaid was meeting with two Russians. There's no reason why someone in the Links Trust would have anything to talk about with some Russians."

"Unless he's in the oil business," Sir Hamish said suddenly. He had been standing next to Mary Jane, listening to our conversation with DCC Wallace with a mix of amusement and interest on his swarthy face. We all swung around to look at him and he laughed softly.

"Well, I mean, it's no secret about the proposed REBCCO refinery, is it?"

"What in the world is a REBCCO?" Mary Jane asked.

"It stands for Russian Export Brent Crude Corporation," Wallace said to her with a smile. "A division of Statoil, I believe. They've announced plans for an oil refinery here on Scotland's east coast. They want to buy our crude oil from the North Sea rigs, and instead of paying to ship it back to Mother Russia, they want to pipeline it direct to a new refinery, process it into gasoline and ship it worldwide from here. Saves them a step in the process and thus makes it more profitable for President Putin and his friends who own the company. Naturally, the environmental crowd is against the idea, not to mention the national security community, and they have enough politicians on their side that it's highly unlikely the proposal will ever get approved."

"And where would this new refinery be built?" I wondered.

"Hasn't been decided yet," Sir Hamish said. "Could be anywhere along the coast from Fraserburgh in the north to Eyemouth, south of Edinburgh. Despite the Greens and the spooks being against the whole idea, a new refinery and associated development could mean billions in new revenue and several thousand high-paying jobs. It would be worth a lot to Scotland in general and whatever community is selected in particular."

"And is this one of the communities under consideration?" Mary Jane asked.

DCC Wallace shrugged. But Sir Hamish was nodding. "Oh, yes," he said. "Especially with the news that the Royal Air Force is considering closing down Leuchars."

"The air base over there?" I motioned in the general direction of RAF Leuchars, which had occupied the sandy point of land directly across the River Eden from the Old Course since the first World War. "It's going to be shut down?"

Sir Hamish nodded. "It's been placed on the short list for decommission," he said. "The Air Force wants to move operations up to RAF Lossiemouth, consolidate some divisions and save money."

"So that would leave a nice big piece of real estate up for grabs," I said. "Interesting."

"I daresay there's a long row to hoe," said Wallace. "Many, many issues to be resolved. Be years in the making…decades even." Sir Hamish nodded his agreement.

"And in the meantime, we still have a local guy killed and dropped into the Bottle Dungeon, and no idea who did it or why. That about right?"

DCC glared at me, color coming up in his cheeks. "I wouldn't go quite that far, Mr. Hacker," he said. "There are certain elements to the case that we have not released publicly and that I will not discuss with you or anyone else. We do have certain leads and we are pursuing them. Vigorously. "

"Right," I said. "Good answer."

His eyes narrowed and his lips turned down. "It has been nice chatting with you," he said. "But I'm afraid I must move along. Have a most pleasant stay with us. Madame," he bowed curtly to Mary Jane. "Sir Hamish." He turned on his heel and marched away.

"How is it," Mary Jane mused, mostly to herself, "That you manage to piss off every policeman you talk to?"

"Boyish good looks and a sparkling personality?" I suggested.

She gave me one of those looks and I let it drop.

Chapter Sixteen

THERE WERE A lot of people tossing and turning the night before the Open Championship in St. Andrews, and I was one of them. My insomnia wasn't due to the tension of a major championship about to be played on an ancient and unforgiving golf course in a stiff quartering breeze that originated somewhere in northern Norway and came sweeping in across the whitecaps of the North Sea. I left that problem to the 140-odd golfers who were scheduled to tee it up. Nor was my problem the dozen or so heavily garlicked and breaded scallops, the fairly incredible amounts of smoked salmon delicately arrayed on triangular toast points, nor the many tart-sized Scottish meat pasties I had consumed at the Gold Standard party. Along with several glasses of champagne and two, or was it three?, pints of ale that I used to wash it all down. Though I'm sure all that didn't help.

No, despite the warning looks from Mary Jane, who had kept up with me for most of the night, my rumbling stomach wasn't the main culprit. It was the Kincaid case. All the rich food may have kept Wee Willie Winkie from sprinkling his sleepy dust on my eyes, but it was the questions popping into my fevered brain that kept me up most of the night. Not so Mary Jane—her warm body next to mine and the soft rise and fall of her breathing were a constant reminder that I was dead awake.

All the things I realized I didn't know kept pulling at me. Who *was* Colin Kincaid? What did he know or do which would lead someone to break his neck and drop him down a hole? Where and how was he killed? How did the killer get him into the Bottle Dungeon, much less without anyone seeing anything? How did Johnnie Swift fit into the picture? Or Lord Cheape? Or Yuri the big bald Russian? Or Conrad Gold, for that matter? And, perhaps most important of all, why did I care, why couldn't I just forget the whole thing, cover the golf tournament, enjoy Mary Jane's company and go home once the Champion Golfer of the Year had been determined?

I didn't really spend much time on the last one. I've never been able to let things go once I got my teeth into them. Despite what Mary Jane thought, I didn't really obsess over this stuff. It just so happened that I was here, I knew or had met some of the players in this little drama and I wanted to find out what happened next. What was so wrong about that? And, having rationalized that part, I began to think of what I should do next.

Which is why the next morning, instead of heading over to the golf course to wait and watch while the opening round of the tournament ground on through its first long day, I decided to visit the offices of the Links Trust, where Colin Kincaid had worked. My two roomies, typical hard-working journalists, had a 10 a.m. tee time at Kingsbarns, the American-built links course a few miles outside of town. That would get them back to the Old Course in plenty of time to watch the afternoon groups straggling in, and plenty of time to file their first-day reports back to their papers in the States. Mary Jane announced that she had her fill of sight-seeing and was planning on spending the day on the couch working through one of P.D. James' excellent Adam Dalgleish mystery novels. "And if I had any bon-bons, I'd eat some," she said.

So I got the car out and drove over to Pilmour House, a modest little cottage set in a glade outside town, where the Links Trust had its offices. The one-story stucco building had parking for six cars and a quiet, unassuming air, like it was pretending to be a doctor's practice or an accountant's office. I thought it might be a good day to drop in, inasmuch as the Open had disrupted most of the usual activity in the town, including golf on the Trust's seven courses. The Old Course, of course, was closed, as were the New, the Jubilee, the Eden, the Balgove and the Strathtyrum. The new Castle course, perched on a seaside cliff to the south of the city, was still accepting paying customers. My roomies were scheduled to play there on the morrow, and I was trying to decide if I should join them.

So it was quiet when I arrived. There were two women talking intently to each other at the front desk. They broke off their conversation abruptly when I came in the door. I introduced myself and asked if it might be possible to get 15 minutes with the director for a piece I was doing for my newspaper. A small fib, but you never know. It's all grist for the mill, one way or another.

The receptionist, a middle-aged woman with flaming red hair, was polite but noncommittal. "The director is not in at present," she said. "He's probably over at the R&A this morning. But perhaps you'd like to speak with Mr. Gordon? He's the director of operations."

I said that would be fine, and she went off to warn Mr. Gordon that a journalist was coming in. The other woman smiled at me but her eyes were red and her face drawn as though she'd been crying.

"Are you okay?" I asked.

"Oh, thank you," she said. "Yes, yes, I'm sorry. My boss died recently. It's so sad."

"Was that Mr. Kincaid?" I asked.

"Yes, yes," she said, nodding, eyes getting watery again. "He was a dear man. Very dear."

"I'm sorry for your loss," I said. She nodded gratefully, unable to speak.

Duncan Gordon was about 45, heavy-set, dressed casually in a navy sweater, white golf shirt and black slacks and he looked wary. "All press inquiries are usually handled by Michael Perry, our press liaison," he said when I was shown into his small but neat office. "Perhaps I should call him for you?"

"There's no need to bother him," I said. "I'm really just trying to get some background on the Links Trust organization and how it works. You know...my editors want a kind of travel piece for the Open coverage, and I want to sound like I know what I'm talking about."

He still didn't look comfortable, but he dutifully explained to me much of what I already knew. The Links Trust had been established in 1974 by an Act of Parliament to manage and maintain the golf courses in St. Andrews on behalf of the Fife County Council, which had taken over official ownership when the town government of St. Andrews itself had been eliminated and folded into the larger county system. The Act had set up a board of Trustees to oversee the organization, made up of appointees which included representatives of the Council, the R&A, citizens of the town, the elected Member of Parliament for the district and another politician appointed by the Scottish government in Edinburgh. The Trustees set overall policy direction for the town's golf courses, all of which were considered public and open to all, and hired the Links Management Committee to run the day-to-day. The managing director of the Links Management Committee also sat on the Board of Trustees and was the chief executive. The Links Management Committee also had an assistant director, the position that had been held by Colin Kincaid, as well as directors of retail and licensing, operations, golf, greenskeeping and finance.

"So you're the nuts and bolts guy," I said, when Gordon had finished his spiel.

He smiled. "Well," he said, "Everyone here has their areas of responsibility that keep the whole working. I can't say that my contributions are any more important than anyone else's. Would you like a coffee or a cup of tea?"

"Tea would be lovely, thanks," I said. He picked up the phone and asked someone to bring two cups.

"Tell me about Colin Kincaid," I said. "Has his death affected the organization?"

Gordon looked worried again. I wondered if I had gone too far and too fast.

"Well of course," he said. "Colin had been here for just over twenty-five years. He was something of an institution, both here at the Committee and in the community as a whole."

"So he was well liked?"

He smiled, a bit ruefully it seemed to me. "Well, I might use the word 'respected' more than 'liked,'" he said. "A great part of his job was to say 'no' to people. Lord Forbes, our chief executive, would be the one people would approach with their ideas and proposals for business partnerships and the like. He would smile and nod and take their proposals and then turn it all over to Kincaid. Colin's job was to tell people 'sorry.'"

"So Kincaid was the designated bastard," I said. "Just like Clifford Roberts at Augusta National."

He looked confused.

"Bobby Jones was always the one people came to with ideas about what they should do at the Masters," I said. "Just like Lord Forbes, apparently, he was approachable and likeable. But it was up to Cliff Roberts to say no. Which he did to almost everything. He called himself the designated bastard."

Gordon nodded. "I see," he said. "Yes, that was Colin's role. One of them, in any case."

The red-eyed woman from the front came in with a tray that held a small pot and two ceramic cups of tea.

"I hope you like it with milk," she said.

"That will be fine," I said, smiling at her.

"Thank you Sarah," Gordon said.

"So it would be fair to say that there were probably a lot of people who didn't like Colin Kincaid very much," I said. Sarah finished pouring the tea, replaced the pot and left the office.

He looked worried again. "Well, yes, I suppose that is true," he said. "But I don't think you can say that there were a lot of people who disliked Colin enough to kill him. I mean, we have to turn golfers away from the Old Course every day. Hundreds if not thousands of them every year. But none of them have ever tried to kill our reservations director."

"Point taken," I said. "And you can't think of any deal in particular that might have really ticked someone off? Like that incident with Conrad Gold?"

He shook his head. "That was way before my time," he said. "Ten years ago. More."

I could see I'd gotten as much as I was going to out of Duncan Gordon. I thanked him for his time and the tea and headed out of the office. Teary Sarah was sitting behind the receptionist desk. The red-haired woman was nowhere to be seen. Despite her red-rimmed eyes, Sarah looked at me sharply.

"Don't you go believing anything bad about Colin Kincaid," she said, voice quivering. "He was a dear, dear man. Not a saint, by any means, but he was a good man."

"Tell me about him," I said, perching on the side of the desk. "Was he married? Did he have a family?"

Sarah plucked a tissue from a box beside the computer keyboard and dabbed at her eyes. She shook her head.

"Nae," she said. "Colin never married. I once asked him why at a Christmas party one year, but he didn't want to talk about it. He rarely talked about personal matters. His life was devoted to the Links Trust."

Her eyes welled up again, and I waited until she got control back.

"Did he have any hobbies outside work? Was he a golfer, for instance?"

She laughed. "Och nooo," she said with a sad chuckle. "He positively *hated* the golf, he did. He told me once that he didn't think he could do his job correctly if he played the silly game. He had to make so many difficult decisions. He was certain that if he played golf, he wouldn't be able to make an unbiased decision."

She paused and smiled a little to herself. "He did like birding, though. He was very keen on that."

"Hunting?" I asked, surprised.

"Och, no," she smiled. "Watching the wee birdies. Y'know…with binoculars and cameras and all that? He was always making weekend trips to the Highlands and out on the Hebrides, searching for this or that. He had a circle of friends he often went with."

"Did he live here in St. Andrews?" I asked.

She shook her head. "Nae, he had a flat over in Dundee," she said. "It's a good solid hour's drive he had to make every day…longer when the bridge was backed up. He was a city lad who loved the countryside, too. He was a dear, dear man."

I hesitated for a moment, then decided to go for broke.

"Is there any chance I could see his office?" I asked. "Just a peek. I won't touch anything. Just want to get a feeling for what kind of man he was."

There was absolutely no reason for her to allow me into Kincaid's sanctum. On the other hand, she wanted me to think well of her former employer. So, with a quick glance back at the closed door to Duncan Gordon's office, she nodded at the corner office, where the door was open.

"Tis there," she said in a conspiratorial whisper. "Be quick about it."

I gave her a finger-gun shot and a wink, playing the role of the fast-talkin' gumshoe from every black-and-white movie the two of us had ever seen, and strolled into Colin Kincaid's office.

It was standard-issue modern executive. Red mahogany desk with knee hole, twin flanks of pull-out drawers with brass handles, tall-backed leather executive chair with wooden arm rests. Two upholstered guest chairs on the other side. Brass table lamp, calculator, telephone, brass nautical clock and a wooden pen holder. Two windows covered with adjustable vertical blinds. A long mahogany credenza against the back wall held the computer screen and keyboard: the guts must have been stored below. The walls were covered with a series of colorful photos of birds, both in extreme close-up, and a couple of wide shots showing steep cliffs rising out of a restless sea, with hundreds if not thousands of birds diving, flying, nesting and otherwise being birds. Among the close-up portraits, I recognized some puffins, with their colorful curved beaks, and an eagle, which had that breed's usual glaring and haughty eyes. There were two stone penguins huddled together atop the credenza.

There was a small door off to the right, beyond the credenza, which I figured led either to a bathroom or a closet. But on a small portion of the wall between that door and one of the windows, I saw two framed diplomas. I stepped over to see them. One was a baccalaureate degree from Glasgow Caledonian University, announcing that Her Majesty the Queen as well as the Faculty and Trustees of said university were proud to award a degree in Language Arts to one Colin Kincaid of Edinburgh. I could not read the other diploma, since it was covered with Cyrillic letters which sometimes resemble our Latin-based characters, and sometimes don't. But it seemed to signify that one Colin Kincaid—those letters were readable—had completed advanced degree work in the Russian language.

I was thinking about that when I heard a cough behind me. I turned around and saw a sandy haired young man in a light grey business suit, arms crossed and a frown on his face.

"Hullo," he said, none too friendly. "I'm Michael Perry, press liaison for the Links Trust. May I ask just what in the hell you're doing in Colin Kinkaid's office?"

There were several answers I could have come up with, none of them very believable. So I opted for the truth.

"I'm just snooping," I said.

He wasn't expecting that, which gave me an opening.

I laughed and said "No, I was just leaving and apparently took a wrong turn. Thank you very much. Good day!" And I just walked past him and out the door. He didn't chase me.

Chapter Seventeen

I WENT BACK to the flat and had lunch with Mary Jane. I filled her in on what I'd learned.

She stuck a thumb in her book. "Commander Dalgleish would say that you have stumbled upon a clue," she said. "Not to mention a recurring theme."

"The Russkis," I said, nodding.

"Quite so," she said. "Johnny Swift is being chased by them, Lord Cheape of Wormwood employs them and now we find that the dead guy—"

"Colin Kincaid of the Links Trust," I said helpfully.

"—whatever...he was apparently fluent in the Russki tongue. That's a lot of coincidences gathered together in one smallish, if auld, grey toon."

"I wonder if Commander Dalgleish would call it the Russki tongue," I said.

"Perhaps not," she said, opening her book and beginning to read again. "But he'd sure as hell grab onto it and start shaking until something came out."

I kissed her on the top of her head and left her to the fictional world of New Scotland Yard, where murder and mayhem always get neatly explained in the penultimate chapter, the murderer is always imprisoned for life and truth and justice is always served.

I walked through the busy streets of town on my way down to the golf course, guided by the occasional bursts of cheers and applause erupting from the giant bleachers and the rings of fans standing along the ropes. From a distance, one could tell the difference between the percussive sounds of joy elicited by birdie putts or great shots and the slow welling of applause that sounded like rainfall on a tin roof, building in crescendo as a famous golfer walked down the last fairway towards the last green.

The weather for this first day of the Open was near perfect: the skies were clear but for a few scudding clouds, the sun was warm and the wind was fitful and mostly calm. It was a good day for going low. The crowds were ten-deep behind the first tee, where golfers were still being sent off every ten minutes. The R&A's iconic tee-box announcer Ivor Robson, known to most of us as The Man with the Iron Bladder, sent each player off with his usual cheerful announcement. "*Now on the tee, from Denmark, Hans Büller!*" Robson stood on that tee for ten hours a day, four days in a row, flawlessly pronouncing everyone's name—including the growing contingent of players from Asia—without stopping for food, drink or a bathroom break. He ought to get an endorsement contract from Depends.

I glanced at the tall yellow scoreboards to see that Zach Johnson, Germany's Heinrich Gruber, and somebody from South Korea named Park had all had good mornings and were currently tied for the lead at four-under-par; closely trailed by the young Spaniard Enrico Paz and the Irish boy wonder, Conor Kelly, who were among a passel of golfers at three-under. The afternoon rounds were just getting underway, so it was far too soon to tell what names might yet appear in the black letters on the board.

Then I turned and looked at the stolid eminence of the Victorian clubhouse of the Royal & Ancient Golf Club, crouched in its place of honor just behind the first tee. And thought, not for the first time, of the dichotomy between that imposing edifice and the power and privilege it represented standing against the populist impulse that long informed the game of golf in its native land.

Golf had already been played for centuries when the 22 Noblemen and Gentlemen of the kingdom of Fife got together and declared themselves a club in 1754, chipped in enough cash to buy a prize in the form of a sterling silver golf club, and scheduled an annual competition in mid-May. In so doing, they announced to the world that they were now an official golf club, following the lead of the Gentlemen Golfers of Leith, soon to be known as the Honourable Company, which had formed ten years earlier down in Edinburgh. Both of these clubs had a lot in common with your local Kiwanis or Elks: a special clubhouse, spiffy uniforms to set them apart from all others, and some kind of secret initiation ceremony. OK, that last part is a lie. I think. And the guys who formed these clubs were generally a little wealthier than your average Elk: they were the landowners and business professionals of their time.

It would be another 80 years before the St. Andrews club became known as the Royal and Ancient Golf Club, when King William IV gave it his royal kiss (bestowed more so on a London actress with whom he had ten illegitimate children, thus leaving his throne to his niece, Victoria); and 100 years before construction began on the current sandstone building with the big windows looking out on the ancient links.

The johnny-come-latelies in St. Andrews in 1754 had been trying to restore a little luster to a town than had fallen on hard times. The anti-Catholic Reformation movement of John Knox had laid waste to the city's position as a great ecclesiastical center and left behind only the burned-out shell of its once-formidable cathedral. The ancient University, which had churned out centuries of clerics, had gone broke and almost moved its operations, lock, stock and berobed dons, up to Perth. St. Andrews in the mid-18th century had all the mojo of today's Detroit.

But the golf course that started and ended in the middle of the old town was still there, and people still went out and played on it, just as they had for hundreds of years. And not just the noblemen and gentlemen, either. Ordinary people, even *poor* people took advantage of the opportunity to avail themselves of what they called the "ancient and healthful exercise of the Golf." It was recreation, sport—interesting, challenging, something anyone could do, and it took people away from their regular problems, like life and death, food and shelter, war and poverty, for at least a couple of hours. That was why the Stewart Kings had earlier tried to ban the game—the common folk much preferred whacking their little balls around the links, and betting on the outcomes, to doing military drills, archery practice and other real-life activities. Who could blame them for wanting to get away, even for just a short time, from their otherwise brutal, short and pretty grim lives?

So these 18th century land barons and titled gentry decided to take over the people's sport. Beginning with the handful of clubs that shared the links at Leith and Musselburgh near Edinburgh, and the ones that soon followed at Bruntsfield, Perth and St. Andrews, these upper-crust dandies began holding regular meetings over lunch or dinner, heavily fueled by flagons of port and barrels of kümmel. They decided that they should all dress the same, in elegant and elaborate waistcoats, breeches and jackets of various gaudy colors, buttons of brass, lapels of the finest silk. The grandees of St. Andrews began to write down the generally accepted rules of the game, because what is a Sport if it does not have Fair Play?

It is to their everlasting credit that the workaday people of Scotland generally ignored the fancification of their game and kept on playing, dressed in their usual tattered tweeds, hand-knit jumpers and hobnail boots. Golf on the Old Course was, until well into the 20th century, pretty much free for any and all who wanted to play, and just about everybody did. Sure, the first tee on the Old Course would be reserved from time to time to allow Lord So-and-So play with Sir Who-sis, and for the annual Spring and Fall meetings of the R&A, when the Prince of Wales would open the ceremonies with a shot from the first tee accompanied by a cannon shot, and the promise of a gold sovereign to the lucky caddie who could retrieve his ball. But if Angus the butcher wanted to play a friendly match against Duncan the fishmonger on a slow Tuesday afternoon, they just showed up and played away, and nobody said they couldn't.

It was Young Tommy Morris who had the best line. Young Tom, a golf prodigy, had not worked his way up through the caddie ranks, as had his father. Young Tom had never carried the clubs for anyone, never searched through the gorse for someone else's missing ball nor ever bent his knee to pat together a little muddy tee for His Lordship's use. He was a *golfer*, by damn, not a *servant*. And one day, walking in the town, he passed one of those "don't-you-know-who-I-am?" types from the R&A who demanded that the young Morris tip his cap to his better.

"If I could see one, I would," said Tommy, looking right at the man.

Tommy's cap remained firmly on his head, but the R&A types, who if they weren't members of Parliament themselves were connected in some way to them, gradually took over the game. Or at least the official parts of it. And they continue to this day to oversee the game's Rules and its progress from inside those thick stone walls behind the first tee of the Old Course. Those walls may keep the riffraff outside the elegantly appointed clubhouse, but they haven't yet figured out a way to keep them off the golf course, nor from enjoying the game itself in any way they see fit, with or without the officially sanctioned rules. And they never will.

I could see the usual collection of old boys up in the Big Room, peering out the tall front windows at the Great Unwashed who had assembled once again in the Auld Grey Toon to watch the world's best golfers tromp their way around the ancient ground, stumbling over the rude Roman bridge across the burn on the Home hole and following their balls into the sooty slate embrace of the buildings of the town that wrapped around that last green.

I always wondered whether those old boys secretly desired to be down here with us, in the great bawdy noisy chaos of the real world, sounding our Whitmanesque barbaric yawps—*Yoodamannn*! and *GetintheHole*!—munching on greasy fried sausages and swilling warm beer, getting burned by the summer sun and drenched by the passing showers, ogling in equal parts the pretty girls and the amazing golf. I very much doubted whether most of the commonfolk yobs down here, looking up at those pinched pale faces, tightly cinched collars and officially emblazoned jackets, would want to change places. I know I wouldn't.

Chapter Eighteen

I WENT BACK inside the media center and spent a few hours doing some actual work. I filed a couple of pages of notes back to Boston even though I was pretty sure my idiotic editor, Frank Donatello, who should be the poster boy for an national anti-obesity campaign, would shitcan the lot and just run a five-graph AP report. Of course, he'd expect my usual lengthy notes page for the Sunday paper—and complain if it didn't include at least one item about the Charles River Golf Club, whose membership had somehow failed to blackball his application. I might get a few graphs of my game story printed on Monday. It really isn't much fun these days being a golf writer for a major metropolitan daily. I'm one of an endangered species, a dying breed. Even if I still get a paycheck. I'm really going to have to learn html one of these days.

I had finished up and was chatting away on the subject of American presidential politics with a less-than-rapt group of Brit writers, when one of them, watching the big screen in the corner where the BBC tournament feed was playing, said, a note of wonder in his voice, "Bloody hell...Will you look at that!"

The rest of us turned to look at the TV screen.

At first glance, it looked like a holiday parade. But when the TV director began cutting in for close-ups, we could all see that we were looking at a mammoth protest march. At the front of the march were two large red-haired men wearing tartan kilts and each pounding on a huge bass drum. Behind them was a long line of people stretched back for a hundred yards, holding colorful hand-lettered signs, flags and banners, or just clapping and shouting a chant we could not hear.

"Turn up the sound," someone yelled. "Where the hell are they?"

The press tent fell silent as finally someone found the volume control and we began to hear the dulcet tones of Peter Alliss, the BBC's perennial and ageless golf announcer.

"...is apparently the handiwork of an organization called Eliminate Golf," Alliss was saying. "It is the brainchild of a university professor here in St. Andrews and he has promised to try and disrupt the proceedings here this week to further his stated goal of eliminating the game of golf and replacing it with...well, we don't exactly know what, now do we? But no matter...here is the demonstration. They are marching down The Scores from the University, and approaching the Bruce Embankment which is just behind the R&A clubhouse here in St. Andrews. There, as you can now see, a line of constables has formed to stem the march and, we are told, try to keep them on the Embankment and away from the golf course proper."

"That's just up the hill," someone shouted and a mass exodus of golf writers began to pour out of the press tent, around the R&A clubhouse and up behind the grandstands to watch the action. I followed along. None of us got very far. The marchers had been stopped at the top of the hill near the Martyr's Monument, the old stone obelisk erected in memory of the Protestant Reformers who had been put to death by those evil Catholics several centuries ago, never mind the innocent Catholics who in turn had been massacred by the evil Protestants once they assumed power. The constables, all dressed in their Day-Glo lemon-lime vests, had linked arms to form a human barrier along Golf Place, the small lane which runs behind the R&A clubhouse and pushed halfway up the hill along The Scores to keep the marchers away from the golf course. Another wing of uniformed cops had swooped in on the seaward side of the small grassy park of the Bruce Embankment, trying to keep the protesters away from the Scottish Golf Museum, the Aquarium and the fancy all-glass Seafood Ristorante perched on the rocky cliffs overlooking the sea.

The E-Go marchers had taken up positions around the Monument and were chanting and beating their drums loudly. Crowds of onlookers from the golf tournament and the town gathered behind the police lines to watch the fun. It was a lovely afternoon for a protest, with the gold sunlight beaming down on a placid sea turned blue under the cloudless sky. Someone in the crowd of marchers turned on some kind of loudspeaker and they began to amplify their chants, in time to the twin bass drums. *Hey, Hey, Ho Ho, the game of golf has got to go!*

This led to some angry buzzing from the golf fans watching from The Scores. A few of them, no doubt deep into their lagers, tried to break through the line of constables to express their disapproval of the E-Go message. For the most part, the long Day-Glo line held fast against the pushing and shoving, and a few dozen more of the men and women in white police shirts were stationed at the ready to quickly subdue any who managed to break through the line.

"How cool is this, Hacker?" said someone just behind me. I turned to see my roomie Mario standing there, red-faced with excitement. "It's like a soccer hooligan street fight! Except it's about golf!"

All I could do was grin back at him. Attracted by all the noise and excitement, the crowd began to swell and, like crowds so often do, to take on a life of its own. Jammed together cheek to jowl, we began to move like a wave, first to the left and then back to the right. It was hard to stay upright, and a degree of panic began to set in. I heard a woman scream, the police began blowing shrill whistles and things turned ugly in a hurry. I heard the first tinkling sounds as glass began to shatter and decided it was way past time to get the hell out of there. I turned and began to fight my way back towards the R&A clubhouse and the press tent beyond. I caught a glimpse of Mario off to the left, doing the same. I began shoving people out of my way as I fought to escape the press of the crowd. There were more screams and more glass breaking. I heard a dull thump and, with a glance over my shoulder, saw a white cloud of tear gas forming halfway up the hill. I turned back and kept fighting my way through the crowd which was still pressing against me as people tried to see what was going on.

I was gasping for breath and almost back to Golf Place when I grabbed someone by the shoulders and began to shove him out of my way. Then I saw his face. It was Johnny Swift and his eyes were wide with fright. He recognized me and almost sagged into my arms.

"Hacker," he gasped. "The Russkis! Right behind me!"

I scanned the crowd nearby, this time focusing on the faces. Sure enough, about ten yards off to the left I saw the bald pate of one of the tough guys, his eyes hidden behind his dark glasses. There was another one, with bushy black hair, next to him. They saw Swiftie and began throwing people out of their way in an attempt to get to him.

"C'mon," I said and, grabbing Swiftie by the back of his belt, began forcing my way through the crowd. Bodies began flying every which way as I finally managed to drag Swiftie down to the corner of the R&A building. With my free hand, I fished my press credential badge out and showed it to the security officer standing there and we broke through to the other side. There were still people trying to exit the grandstands and pressing to see what was going on up on the hillside, but we managed to dodge through them and made it to the entrance of the press tent. There were two more security guys standing there, but I just pushed past him waving my credentials, keeping a firm overlapping Vardon grip on Johnny Swift and made it into the tent.

Mindful of the goons behind us, I dragged Johnnie past the long rows of tables facing the giant scoreboard and into the back section of the tent, where temporary offices and studios for the broadcasting boys had been set up. One of those rooms was dark and empty, so I dragged Swiftie inside and thrust him into a chair. "Stay," I ordered, as if talking to an incorrigible corgi. Then I walked quickly back to the tent entrance. I kept off to one side and peeked outside.

Sure enough, the two goons were standing there, in a heated discussion with the security official, who was not going to let them in without the required media credentials. They were arguing and I saw the bald-headed goon reach into his coat pocket and pull out some bills, which he offered to the gatekeeper. He was waved away. The black-haired one grabbed Baldy's arm and pulled him away, as some other journalists had stopped to watch the encounter. The two goons left, disappearing into the crowds of people milling about outside.

I went back to the dark studio where I had stashed Swiftie. Amazingly, he was still there, smoking a cigarette as if he had not a care in the world. I didn't tell him that the press tent was an official no-smoking area. Nor did I ask if I could take a drag. But I thought about it.

"Och," he said when he saw me. "They didna get ya, I see. Good on ya, lad."

I pulled up a white folding chair and placed it in front of him. I sat down. "OK," I said, "Why are you being chased by these guys? No more bullshit, Johnny. Tell me the truth."

He stroked his chin thoughtfully. It had about four days' worth of growth on it, and I could almost hear the scratchy sound.

"Hacker, me lad," he said, "I dunna want to get you into the soup with ole Johnny Swift. From what I hear, you dunna want these Russkis a-chasin' you, especially with your lady friend near at hand."

"It's a little late for that, John," I said. "Whoever they are, they've seen me with you at least twice now. I suspect they know that you and I are friends at the very least. So tell me. Why are they chasing you? What do you know?"

He sighed. Then he stood up and began to pace back and forth the width of the small room, little white clouds of cigarette smoke trailing above his head like steam following a train engine. I kept silent. He had to work this out for himself.

"Hacker," he said finally, looking at me with his doleful, rheumy eyes. "Have y'ever seen a man killed?"

I thought about that for a minute. I've seen plenty of dead bodies, both from my days as a police reporter in downtown Boston, and even during my stint as a golf writer. And there was that time in Miami, when the husband of LPGA star Big Wyn Stilwell reached his limit of spousal abuse and blew her away in front of me.

"Was it Colin Kincaid?" I asked. "Did you see him being killed?"

Swiftie shook his head. "Nae, nae," he said. "Twas not that poor sod I seen go to meet his maker. Twas another poor sod."

It had been a night in early June, he explained to me. After working his dishwashing shift at the restaurant kitchen near Kingsbarns, Johnny had walked down the coast about a mile to the Balcomie Links at Crail, a lovely little seaside course wedged in between the cliffs and the rocky shoreline. He knew a place just off one of the promontories there where he could safely scramble out onto the mossy rocks and cast a line into the cold sea in search of night-feeding codlings and flounder. The sea was shallow there before dropping off a deep shelf, and the fish liked to come near the shore at night and forage.

Johnny said that many times some of his fellow caddies would be out on the rocks, especially if the moon was full, casting with long poles out into the black sea. But that night, he had been alone. The sky had been covered in cloud, he remembered, and even with the lingering summer twilight, the night had been quite dark. Johnny didn't mind being alone, in fact he enjoyed the solitude, and because he had been fishing there for almost his entire life, he wasn't afraid of slipping and falling on the wet rocks. There were some large boulders lying atop the rocky shelves that extended outwards into the sea, and those provided some protection for him against a cold wind which knifed in off the North Sea.

He remembered that he had been quite successful that night, hauling in a good catch of fix or six plump cod, and had taken a break behind one of those boulders to smoke a cigarette. The lighthouse on May Island to the southeast blinked at him from time to time to remind him that he was not alone on the planet, an easy feeling to have out there on the far edges of the East Neuk.

While he was smoking, he had heard the faint puttering of an engine out in the sea. He looked out but could see nothing. The sound grew louder and louder, and eventually he caught a glimpse of a large inflatable dinghy, with three men inside. The boat carefully made its way toward the shore not far from where Swiftie was standing, with one man leaning over the bow flashing a torch into the water to help the helmsman steer between the rocky arms and up onto the pebbly shingle beach.

As soon as the boat had landed, the three men jumped out. It was too far away and too dark for Johnny to see any of their faces. He heard a soft whistle just to his left, and saw a fourth man come down the rocky beach to join the other three. He heard them whispering, then talking aloud, but he couldn't make out anything that was said as the wind carried the sound off into the ether. But Johnny could tell that things began to get a little heated when he saw one of the men from the boat angrily shove the man from the beach backwards. The shoved man regained his balance and charged forward, fists swinging wildly. But one of the other men from the boat had circled around behind him.

"He stabbed that poor bastard in the back," Johnny told me, his eyes serious now. "Then he reached around and drug that shiv across 'is neck." He made a cutting motion with his hand across his own neck and shuddered at the memory. "He made nary a sound, Hacker, not a peep. Just collapsed like a sack of rags of a sudden onto the beach."

The other three men had dragged the body of their victim to the edge of one of the deep, rocky pools and shoved it into the sea. Then they dragged their dinghy further up onto the beach, tied it off and disappeared inland, in the direction of a large barn that housed the heavy equipment used on the Balcomie golf course.

"Once they was gone, I skedaddled out of there fast as my feet could go," Johnny told me. "I was so scared, I even left me fishies behind! I went in the other direction, climbed up a cliff and cut across the golf course, passed by the go-kart track and found the main road. I thought sure I was home free. Me hands were shakin' so hard, I couldna get me fag alight," he said.

But he had walked no more than half a mile, looking like a Scottish Huck Finn with his fishing pole over his shoulder, when he heard the throaty growl of a car coming up behind him. The driver saw him, flashed on the high beams and the car drew up next to him in a cloud of dust.

"Twas a big black Land Rover," Johnny recalled for me. "Windows all tinted black as well. The driver rolled his window down and looked at me. I couldna see inside, but I smiled and nodded and said 'Evenin' gov'ner,' and kept on walkin'. They let me walk in front of them for ten, twenty yards, Johnny Swift in those bright headlamps, fearing for a knife in me back, or for that car to jump forward and run me doon."

But they didn't. Maybe they were debating. Arguing. But it was Johnny's great good luck that a farmer he knew came poking down the road from Crail Harbor in his rusty old Toyota pickup, belching smoke, passed the black Land Rover idling at the side of the road and saw Johnny and his fishing gear walking along. He must of recognized him, for he stopped, honked, and yelled out a greeting.

"Johnny Swift, ya right bastard," the farmer had shouted. "Out poaching the Queen's fish agin? Get in the truck, ya bloody wanker and I'll gie ya a lift inna town, I will."

Johnny had stowed his fishing rod in the back and gratefully clambered into the farmer's vehicle and they set off towards St Andrews, followed the whole way by the black SUV. The farmer had asked Johnny who the hell it was following them so close, but Johnny had said he didn't know. The farmer knew where Johnny lived, and was going to take him there, but Swiftie, realizing that the Land Rover contained the men who had knifed the poor bastard on the beach, asked to be dropped on the South Road, near one of the university quads at an entrance to one of the many winding medieval alleys that snake through the ancient town. He thanked the farmer, got out of the truck, waved cheerfully and turned into the alleyway.

"I left me fishin' rod with the man, and I haven't yet gone to retrieve it from him," he said sadly. "I had that gear for near twenty years now. But it woulda had me dead if'n I'd kept it."

Swiftie took off into the dark night, running for his life. He could hear the door slams of the Land Rover as the men inside got out to chase. But there are few men alive who know the streets and alleys of St. Andrews better than John Swift. He had lived there all his life, the street plan embedded in his brain. He ran like the wind, he said, zigging and zagging through the old quiet streets, let himself in through the back door of a rickety old garage owned by a pal and listened carefully to see if he had been followed. He hadn't, but he decided not to chance fate again, found a dry corner and slept the night there.

"They've been at me ever since," he said sadly. "They must have heard the farmer call out my name. I didn't even know they were Russians, until later. They've been to my wee flat. Turned it upside down, they did. You saw them at the restaurant. They've asked the caddie master where I might be. So far, I've been a step ahead. But Johnny Swift is nae as young as he once was, Hacker, and I'm a'feered me days in this old world is numbered. The Russkis want me dead and dead I shall be, mark my words."

"Did you report the crime to the police?" I asked when he was finished with his story. "Did a body turn up?"

He shook his head. "Nae, nae. The police would think Johnny Swift had been drinkin' the poteen again," he said. "The water off the point there falls into the deep pretty quick. If I recall, the tide had turned outwards. So I expect the body was carried out a ways and like as not sank like a stone."

"Do you have any idea who it was who got killed?" I asked.

He shook his head. "Too dark, too far away," he said sadly. "I couldna see the man's face nor hear a word that was spoke."

"And where had those men come from?" I asked. "Isn't there a small harbor down at Crail?"

He shook his head again. "Aye, there is," he said. "But I'm bettin' they come off a Russki submarine. Plannin' the big invasion, you ask me."

I smiled. "I don't think the Russians have any plans to invade Scotland," I said. "There are many easier countries they could invade, if they had a mind to. Which, so far as I know, they don't."

Outside, the first day's play was nearing its end. Looking at the big television screen, I saw that the police had managed to restore order on The Scores, keeping the noisy protesters hemmed in and keeping the beer-crazed spectators hemmed out. Without the further threat of violence, the excitement had died down and people were filtering away to the town's pubs and restaurants. There were perhaps six or seven groups left on the course, slowly straggling toward the Home hole, none of the players a big name and none looking like they were going to seriously contest for the Claret Jug.

But now I had a problem. How was I going to get back to my apartment with Swiftie? I was relatively sure that the Russkis, if that's what they were, would be waiting in ambush for us somewhere out in the faceless mass of the crowd. With Swiftie by my side, I went in search of Bernie Capshaw, the R&A's press secretary. He was standing near the interview area, where the players who had shot good rounds, within two or three of the leader, were ushered in, plunked down behind a table with a microphone and waited to be interviewed by the media gathered in the theater-like space. Bernie's lovely red-haired assistant, Fiona, who was much more photogenic than the perpetually disheveled Bernie, sat next to the player, asked him to "take us through your excellent round today" and helped select the follow-up questioners.

"Bernard," I said, "I need a favor."

"Sorry, Hacker," he said, "But Prince Andrew is not giving interviews this week."

"Why in the hell would I want to talk to a guy who's about six slots away from being the King, if his mother ever dies?"

Bernard shrugged. "I dunno," he said. "But that's what every Yank writer has been asking me this week so far."

"Oh," I said. "Well my favor is slightly different. Is there a back door to this place?"

Bernard looked at me, then at Swiftie. Then back at me.

"Look," I said, "My friend John, who by the way is a senior caddie here, has gotten himself into a bit of a pickle and there may be some gentlemen outside who wish to do him bodily harm. And me, too, if I happen to be standing next to him."

"Uh-huh," Bernie said.

"So we need to find a way to get out of here without being seen," I said. "Disappear into the crowds, as it were."

"They'll be cuttin' our throats, they will," Swiftie said. "Wssst!" He made the sound while drawing a finger across his throat.

I looked at Bernie and rolled my eyes. He grinned. "Well that's about the most original request I think I have ever had at an Open Championship, and I've been doing this for more than twenty years," Bernard said, chuckling. "Let's see what we can do."

Crooking his finger at us to follow, he set off towards the dining area of the huge tent. Throughout the day, the hard-working journalists covering the Open could wander into the dining area, shuffle down a line of steam tables filled with all kinds of food, including hot dishes kept hot in rectangular metal chafing dishes, and eat to heir heart's content. All free of course. Covering a golf tournament, which for most of the journos in attendance meant sitting at their desks with laptops and watching the big-screen TV all day, can be hungry work. The food area is always full of photographers, too, who are the ones who actually have to get outside and onto the golf course, following the people who are actually playing the game and recording their shots for posterity. That's an activity guaranteed to burn some calories. Now, at the end of the long day, there were just a few stragglers, and most of the food had been taken down, save for a tray or two of cookies. There were a few white-coated food service workers, all wearing their distinctive plastic gloves, cleaning up.

Bernard led us through a flap to a staging area, where several small white vans were parked, back doors open and boxes and cans being loaded. He went up to the driver of one van and spoke quietly into his ear. The man, dressed in a blue workman's jumpsuit, nodded. Bernie turned back to me.

"OK, Hacker," he said, "You and your caddie friend can climb in the back. He'll drop you off in town, unless you want to ride all the way to Cupar."

"Town will work fine," I said. "Thanks, Bernie. I owe ya one."

"More than one, Hacker," he said. "More than one."

We squeezed in beside the vats of cole slaw and bags of crisps, and the driver closed the door behind us. John was munching happily on one of the cookies he had liberated from the tray; I'd bet he had a few more stashed away in the pockets of his dirty parka. There was one small window for light. But it was pretty airless in there. The truck vibrated when he turned the engine on, and we had to find something to grab onto when he pulled away. Even though traffic was mostly banned in the area, it was still a long, slow ride with all the people wandering on the street. We circled around behind the R&A clubhouse and had to wait while people got out of the way. Peering out my small window, I saw the two goons standing behind the Victorian caddie pavilion just behind the towering grandstand erected behind the last green. They were studying the passersby, looking for either Johnnie or myself. I nudged Swiftie and he took a quick look and then ducked back.

"Them's the Russkis, them is," he said.

In about ten minutes, the truck had made its way into the heart of town. When he stopped at a red light, I knocked on the cab wall, opened the rear door and Swiftie and I got out. I went up to the driver and passed a tenner through his window. "Cheers, mate," he said, nodding.

I took Johnny home with me.

Chapter Nineteen

EARLY THE NEXT morning, I paid a visit to the Fife District Constabulary station on the North Road and asked to see DCC Wallace. I wanted to bring Swiftie with me, but he declined the opportunity, being somewhat allergic to the police. He had spent the night on our sofa, at Mary Jane's insistence, but set off into the city on his own after downing a couple of cups of coffee and a muffin.

"John Swift is na' burden to his friends," he said. "I'll be fine as rain." We tried to talk him into staying, but he insisted on fending for himself, even against the dreaded Russkis.

After cooling my heels in the outer office for half an hour, a female officer in her white blouse with black epaulets came out and showed me into Wallace's office. It was small and official looking, with a Scottish flag standing in the corner and a color photograph of Her Majesty on the wall behind his chair. His gray metal desk was spotlessly clear, save for a blotter and a telephone, and he was sitting ramrod straight behind his desk, also in his white shirt sleeves.

"Good morning, Mr. Hacker," he said when I walked in. "How can I help you?"

"I've come to report a murder," I said.

"Indeed?" he said, eyebrows raised a fraction of an inch. "And did you commit this crime?"

"No," I said. "My friend John Swift witnessed it."

His eyebrows went up another notch and he waited. I told him Swiftie's story. He listened without interruption. When I was finished, he reached into his file drawer and pulled out a manila file folder. He placed it in the center of his desk blotter and flipped it open.

"Boris K. Kasyanov," he read out loud. "Russian national, working in this country with a special immigration permit. His body was found by a fisherman approximately two miles north-northwest of the Isle of May on June 23 last. Body had decomposed to a great extent, but the coroner found evidence of knife wounds in the back and throat."

"Aha," I said. He looked at me. "It *was* the Russkis."

"And where is Mr. Swift at this moment?" he asked.

I shrugged and nodded towards the street outside. "He's still hiding," I said. "From you as well as the Russians. He's not a big fan of the constabulary."

"And for good reason," Wallace said. "He's been something of a regular customer for us over the years."

"But he's got a good heart," I said. Wallace shrugged noncommittally.

"There were three others in the inflatable?" he asked. I nodded. He made a note in the file.

"Have you discovered yet why Kincaid went off with the two Russian gents who invaded his office?" I asked. "I haven't been able to figure out what the connection there was all about."

He sighed. He obviously didn't much like sharing intelligence with a member of the media, even it was only the golfing media.

"We have discovered that Mr. Kincaid had previously been married," he said. "He met a woman when he was studying the Russian language at a university in Moscow, some thirty years ago. They said they were married, but Her Majesty's Customs and Immigration Service could not satisfactorily establish that they were, in fact, legally married. So her entry into the country was denied." He paused, thinking. "It was different times, of course," he said. "The Russians were still considered the enemy, as it were. In any case, she never came to this country, and as far as we know, Kincaid never went back to Russia."

"So how do those two bald-headed goons fit in?"

"We cannot be sure, since Mr. Kincaid is now deceased, but we believe they may have offered Kincaid some information about the woman, perhaps even saying they had a message from her," Wallace said. "It is the kind of thing Russian operatives are wont to do."

"And then?"

"Perhaps they felt Mr. Kincaid might have been able to offer some assistance in their plan to obtain the land in and around Leuchars," he said. "Maybe to somehow use the name of the Links Trust, which has been actively buying land and building new golf courses in and around town for the last decade and more, to help them acquire the land without anyone knowing who the real owners were. Real estate developers have been known to be less than forthright about such matters."

I nodded. It sounded plausible. After all, Kincaid had tried to pull a fast one on Conrad Gold years ago. Maybe Kincaid saw euro signs for himself by working with the Russians. "What do you do next?" I asked.

He wrote something else down in his file. He looked at me. "We will add your information to the investigation file," he said. "It would be most helpful if Mr. Swift himself came forward to be interviewed. Perhaps you could convince him of the importance of his testimony?"

I shrugged this time. "I'll try," I said.

He flipped the file closed and replaced it in his desk drawer. "Is there anything else?" he asked, folding his hands on the blotter.

"I guess not," I said, standing up. He stood as well. "Guess you guys had your hands full with the anti-golf demonstration yesterday. Did you slap the cuffs on Professor Knox?"

He smiled, and it was not a friendly smile. "The Eliminate Golf organization was issued a legal parade permit," he said. "The demonstration was supposed to be held only on the grounds of Kinburn Park, outside the Museum of St. Andrews. Professor Knox said that unruly elements of the crowd left the park and began to march down The Scores. He said he tried to stop them, but failed. All further permits to the group have been cancelled."

"So they were going to do it again today?"

"Apparently," Wallace said, nodding. "We have doubled our manpower for this afternoon. And we have given Cecil Knox a stern warning that any further activity of that sort will be met with a strong police response."

"I'll bet he didn't like that very much," I said. "Did he accuse you of being unbridled fascists stomping on the grapes of freedom, or something like that?"

"Oh, of course," Wallace said, smiling again. "I believe you'll find his comments dutifully reported in every newspaper in the kingdom this morning. I've been told that he compared me to both Josef Stalin and Pol Pot."

"Just for the record," I said, "I don't think you look like Pol Pot at all."

He inclined his head slightly in acknowledgment and I left him to get back to his work. For one of the police brass, DCC Wallace wasn't a bad bloke at all.

I stood on the sidewalk outside the police station and breathed in the heavy, salt-laden air. It was cloudy and the wind seemed to be picking up. It was coming out of the east, all the way from the Russian steppes, across the cold Baltic, over the rocky Danish coast and on across the North Sea. The easterlies meant bad weather, as the cold wind collided with the usual warm westerly flow of the Gulf Stream. In the winter, the easterlies meant blizzards and freezing conditions. In the summer, just periods of heavy rain and steady, chilly breezes. It was likely that the players in the morning draw would have much better luck with the weather than the afternoon players, but all would have to deal with a golf course much more formidable than the Old Course they had seen yesterday in the bright sunshine and mild breezes.

I wandered down to the golf course, and stood for a while in the opening between the massive grandstands and the R&A clubhouse, watching some of the groups teeing off, and some of the early groups coming down the Home hole. Applause rippled through the air and over the brownish green fairways, sounding like sudden outbursts of rain on a tin roof. The grandstands that extended for several hundred yards down the side of the first hole were about half full on this chilly, rainy morning, but the fans were no less enthusiastic in applauding for their favorites as they were announced on the first tee. The occasional Scottish-born player, Paul Lawrie, Derrick Montrose, Ian MacCrae, all got loud raucous cheers along with the applause.

I kind of got lost in the pleasure of it all. The sounds, the sights, the palpable edge of tension in the air, the bursts of birdie cheers rolling in from some distant hole on the course. There is nothing like the atmosphere of a major golf tournament, and nothing at all like an Open in St. Andrews, where the gray slate buildings of the old town echo and amplify the sounds of the cheers, tossing them back into the arena where the wind catches them and carries them off into the ether.

Which is why I wasn't paying close attention, and was surprised when a hard and heavy hand grasped me by the shoulder and pulled me around, and back a few steps under the cover of the grandstands above. I came face to face with the bald Russian goon, his ears sticking out from his round head. He didn't have dark glasses on today in the cloudy and dark conditions, and his black eyes were narrowed and sharp. He kept his hand on my shoulder, gripping it in a meaty fist that came just short of being painful.

"You!" he said in a guttural accent. "Where is friend, John Swift? Tell me now."

I paused for a moment. I could see the other goon looming just over Baldy's shoulder. That meant if I tried doing something like kicking the guy in the nuts, the other goon would be on me in no time. So I went with Plan B.

"Help!" I yelled as loud as I could. "Thief! Pickpocket! Get your hands out of my pocket! Help!"

Baldy's hand flew off my shoulder, so I began waving both hands and shouting some more. People began to gather, interested in the little drama I was creating under the grandstands. Within a few seconds, a woman officer in her starched white blouse with epaulets, wide black-and-white checked necktie and stylish little fedora-like cap appeared at my side.

"What seems to be the trouble, here?" she asked, trying to step between Baldy and me, to edge us apart. Baldy didn't like that and made the mistake of giving her a shove out of the way. It was a mistake because as soon as he touched the lady cop, about a half dozen men had him and his friend down on the ground, hands tightly bound behind his back in white plastic cuffs. Only two of the crowd that had descended on our little scene were wearing official uniforms. The other four or five were plainsclothesmen, all dressed in jeans and light jackets that came down far enough over the hip to hide the guns each man wore on his hip, or tucked in the waistband of his pants. I had figured that security in and around the golf course that morning was likely to be tight, given the near-riot of the previous afternoon. So creating a ruckus had turned out to be a pretty good way of summoning help in a hurry.

The lady bobbie pulled me away from the two trussed goons who were waiting for a paddy wagon to take them away. Once we were a few yards removed, she whipped out a small black notebook and pencil and said "Right then, sir, please tell me what happened."

I spun a pretty good tale of feeling a hand trying

to extricate my wallet from my back pocket and confronting Baldy and his pal. It all sounded plausible, and she wrote down all the details as fast as I could make them up. I figured it would keep Baldy and company tied up with the police for most of the day. If I was lucky, they might have records or pending warrants or something and get stuck in jail for a long time, or at least until the tournament ended and I got out of town. But even if the cops eventually let them walk with a severe warning, they might be a little less enthusiastic about trying to brace me in a public place for Swiftie's whereabouts. Maybe. I tried not to think about what they'd do if they caught me in private.

The lady cop finished taking notes and handed me a business card with her name on it. "Please don't hesitate to call if you think of any other details," she said. "Are you in town for the golf?"

I said yes and told her who I was. "Will I need to come back for a trial?" I asked.

She shook her head. "Nae, nae," she said. "We'll probably have them on up charges of attempted petty theft. A magistrate will either fine them or remand them for a week or so. Your testimony will not be required." We shook hands and I made for the safety, I hoped, of the press tent.

Chapter Twenty

"So, Almighty Hacker of the Great Golf, who's gonna win this thing?"

Mary Jane and I had managed to find one of the small wooden booths in the back of the Central Pub. The booth was just wide enough for two people sitting across from each other, although I have seen students from the University manage to cram four people aside, although none of them looked happy at the time. Mary Jane had made a nice chicken Caesar salad for dinner, along with some warm french bread and an inexpensive bottle of a Spanish red that wasn't bad at all. The roomies were nowhere to be found, no doubt painting the town red, or some other color. So afterwards, we had washed the dishes and put them away, then decided to go for a walk. The air was still thick and heavy with clouds, and a chilly mist blew through the narrow streets as we walked. I had felt Mary Jane shiver, so suggested we stop in for a quick bracer at my favorite pub in town. Even though the joint was jumping with all the golf fans still in town for the fun,

I spotted the empty booth in the back left corner and steered Mary Jane over in time to claim it as our own. I bought a pint of local ale for me and a half-pint of lager for MJ, brought them back to the booth and that's when she asked the question.

"Haven't got a clue," I said. "I'm a golf writer, not golf clairvoyant. Casey could run away with it, or someone could come out the pack from ten strokes behind. That's why they play four rounds, so the winner can emerge." At the end of the second round, Paul Casey held a two-shot lead over American Dustin Johnson, the Dane Thomas Bjorn and a German, Heinrich Gruber. But the buzz had been growing all day as the two young European studs, Conor Kelly from Ireland and Enrico Paz of Spain, had each played steady golf all day long and were tied for third, four shots back. They would play together tomorrow, a match everyone was looking forward to watching.

"Doesn't help a girl much if she's thinking of betting a few quid," Mary Jane said, with a devilish smile playing at the corners of her mouth.

"Who is the girl in question thinking of wasting her money on?" I asked.

"Well, that's why I asked, isn't it?" she said. "I thought all you pundits sat around trying to decide who was going to win."

"You must be mistaking me for some airhead who talks on television," I said. "Their job is to sit around and jabber on for hours about who might win and who might not. I just watch and report, lady."

"In that case, I guess I'll have to bet on the one with the cutest butt," she said with a giggle.

"Child," I said, stealing a line from The Wizard of Oz, "You cut me to the quick! Which one has the cutest butt?"

"Oh, I think Conor is a dreamboat," she said, thinking with head cocked to one side. "But Rikki isn't half bad in the butt department."

"Rikki?"

"It's what everyone calls him," she said. "Don't you know that? Enrico is so formal. He's much more of a Rikki, with that spiky black hair and that smooth olive skin and that delicious little round …"

"Okay," I said. "I think you should stop now. I'm beginning to get jealous and I'm supposed to be an objective journalist."

She laughed. "You know I only have eyes for you," she said, her eyes bright and alive with an excitement I suspected I had no part in whatsoever. But what could I do? Both Conor Kelly and Enrico…*Rikki*…Paz were young and healthy specimens. They ran miles every week, worked the weight room for hours and hit thousands of golf balls. They looked like what 25-year-old professional athletes should look like: tanned, handsome demi-Gods with flat stomachs and narrow waists who made men jealous and made women think of sex. And they probably tooled around in Ferraris. It reminded me of an Irish stud farm I had visited during a golfing trip to the Emerald Isle some years ago. Led on a tour of the stables at this farm filled with magnificent thoroughbred race horses, I had been introduced to Ted the Teaser. Ted was an old gray stallion getting on in years. His back was swayed, his muzzle was shaggy and there were stray hairs poking out of his ears. And his eyes…I will never forget the haunted look on this horse, as if he had peered into the Great Horse Abyss and seen what Fates awaited him. Then they told me that Ted the Teaser's job was to be led into the stable of a filly about to be impregnated, let his normal stallion pheromones get her natural filly hormones in an uproar and then, just as he has signaled *Now, darling?* and she has replied, *Oh, yes…yess…now!* Ted the Teaser is yanked away and the million-dollar stud is led in to do the actual deed. Back in his empty, fly-filled paddock, poor Ted the Teaser is left to ponder what might have been, if not to ask what the hell just happened here?

Compared to the likes of Conor Kelly and Rikki Paz, I was that old, swaybacked stallion, long in tooth, ears full of stray hairs, left with not much beside memories of a time when we had been a contender. For so many things in so many ways.

Mary Jane must have seen something in my eyes, for she reached over and grabbed my hand in hers. "Oh, Hacker," she said, "Those two boys might be good looking and all, but I'll bet they are dumb as stumps. There's more to attraction than just the shape of one's rump."

"There is?" I asked. Then I had to duck as she tried to land a left cross. But I kept hold of her other hand, and we smiled at each other.

"So how's your case going?" she asked.

"My case?"

"You know," she said, snorting a little. "The dead golf official and the Russian mobsters murdering someone down by the sea and chasing poor Johnny Swift around town."

"Oh," I said, "*That* case." I took a sip of beer. It was warmish, but surprisingly tangy. I'm not so sure a Budweiser would taste good at just under room temperature, but the local ale was quite tasty that way. I wondered, not for the first time, if the Brits didn't have this beer thing figured out rather well after all.

"Well," I said finally, after thinking about beer for a few seconds, "I don't think my so-called case is going very well. Which is to say, I seem to have more questions than answers at this point, and that's never a good thing for a so-called sleuth."

"Poor baby," Mary Jane said, patting my hand again. "Tell Mama what you know and what you don't know. You usually get an idea of what to do next when you do that."

I took a breath and let it out. "Okay," I said. "We know that Colin Kincaid was killed."

"That's a good start," she said with a smile. "At least, for a murder case."

I forged on. "We don't know who killed him. But we do know that he was probably killed somewhere near the River Eden, based on the seeds and other plant material found on his clothing. We also know that he was killed with a very efficient breaking of his neck. That could mean that he was killed by someone who knew what he was doing."

"Or she," Mary Jane said.

"Don't complicate the complicated," I said. "A neat, clean fracture of the cervical structure is the hallmark of secret agents, paramilitary types or special forces."

"Like the Russians?"

I shrugged. "Well, maybe. There do seem to be a lot of Russians around this case, and there certainly are a lot of former Soviet special forces operatives working for the Russian mafia gangs around the world. It's not dispositive, but when you also consider that Kincaid's body was neatly deposited in the Bottle Dungeon, which is kept under lock and key, it seems to point to someone with special, er, knowledge."

"What do we know about Kincaid?" she asked.

"He was the designated bastard at the Links Trust," I said. Seeing her eyebrows raised, I explained. "His job was, among other things, to turn down hare-brained deals and proposals. That would have the unfortunate side effect of making him unpopular with a lot of people."

"You'd have to go through all those proposals and interview them all to see who was mad enough to kill the man," Mary Jane pointed out sensibly. "You're not thinking of trying to do all that, are you? I'm supposed to be back at work next Tuesday."

"No way," I agreed. "Hopefully Deputy Chief Commander Wallace is doing all that legwork."

"Good," she said. "What else?"

"Well, we know that Kincaid was a bird watcher and he was apparently fluent in Russian. And, he lived alone in Dundee."

She thought about that. "Only the Russian language thing is interesting," she said. "What with all the Russkis suddenly floating around."

"And the birdwatching," I said. "Could explain why his clothes were covered in stuff from the fields and all…"

"Maybe a big bird didn't like being watched, jumped on him, broke his neck, flew him off to the castle and dropped him down the hole into the dungeon," she said, smiling.

"More likely it was a big Russian in an inflatable dinghy," I said. "Kincaid might have seen something he wasn't supposed to see."

"And who are all these Russians?" Mary Jane asked next.

"Dunno," I said, shaking my head. "But we've got Colin Kincaid as a student of the language. Also, he had a secret Russian wife, although that may have just been a youthful mistake. We've got Sir John Cheape trying to do business with Russian firms. And his Man Friday is a Russian named Yuri. We've got the rumors of a big new Russian investment pending somewhere on the Scottish coast. Kincaid himself may have been trying to help the Russians secretly acquire land at the Leuchars airbase across the river. And we've got this supposed hit squad in the inflatable dinghy, tooling around the coastline in the middle of the night. And the same guys, as far as we can tell, have been trying to find Swiftie and I doubt if it's to give him a nice tip for his caddie services."

"Add it up, and what do you get?" she asked.

"Bupkis," I said sadly. "There's gotta be a connection in there somewhere, but I'll be damned if I can find it."

Mary Jane held up a finger, then turned and began to dig into her purse. She pulled out a little blue spiral notebook, flipped it open and began to parse through the pages. "Here it is," she said. She looked at me. "I went to the university library this afternoon," she said. "Did a little research on this REBCCO refinery thing. Found some interesting stuff."

I looked at her admiringly. "You went to the library?" I said. "Why, that's…that's…" I couldn't find the right words.

"Intelligent," she said, supplying the right word. Might not have been the one I was searching for, but it worked. "Here's what I found out. REBCCO initially floated the proposal to build this refinery back in 2010. It was immediately rejected by the Scottish executive—that's the head of Scotland's government, which, I've learned, is different from the British government down in London. These people love their layers of government." She stopped and tapped her pencil against her teeth thoughtfully. I waited.

"Anyway, the deal seemed to be dead in the water at that point. But then, about a year ago, the Scottish Board for Economic Development, which is called in the newspapers a 'quasi-governmental organisation,' voted to officially take the idea of a Russian-built oil refinery on the Scottish coast under advisement. And guess who chairs the board?"

She looked at me triumphantly. I shrugged.

"Sir John Cheape of Wormwood," she said. "Who we know is rich in land, poor in cash, has lots of Russian business contacts and even employs one to run his estate."

"Verrry interesting," I said, nodding. "Maybe he thinks he can swing a deal with the Russians and the Brits to bring the refinery project to the old Leuchars air base. What do we know about the closing of the base?"

Mary Jane beamed at me, as she flipped a few more pages in her notebook.

"I knew you would ask me that, so I looked it up. You will never in a million zillion years guess what I found out, regarding the owner of the land at Leuchars."

"I'll bet it's our very good friend Johnny Cheape," I said.

"How in the hell did you know that?" Her face fell. She had been planning for the big reveal.

"Well, it makes sense, doesn't it?" I said. "The Cheape family purchased all the land on this side of the River Eden way back when. Why wouldn't they also buy the land on the other side? Isn't that how these aristo families got to be so wealthy and powerful? Buying up land and charging rent for its use?"

"Shit," Mary Jane said. "But you are absolutely right. Johnny Cheape's great-great-grandfather bought about two thousand acres at Tentsmuir in the Howe of Fife just before the turn of the last century. He bought basically all the land between Leuchars and Tayport. The estate contains one big old drafty castle, at Earlshall, a dozen or so small farms, and the land underneath the runways at RAF Leuchars. So now the fighter jets are being re-assigned up the coast at Lossiemouth, there's a nice big parcel of empty land on the north bank of the River Eden, owned lock, stock and gorse bush by Johnnie Cheape of Wormwood. Should be worth quite a bit of cash should, say, some Russian company need a place to build an oil refinery."

"Do we know who owns REBCCO?" I asked.

She looked in her notebook again. "Yeah, here it is. The Russian European Brent Crude Co. is a subsidiary of Rusoil, which is the national oil company of the Russian Federation. When the Commies got the boot, Rusoil was sold off to one of the oligarchs. But when Putin took over, he wanted it back, so he had the guy shipped off to Siberia on some lame excuse and put his own lackey in control. So both Rusoil and REBCCO are basically under the control of the Kremlin."

"Which means they can also hire all the strong-arm muscle they want," I said.

"But why would they want to go around Scotland killing people?" Mary Jane asked. "Wouldn't that effectively screw the pooch, as far as getting approval for their plans?"

I thought about that. "Yeah, that doesn't seem to make sense," I agreed. "Maybe the goon squad is entirely separate from the business deal. But what are they after?"

Mary Jane yawned. “I dunno, bucko, but all this sleuthing is making me sleepy. Take me home.”

And so I did. I tried to stay alert in case any Russian goons were lurking, but the streets were mostly empty, the night was warm and I was happy to be walking arm in arm with my favorite person in the world.

Chapter Twenty-one

NONE OF US in the flat was up early on Saturday. I woke before dawn, heard sheets of rain pelting down against the window, thought *that won't be fun to play in,* turned over and went back to sleep. When I next awoke, it was after ten and when I looked out the window, the rain had stopped, the sun was struggling to break through the clouds and a gusty wind was rattling the panes of glass in the window. It was the kind of day that promised to wreak havoc on low scores. *Oh, goody,* I thought, *now we have ourselves an Open.*

Out in the lounge, I found I was the last one up. Someone had gone out for the morning papers, and the sports sections were spread everywhere. I picked up a news section and learned that Israel was warning Iran, Pakistan was warning India and the German bankers were warning Greece. In other words, the world was pretty much operating at normal, that is, most people in it didn't give a damn about what was going to happen that afternoon on the Old Course.

When I finally managed to grab a cup of coffee and an unread sports section, I discovered that Professor Cecil Knox, head of the Eliminate Golf group, had disappeared. Or, at least he had stopped talking to the press, which in his case amounted to the same thing. One of the London sports columnists huffed in print: "If the Professor does not care to come forward and argue his case, as inestimably silly as that case may be, then the rest of us may be excused if we simply ignore this man's rot and go back to watching golf as we always have. What a colossal waste of time this man has been. I hope the Fife District Constabulary sends the professor, and his University, a nice hefty bill for reimbursement of their services the other day in preventing a mob of hooligans from putting the sack to an innocent town."

Mario saw me reading the piece. "Don't you just love the writing?" he said. "Rot and putting the sack to the town. Why can't we write like that? Guess E-Go was an epic fail. Guy got his fifteen minutes of fame, then took a powder."

I shrugged. "I don't know," I said. "It may not be over yet. Something tells me that the mad Professor may have something else up his sleeve. After all, there are still two rounds to go."

"No way," Mario was convinced. "The place is crawling with cops and security. Someone told me yesterday that there's like several platoons of military guys on call over at the air force base in case something breaks out. Naw, I think this idiot learned that you can't mess with the game of golf in St. Andrews. So he's decided to go on vacation. Probably to Moscow or someplace where they like his kind of thinking."

I looked at Mary Jane and she looked back at me, nodding. Mario had just been throwing out one of his typically sarcastic comments, but something he said had clicked into place. I had wondered why Sir John Cheape had invited someone like Professor Knox to dinner the night Mary Jane and I had joined them. Sir Hamish had scoffed at the idea of Cheape having enough spare cash lying around to contribute funding for the E-Go organization. But what if Cheape had helped arrange financing through his Russian associates? If those associates were the ones trying to gain approval for an oil refinery on the Fifeshire coastline, taking over the seaside real estate now occupied by Her Majesty's air force base at Leuchars, across the River Eden from the golf courses of St. Andrews, there might be some value to disrupting the Open Championship. But what?

"Why would they want to goober up the tournament?" I asked out loud, speaking mainly to Mary Jane, who understood the question. "What do they gain?"

"Maybe they're hoping the R&A will decide to take St Andrews off the rota of courses used for the Open," Mary Jane guessed. "That would solve some problems, no?"

"Hey!" Mario stood up suddenly and almost shouted at us. "Goddam it! How did you guys get my Sunday column? I haven't even printed out a copy yet."

"What are you talking about?" I said to him. "We were just thinking out loud about something else."

"No way," Mario was pacing now, arms gesticulating wildly. "Mary Jane said something about the R&A taking the Old Course off the rota. That's what my column is about. I thought I had an exclusive!"

I laughed and told Mario to calm down. I explained that we had been talking about the professor, the E-Go organization and a possible source of financing from Sir John Cheape's Russian partners.

"But tell me what you found out," I said. "Off the record, of course."

"You steal a word of this and I will personally de-ball you," Mario said a finger waving at me menacingly, although I knew he was really a pussycat. He told us that he had been talking with someone fairly high up in the R&A hierarchy who had told him there had been internal discussions about taking the Old Course off the list of courses traditionally approved for hosting the Open Championship. "They think it's not really long enough anymore for a major championship," he explained. "And unless the weather is really awful, like today, for instance, they know the scores will be low. While the R&A has never cared as much as the U.S. Golf Association about keeping the score for its national championship under control, they really don't want to see some future championship where the winning score is twenty-two under par or something, and they're afraid that's going to happen. There's not a whole lot they can do to this golf course to make it longer or tougher. It is what it is. On the other hand, there's all the tradition and history and crap that they love so much. My source told me that the debates on the topic so far have been pretty heated on both sides."

"Lord Cheape would have been aware of these discussions," I said, speaking mostly to Mary Jane again. "Even if the R&A was holding super-secret talks deep in the bowels of the clubhouse, word would have to leak out. St. Andrews isn't that big a town and Cheape is still a R&A member, and something of a big swinging dick in this town. And if it would help his clients get their refinery approved, he'd be glad to give a little push to the side that's in favor of taking the championship away. It would increase the value of his land across the River

Eden. And if the R&A sees that there will be marches and protests and such every time they stage the Open here, they might think twice about it."

"That sort of makes sense," Mary Jane agreed.

"Not to me," Mario said. "I'm lost."

I explained. "The Russian state oil company, or an offshoot of it, wants to build a big new refinery somewhere on the Scottish coast, the better to process and ship petroleum from the North Sea back to the Motherland," I said. "Lord Cheape, the local bigwig, has been trying to help the Russians get approval for the deal. He's said to be in rather dire financial straits personally, so he would likely stand to benefit handsomely if the deal goes through."

"And he's the chairman of the economic development board that is considering the proposal," Mary Jane piped in. "Plus, he owns the land currently occupied by the RAF base across the river, and would make a fortune selling or renting to an oil refinery."

"Ah," Mario said, "Classic political corruption. Sounds like something that happens every day in Jersey. OK, I get it now."

"Right," I nodded. "The RAF is decommissioning the air base across the river, the Russians want to move in and build the plant there. But the locals here at the home of golf would likely protest having a smelly oil refinery over there. So Cheape and his Russian backers have helped Cecil Knox organize his little protests against golf during the Open. Marches, riots…and whatever he has planned for the weekend. That creates bad publicity, tosses egg on the face of the R&A. Which, as you found out, is already wondering if St. Andrews is still a good place to stage a major championship."

"It's the bloody Old Course," Mario said, waving his hands. "They've been holding championships here for what, a hundred and fifty years now? You really think they're going to stop?"

"No," I said. "Probably not. But maybe instead of coming back here every five or so years, what if they decide to hold the Open here once every twenty years? Especially after this year, maybe they decide to have a little hiatus, let the controversy die down, try to figure out ways to make the course longer or tougher…"

"It's the bloody Old Course," Mario said again. "It's like the Sistine Chapel or the Louvre or something. It's the Holy of Holies."

"I know, I know," I said quickly, cutting him off. "But bear with me. They announce that after this year, it'll be another ten or so years before they come back. They can roll out an excuse, like there are lots of new and worthy golf courses in Great Britain that ought to have a chance to host an Open. So they start working them in. That gives the Russians time to get their refinery built and operating, bringing lots of economic boon to the area, and people will have time to get used to seeing it over there. Hell, most of the fanciest golf courses in this country have campgrounds and RV parks just outside their gates. So even a refinery away across the river would hardly be noticeable. Except for the smell and the smoke and the huge tanker ships lined up to get their loads. But maybe the new generation of refineries don't reek so bad."

"They reek pretty bad over in New Jersey," Mario said.

Brad had been quiet through all this, listening while he sipped his coffee. Now he stirred.

"There's no way in hell they will ever take the Open out of St. Andrews," he said. "Not a chance."

"Not even if they routinely have scores in the minus-twenties?" I asked.

"Nope."

"Or the threat of more political protests?"

"Nope."

"Or if the players or the sponsors decide it's not a good thing to have it here?"

"Nope."

"Because?"

He sighed. "Because, like Mario said, it's the bloody Old Course," he said. "It's the freaking mythological home of golf. It doesn't matter what they score here, or even what's built or not built around the place. They could line the fairways with condos, hire Conrad Gold to add a casino or three, or build another Disneyland over on the East Sands. Wouldn't matter. It's the Old Course. They've been playing the game on it for five hundred years. Every generation since time began has come up with some new kind of golf equipment or technique or something to improve the game, but the Old Course stays the same. It doesn't matter what the score is, it only matters who figures out how best to solve the problems out there. The bumps and the hollows and the bunkers and the wind. Those ridiculous goddam ocean-sized putting greens and the sideways rain. It's the salty air and all the nice red-cheeked people who understand how difficult it is to rope a five-iron around that bunker on seventeen and two-putt for par. Especially on Sunday afternoon at the Open, when the pressure is ramped up to eleven. It doesn't matter what the score is. The point of playing here is to test yourself against a golf course that really hasn't significantly changed since the days when the shepherds were knocking round rocks around with their crooks. If it took one of them 100 whacks to get his rock to fall into a rabbit hole, the next guy tried to do it in 99. That's what the game is all about. Allan Robertson shot a 79 with hickory clubs and a ball stuffed with feathers in the 1850s. Probably the single greatest round of golf of all time. Old Tom Morris was the first to break 80 with the gutta. But in the Open, no one shot lower than 80 here until J.H. Taylor in the second round in 1895. But so what? Back then, the pros went out and shot 85s and thought they were the greatest of the great. Now they shoot in the low 60s and think the same thing. So what's changed? What's different? When it comes right down to it, *nothing*. You still have to drive the ball in the fairway, hit the ball on the green and get it into the hole. If you can do it in fewer strokes than anyone else, they engrave your name on the Claret Jug. That's what it's all about. They're never going to take the Open away from this place. They can't. It's the fabric of the game. It's the beating heart of golf. Golf can't live without this place. Simple as that."

None of us said anything. For what else was there to say?

Chapter Twenty-two

I GOT DOWN to the golf course after lunch. Now that the field had been cut to the low 60 golfers, they started sending players out around ten, and the leaders were scheduled to hit the first tee around three in the afternoon. Everyone in St. Andrews was looking forward to watching the match that would tee off third-from-last: the two young guns, Enrique "Rikki" Paz and Irishman Conor Kelly. The British press was calling it the "Match of the Next Century" as these two talented young stars were expected to carry the banner of European golf for the next twenty or thirty years. The two were tied at two-under and everyone in the press tent had a different opinion on how these kids would hold up under the pressure of a major on "moving day," when the goal is to get into contention for Sunday's final dash to the finish.

I went out to watch them tee off, just after two thirty. The rain had stopped and the sun was shining, but a strong wind kept blowing clouds across its face and the shadows that raced across the corrugated surface of the famous old course looked as if they were being blown by the gusts coming down from the mountains of the Highlands. "Tis a grand day for golf, is it not?" an elderly gent dressed in a tweed sport coat of gold and green asked me as we crowded around the ropes at the first tee. "Grand," I agreed, nodding. It was certainly a day when the Old Course was showing her teeth, and they were pointed, sharp, and ready to tear away strokes from any golfer who let his attention wander. The conditions had been gusty since the morning, and the early scores coming in had been high.

I looked up at the Big Room window in the R&A clubhouse and saw the usual collection of Old Boys, drinks in hand, staring out at the magnificent scene. How could they think about taking the tournament away from this place? I wondered. This is what it's all about. A championship. A golf course. The weather. Eighteen holes, long and short. Seven straight out, with the wind helping from the left. The loop of four at the far end and then seven more straight back into town, this time against the gusts. Unless the wind changed with the tides. Or picked up. Or laid down. Or if it started to rain. Or snow. Those great uncontrollable unknowns were also part of what made this place, and this game, so special. Just as in life, nobody really knew what was going to happen next. So the journey, over the next four and a half hours, was going to be fun to watch.

The crowds packed in around the tee, as well as those gathered in the towering grandstands behind the tee and down the first fairway, seemed to be evenly divided between supporters of the Irish kid and the young Spaniard. Flags were waving back and forth, chants and cheers split the air as each golfer was introduced by the diminutive Ivor Robson. *Now on the tee, from Ireland ...*

Conor Kelly! Kelly had the honor and hit a three wood straight and long down the middle, where it stopped about fifty yards short of the Swilcan Burn. *Now on the tee, from Spain...Enrique Paz!* Rikki Paz followed suit, going a little further left, and they were off. Thousands and thousands of fans pushed along with them, outside the ropes. You could feel the excitement in the air. It really was a grand day for golf.

I decided to let them go, and catch up with them on the back nine, if they were still in contention. I went back inside the tent and got some work done, sending off notes and beginning a draft of my column for Sunday's paper. Like almost every other golf writer, I was planning to write about the Match of the Next Century and what it meant. And I was hoping neither one of the young guns would collapse under the pressure of the day, or I'd have to come up with another brilliant idea.

The tent was quiet and mostly empty, which was strange. Many of my colleagues had apparently decided to follow the young stars around the course. That was unusual for golf writers, who usually never walked further than the commissary at the far end of the press room during a tournament, relying instead on the wall-to-wall television feed and the after-round packaged interviews with the players to get their material. That was fine with me: I was able to concentrate on my work without the usual interruptions and inane discussions and after an hour or two I was pretty much finished. Once the day's play had ended, I could wrap things up in my column, write the day's game story and send it all back to Boston, where the understaffed copy desk and the overstuffed executive editor would likely butcher my syntax and rewrite the lead. Bastards.

I glanced at the TV screens and saw that the dynamic duo had just finished the seventh hole, and were heading for the par-three eighth on the loop holes. Each of them had made a birdie and a bogey so far, while the two groups of leaders behind them had struggled with the wind and dropped some shots, so that there were now at least ten or twelve players within shouting distance of the lead. It was shaping up to be a fine day. Grand, even.

Suddenly, the TV went black. The overhead lights in the tent flickered and went out. I heard a soft beeping alarm begin to sound. I stood up and walked over to where Mario was typing furiously away in the semi-dark.

"Somebody must have blown a fuse," I said. Mario shrugged. He was on a roll, fingers flying across his laptop's keyboard, a deep frown on his face, oblivious to anything going on around him.

A group of policemen began swarming in through the front doorway. Two of them had black labradors on leashes. There must have been at least twenty cops, milling about looking serious. A lady bobbie pulled out a megaphone.

"Attention please," she broadcast to those of us in the tent. "This area is under an evacuation order. Please gather all personal belongings and leave at once. Repeat...please leave this area at once. There has been a security incident and this area must be secured." She repeated the message a few times to make sure everyone, even the small city of Asian journalists down in the far corner, got it. We did. I folded up my laptop, stuffed it into my briefcase and headed for the door. Outside, I went up to one of the policemen.

"What's up?" I asked.

"Bomb threat's been called in," he said, eyes giving me the up-and-down that cops do so well.

"Someone wants to blow up the press tent?" I asked, sounding as incredulous as I felt.

The cop smiled. "Nae, lad," he said. "It's the big one over there." He nodded over his shoulder at the R&A clubhouse. "Supposed to blow any minute now. Probably just a crank, someone trying to be funny. But if it does go off, there would likely be some pieces of building raining down over here..." he nodded this time at the press tent. "So it has been decided to evacuate both places just to be safe. And some of the grandstands. Our canine sniffers are going over both places. Shouldn't take too long to clear the area, I wouldn't think." He smiled somewhat ruefully. "Unless she does blow, of course. You should probably stay well clear, just in case."

I looked up again at the big window on the second story of the clubhouse. The Old Boys were still up there, drinks in hand, ties in place, blazers buttoned. I couldn't tell if their eyes were glazed, but I suspected as much.

"How come they're not clearing out?" I asked the cop, pointing at the R&A. "They don't want to miss a shot?"

He looked up and shrugged. "Most of the old buggers up there are retired military," he told me. "They probably consider it their patriotic duty to go down with the ship. Imagine it would take another stick of dynamite up their bottoms to make them leave."

"That's why there'll always be a Britain," I said with admiration.

The cop shrugged. "Unless she does blow," he said. "In which case there'll be a lot of bloody patriotic body parts flying around. And guess who gets to pick them up?"

Another phalanx of bobbies was trying to usher people out of the grandstands behind the last hole, without much success. Many of the fans had arrived before dawn to secure a place there, and they didn't want to leave, despite the threat of flying chunks of sandstone or the heads, along with the torsos and legs of a couple dozen of Her Majesty's Major Generals, (Ret.). But the bobbies were insistent and, eventually, they got the stands emptied. After some deliberation, it was decided to let the grandstand fans and anyone else who wanted to gather out on the massively wide fairway that served the first and last holes, and play was temporarily stopped after the groups finished the seventeenth. A ring of officials took up positions around the edge of the last green to keep people off the actual putting surface, but thousands of fans gathered on the tightly cropped fairway in something of a carnival atmosphere. Kids were turning cartwheels and people were taking each other's pictures as if they were on holiday. *Here's Fred and Magda just before the roof blew off and killed them both. Doesn't she look happy?* The waves of Day-Glo police eventually managed to push everyone back across Granny Clark's Wynd, the narrow little public street that cuts across the fairway about 100 yards from the green. And then we all waited. And waited.

It was about forty-five minutes before the sniffer dogs and the bomb squads had inspected every square inch of the R&A clubhouse. I heard some wag near me comment that they probably were enjoying some G&Ts at the Members' Bar. Somebody finally rang a loud bell for the all-clear and several thousand spectators began rushing back to take up their former positions in the grandstands. After another half-hour or so of madness, they cleared the fairways, let the first of the six or seven twosomes waiting on the last tee play away, and things slowly began to come back to normal.

I went back inside the press tent, and stored my briefcase again at my work station. A group of writers had gathered around Bernie Capshaw, the press secretary, and he was explaining what he knew.

"A phone call came in at about three-thirty," he was saying. "Said a bomb had been placed in the R&A clubhouse and was scheduled to detonate at approximately four p.m. Special police forces had been on call nearby and they were brought in to take over the situation. The R&A building was searched, as was the press area, and the caddie house underneath the grandstands, and nothing out of the ordinary was found. The authorities are continuing to investigate this incident and if they learn anything further, we will let you know. That's all I have at the moment."

"Do you think it was the E-Go people?" I asked.

Bernie shrugged. "Pure speculation at this point, Hacker," he said. "I'm sure the authorities will check into that possibility. But it could have been any crank with a belly full of lager and a telephone."

Speculation or not, I suspected Professor Knox for the bomb scare. But I had work to do. I wanted to watch the tyros fight their way back to the clubhouse. So I left the press tent and began the long trek down the course to the loop holes at the far end. The wind was still brisk enough for most of the spectators to wear a windbreaker or a light sweater. The row of international flags atop the main grandstand to the right of the first hole were all stretched out flat, snapping in the wind. But I noticed the wind had shifted around a little and was now coming out of the southwest, a bit of a change from the morning. That meant that the field would be battling the strong breezes all the way home to the final hole.

Kelly and Paz were putting out on the par-three eleventh hole when I made it out to the bank overlooking the River Eden. I waited for them near the 12th tee, looking out across the mudflats. It was low tide and the river had withdrawn into its narrow, snakey little channel several hundred yards away, leaving the mud covered in sea weed and other detritus. Wading birds were scuttling around picking at things, looking for revealed delicacies in the barren landscape.

The golfers arrived on the tee, with their caddies, the rules official, the scorer, the kid with the score sign, a few security types, and about a half dozen media, both writers and photographers, who had been authorized to walk inside the ropes with the group. Spectators came rushing over from the last hole and took up positions against the fairway ropes. Within seconds, the gallery was ten deep. Conor Kelly was now at five-under par, one ahead of his Spanish rival. The German, Gruber, was leading the tournament at seven-under, and he was now playing the tenth.

Number twelve at St. Andrews is a short par-four, the fairway moving slightly diagonally to the left. On a day when the wind is shrieking out of the north, it is a driveable hole, especially for the pros. But today, the wind was against them, and slightly across from right to left. That brought the smattering of bunkers across the fairway into play, especially the one small and deep one situated just in front of the green. I watched as both players consulted with the caddies, studying their yardage books and trying to decide on the best strategy. Kelly finally reached into his bag for the driver. Given the conditions of the day, it was not a bad choice. He probably couldn't reach the green, but if he managed to hit a straight shot, chances were good he would fetch up on the fairway with but a wedge left into the narrow green perched atop a high shelf and surrounded by a steep dropoff in the back and some nasty looking clumps of gorse. He made a beautiful pass at the ball—I recalled the conversation about poetry—and sent it flying down the middle of the fairway. The wind pushed it a little to the left, and we watched as it safely hit the green turf, took a hard bounce further left and skittered into the short rough. Unless he got truly unlucky, he would have a good look at the pin.

Rikki Paz went through the same routine with his caddie, but he eventually decided to hit a hybrid iron. He started his shot more down the right and the wind curved it back to the center, where it hit and ran like one of the rabbits that once roamed mostly freely out here. There was applause from the galleries at the green, so we knew he had safely found the fairway. The golfers set off together down the fairway and the huge gallery oozed its way after them.

Both golfers parred the hole, although Kelly's approach from the rough ran slightly over the back of the green, and he had to work to get up and down with a deft little chip. Paz's approach ended up about twenty feet left of the hole and he got it down in two.

Thirteen, Hole o' Cross (In), is a strong par four of some 465 yards. The main problem on this hole is the series of three deep cross-bunkers called the Coffins, and they sit out on the left side of the fairway, just where one's drive is supposed to go. There's room to the right side, but that leaves a mostly blind approach to the green, tucked behind some bunkered hills. Both Kelly and Paz did what most of the pros do on this hole: smashed a driver way left of the Coffins, onto the rolling turf of the shared sixth fairway. Since both of the young guns had plenty of power, and with the help of the pushing winds, they both found short grass way to the left and both knocked their approaches onto the green. Two putts each, two pars.

Fourteen, the inward nine's "Long" hole, had been lengthened a few years ago to a brute of more than 600 yards. Kelly cut a driver up against the wind to keep his ball out of the Beardies, another nasty nest of bunkers on the left side. Paz tried the same maneuver, but overcooked his fade and his ball drifted right into some deep rough. Kelly smashed a three-wood over the high lip of the fearsome Hell bunker, which sits a hundred yards or so in front of the green, but Paz, with a bad lie, hit a long iron and immediately began begging for it to carry. It needed about one more yard, but struck one of the crowns atop the huge, U-shaped bunker and fell into the soft sand. Hell is never a good place to be, but especially so at the Old Course, where the sodded vertical walls are about eight feet deep, plus another foot or two of hillock atop that.

When we got to the bunker, we saw that Paz had been slightly fortunate, in that his ball had rebounded backwards a few yards, so he wasn't tucked right up against the face. But he had to hit his most lofted wedge to clear the wall, and, with the quickening breeze in his face, there was no way he could reach the green. He laid up his third in front of the green and prepared to try and get up and down for his par. From about forty yards out, Paz nipped a sand wedge over the steep rampart of the front of the green and we watched as it hit in front of the pin, bounced once about ten feet past and then stopped. But the green is canted away from the fairway and his ball continued to trickle away from the hole for another four or five feet. It was a lovely shot under the conditions, but he still had work to do for his par.

Kelly, who had almost reached the green, decided to nip a little chip-and-run up and over that four-foot rampart, and judged the shot well enough to leave himself a five-footer for birdie. After Paz hit a beautiful putt that just rimmed the edge of the cup and spun out, Conor calmly dropped his birdie for a two-shot swing. Kelly was now one shot out of the lead for the Open Championship and three shots ahead of his young Spanish rival. The crowds went ballistic.

Fifteen is another tough driving hole against the wind, which was beginning to get even stronger as the sun began to sink towards the west. The huge Pilmour bunker looms in the distance, but the pros can easily fly it, even with the wind against. But it's the second bunker, unseen from the tee, that they worry about. It's called Sutherland and the legend has it that in 1869, after the course officials filled in the little pothole, it magically reappeared three days later. I would have called it Resurrection Bunker, but it was instead named after the local golfer who is supposed to have snuck out onto the course in the dead of night and dug it out again. In any case, that little pothole bunker collects many a fine tee shot that climbs over Pilmour, and when a golfer who believes he has striped one down the middle finds his ball nestled in its evil depths, it gets called many other names, mostly unprintable.

Both players managed to avoid Sutherland, one left and one right. Rikki Paz hit a fine approach shot to ten feet and dropped the putt, gaining back the shot he had dropped on the last. Conor Kelly made a routine par.

The sixteenth is a dangerous hole from start to finish, with a wire fence that defines the out-of-bounds line running all the way down the right side and close to the fairway. Because of that OB, the safe play is always well left of the Principal's Nose, a grouping of deep bunkers in the center of the fairway some 260 yards out. But Rikki Paz, on the strength of his birdie, was feeling frisky, so he elected to thread a tee shot down the narrow ribbon of fairway on the right side, between the OB fence and the Nose. And he managed to pull it off, using the wind to keep his ball from drifting over the out-of-bounds fence. When his tee shot stopped on the fairway, the gallery gave him an extra-enthusiastic round of applause for his courage and his skill. Kelly, on the other hand, laid up to the left of the bunkers, the more conservative but certainly warranted play on a day like this. He knocked his second onto the green, but a good forty feet from the hole. Paz took a long time with his approach and finally hit a lovely low burning shot that climbed up into the teeth of the wind, seemed to hang at the top of its parabola for the longest time, and finally dropped down softly next to the hole, less than two feet away. It was a gorgeous shot, especially under the conditions, and the admiring applause from the galleries was deafening. Kelly's long birdie try scared the hole but missed, and when Paz drained his bird, the excitement ratcheted up another notch.

The two players had to wait a bit on the tee of the famous seventeenth, the Road Hole. The holdup after the bomb scare had backed up play a little. I managed to push my way to a place near the back tee. Conor Kelly came over and put a hand on Rikki's shoulder. "Nice birdie!" he told him. "Well played." Paz smiled back. "Theese is fun, no?" he said in his accented English. Kelly dug into one of the pockets of his staff bag and pulled out some energy bars. He held one up at Paz and asked the Spaniard if he'd like one. "Si, gracias," Rikki said and Conor tossed it over. A little boy, standing near the ropes in the gallery, piped up in his sweet, high voice: "I'd like one too, please!" His embarrassed father tried to shush the lad as the gallery laughed. Conor Kelly laughed too, reached back into his golf bag and found another bar, which he walked over and handed to the kid. "Oh, thank you!" the boy said, the tone of wonder and admiration in his voice telling everyone that Conor Kelly had just made himself a fan for life.

Finally, the marshals down the fairway waved their flags to give the all-clear. The Road Hole at St. Andrews is always ranked as the most difficult hole at the Open, or any other tournament held on the course. It's a long bastard at some 490 yards, the tee having recently been shoved backwards 40 yards or more. The drive is mostly blind, cutting across the edge of the Old Course Hotel property where facsimiles of the old railroad barns have been erected to maintain the same look golfers have faced since the Iron Horses were first added to the landscape. One picks one of the letters on the hotel's logo, painted on the side of those sheds, and uses it as the aiming point, launching a drive up and over and hopefully finding a flattish piece on the rumpled fairway that turns sharply to the right, once around the bend. The drive has to be perfect, for the next shot is one of the toughest in the game. The long, skinny green curls lasciviously around the infamous Road Hole bunker in the front, and drops away in the back onto the unyielding macadam surface of the eponymous Road, all of which is in play—no free drops—bordered by a narrow strip of grass and a three-foot-high stone wall. Assuming one has found the fairway from the tee, the assignment is to hit a long-iron approach into that green, avoiding that magnetic front bunker at all costs yet simultaneously trying to stop the ball on the narrow green so it doesn't roll over onto the road or, worse, hop across it and up against the wall. All while the wind is howling along with twenty thousand golf-mad Scotsmen gathered about and sitting in the tall stands looming beyond the road. It is no wonder that so many players, whether on purpose or not, end up bailing out to the right and short, relying on their short game to try and get up and down for a hard-fought par.

Fortified by their short break and energy bars, both golfers hit beautiful tee shots. Kelly's ball bounced right into some shortish rough while Paz found the fairway, although his ball came to rest on an upslope. One rarely gets a nice flat lie on the Old Course, and this one was anything but. Kelly was away and he hit a nicely controlled burner low through the wind. His ball landed well short of the green, but ran quickly forward and ended up on the right edge of the green, a good hundred feet from the hole. Because he had controlled his distance so well, and had avoided the depths of the Road Hole Bunker, the fans gave him a well-deserved round of applause.

Paz worried over his uneven stance. The uphill slope would tend to throw his ball up into the air and into the breezes where anything could happen. He went back and forth between a five-iron and a six, talking animatedly with his caddie. They finally decided on the five, and Paz launched the shot high into the air. We all waited and watched as the shot hung in the air for several seconds before it landed ten feet behind the pin, bounced once and spun to a stop. The ground shook with the cheers that rent the air. "Bloody hell," said a young guy standing next to me. "That wee fucker can play this game!"

On the green from a hundred feet away, Conor Kelly just wanted to two-putt, take his par, and head to the home hole. He looked over the line, which went left, up, over, back to the right and down, and shook his head. The look on his face said "no way." "C'mon, Irish!" came a woman's voice from the grandstand, followed by titters and people trying to hush each other. Finally, the crowd fell into that amazing golf tournament silence, which seems to swallow all perceptible sound, like someone unseen has clamped a glass dome over the world. Kelly went through his routine and finally settled over the ball. With a smooth and calm stroke, he sent the ball rolling across the green. The silence held while the ball took the break at the front to the left, climbed up onto the next shelf and then, as the ball began to turn back to the right and down towards the hole, a slow hum began. It got louder and louder as the ball kept curving. In the last ten feet, as the ball made its way straight for the cup, momentum dying yet the ball still rolling ever forward, the hum turned into a roar and when the white ball disappeared into the blackness of the hole, the sound could have rattled windows back in Edinburgh. Kelly leaped high into the air, his putter held aloft, then pumped his fist and let loose his own shout of excitement.

Rikki Paz, watching calmly from the back of the green, could only smile and shake his head as the sound of the cheers continued to roll over the ancient golf course for a solid minute or more. Finally, exhausted, the galleries fell silent once more. Now Paz stalked his twelve-footer, a tricky little downhiller with a slight move to the right. He and his caddie looked at the putt from every angle, discussed what they had seen with each other and, finally, Rikki settled in over the putt. His stroke was pure, his speed perfect and the ball ran into the cup with all the inevitability of youth. Once again, the crowd exploded with concussive cheers. Rikki Paz picked his ball out of the hole, handed it to his caddie and then took off his cap and waved to the crowd. Conor Kelly walked over and they exchanged a high five. The young guns both knew they had put on an amazing show on the back nine of the Old Course, one to rival those that had gone before: Old Tom against Old Willie Park, Braid against Taylor, Jones v. Sweetser. Two young men from different parts of the world had played beautiful golf, controlled, strategic, occasionally heroic. It had been totally engrossing. All of us watching looked forward to seeing these two play the game together for the next twenty or thirty years, even if we all understood that perhaps never again would the situation, the course, the event and the players all fall into the perfect alignment that had occurred on this windy afternoon in St. Andrews.

Both men parred the final hole. Kelly, still pumped on adrenaline after his massive cross-country putt, drove his ball all the way into the Valley of Sin, that sand-free depression in front of the last green. Paz, still pumped as well, hit his tee shot even further, but a bit to the left, where it ended just about hole high, some ten yards left of the putting surface, but on level ground. Kelly putted his ball out of the Valley, but, as often happens, gave the putt a little extra zip to make sure it climbed that steep wall of grass and his ball finished ten feet above the hole. Seeing that, Paz's chip across the green finished an equal distance short. Both just missed their birdies, tapped in, and left the green arm-in-arm to a loud, sustained and well-deserved final ovation from the massive galleries in the looming stands and jammed in around the last green. Behind them, the German Henrich Gruber had been playing steady if unspectacular golf and still had a one-stroke lead. But the final round on Sunday promised to be an exciting day of golf.

I pushed my way through the crowds to the media tent, my mind already working on the column I was about to write summarizing the day's events. I thought of the series of mano-a-mano matches that took place in the mid-nineteenth century between the two greatest golfers of that era: Old Tom Morris and Willie Park, Senior. The man from St. Andrews versus the man from Leith, the small suburb of Auld Reekie, Edinburgh. The purses had been for the unheard of sum of one hundred pounds, winner take all, and the matches had attracted the attention (and additional wagers) of the entire nation. Indeed, one of the matches had ended in bitter dispute when the galleries crowding in around the players had become unruly and ugly, causing play to be suspended. Those challenge matches—there had been four over the men's prime years—had really launched the idea of professional golf as a sporting spectacle that people would actually pay money to watch. Today's amazing events had just written another chapter in a story that began with Old Tom and Old Willie.

I found my desk, popped open my laptop and had just begun to picture the elements that would form my lede graph when I felt a tap on my shoulder. I looked up impatiently—don't mess with a writer at work!—into the face of Bernie Capshaw, the R&A press secretary. He looked a little unsettled, which, for the normally implacable Bernie, was different.

"What?" I snapped. "I'm trying to work here."

"Terribly sorry, Hacker," he said, and he looked contrite. Bernie does understand what writers go through, having been an excellent golf and sports reporter for the Daily Telegraph before moving over to the Dark Side of public relations. "But I have been asked to have you follow me. I … er … can't tell you anything more than that right now." His face was red and his eyes implored me not to make a scene. I cursed, mostly under my breath, and slammed my laptop shut.

"This better be fucking good," I muttered and followed Bernie out of the media tent, under the stands and into the side entrance to the clubhouse of the Royal & Ancient Golf Club of St. Andrews. Inside the small foyer, there was a desk with a uniformed guard, flanked by two heavy-set police officers bristling with ear buds, armored vests and lethal-looking sidearms. The guard behind the desk recognized Bernie, nodded at him and then turned to look to his left. A man stepped out of the shadows of the room and came forward, holding out an identification badge. He was dressed in a blue suit, white button-down shirt, shiny black shoes, nice rep tie and gold cufflinks, and his reddish-hued hair was short and recently trimmed.

"Mister Hacker?" he said, in well-clipped tones. "I am Ian Cox. MI5. If you don't mind terribly, we'd like to have a little conversation with you."

"About what?" I said peevishly. "I'm on deadline."

"It's a matter of national security," Cox said. "Please follow me."

Chapter Twenty-three

Ian Cox led me upstairs, all the way to the third floor, and ushered me through a set of glass doors into a long, narrow office. It was painted yellow, had a dingy blue-gray carpet on the floor and a long conference table down the left wall, with enough plush blue chairs to seat half of Parliament. Opposite the conference table was a huge wooden executive desk, completely bare on top, with black leather executive chairs tucked into the central knee holes on either side. The ceiling was arched, giving the room something of the look of a fancified Quonset hut, albeit with nice contrasting molding.

Never having been allowed inside the Holy of Holies in St. Andrews, I wondered where we were, until I saw the view from the windows on the far end of the room. They were all floor to ceiling with a large glass door in the center, and the windows provided an amazing view down the first fairway, ringed with grandstands on one side, and the old sooty gray buildings on the other. The door led to a concrete porch with elaborate Victorian wrought iron decorations sprouting from the metal posts growing from waist-high concrete plinths.

When I saw that view, from that porch, I knew where I was: this was the office of the R&A's chief executive. Just below us would be the Big Room, where the members gathered, drinks in hand, for the Big Events, like the Open Championship, peering out at the chaotic scenes below.

The guy from MI5 was nice enough to let me gawk for a while. He then pulled out one of the chairs at the end of the conference table and motioned for me to sit down. I sat.

"Well, Mister Hacker," he said, smiling at me. "You've had quite the week here at the Open."

"I have?" I decided to be noncommittal.

"Oh, yes," he said, nodding. "You've made inquiries about a murder case, insulted a peer of the realm, and managed to evade a fairly deadly assassination squad from the FSB. That's the Russian secret service, in case you didn't know. And here we all thought you were just a golf writer from Boston."

"I am just a golf writer," I said. "And which peer of the realm says I was insulting?"

"That would be the Marquess of Wormwood," Cox said. "He called us to complain that you were being nosy and pushy."

"Johnny Cheape said that?" I was surprised. "I thought I was the very picture of tact and diplomacy the night we dined at his estate. Interesting, though, that he called MI5 to complain about me. You guys go way back, or what?"

Cox smiled at me, like I amused him no end. "Personally? Never met the man," he said. "But of course, when a marquess calls, one must try to address his complaints. And, of course, it is entirely possible that this marquess had been on our radar screens for some time."

"Ah, yes, I could see that," I said. "Probably not often that one of the aristocracy tries to transact some funny business with the Russians."

"Oh, good Lord," Cox said, laughing out loud. "Have you never heard of Philby, Maclean, Burgess, Blount and that merry gang of spies? I shudder to think what would come out if he we held every member of the House of Lords upside down and gave them a good hard shake. No, Mister Hacker, we are quite used to aristos who play games with foreign interests."

"So it's true—Cheape is trying to help the Russians get their petro plant over there in Leuchars," I said. "Thanks. That will make a good story."

"Yes, I am sure it would," Cox said. "But unfortunately we cannot allow you to publish it at this time. Or, frankly, at any time in the foreseeable future."

"Ah," I said. "I don't suppose I can claim freedom of the press?"

"No, alas," he said, cocking his head to one side and still smiling. "We don't have that here in the United Kingdom."

"Can I see a lawyer?"

"No," he said, still smiling. "You may not."

"My ambassador?"

His smile turned into a broad grin. "I could actually arrange that," he said. "I believe I saw the American ambassador downstairs in the Big Room gathered together with the members of the club. I think he's deep into his third G&T by now. Shall I drag him up here for you?"

I thought for a moment. "Nah," I said. "He's from the wrong party, anyway. He'd probably offer to have me taken to Leavenworth. If not Gitmo."

"Quite so," Cox said. "Although I don't think we'd agree to let you out of the country. We'd probably recommend you be sent to Wakefield Prison. They call it the Monster Mansion. Mostly lifers there."

"OK," I said. "Enough with the foreplay. What do you want?"

"We want you to help us with something," he said.

"What?"

Cox didn't respond. He reached into his pants pocket and pulled out some kind of clicker device. He mashed the button. A few seconds later, two large uniformed police officers came through the office door. They were each holding onto an arm of John Swift, who began to grin from ear to ear when he caught sight of me. I looked at Cox, who was smiling at me again. I was beginning to dislike his smile in a big way.

"More 'who' than 'what,'" Cox said. "We need your help with Mr. Swift here."

"Oh, God," I said, mostly to myself.

The beefy guards sat Swiftie down in a plush chair next to me and went to stand by the door. He sat down quietly and looked at me with a forlorn expression on his face.

"They got you," I said to him. "How'd that happen?"

"I was sitting on the loo," he said, rolling his eyes. "Things have come to quite a point in this country where a man canna even enjoy his time in the lavvie without being arrested."

Ian Cox chuckled. "You are not under arrest, Mr. Swift," he said. "We are here to respectfully ask for your cooperation."

"Let me finish my business and we can talk about cooperatin'" Johnny said, glaring at the man.

"Hush, Swiftie," I said. "Let's hear what the man has to say."

Over the next thirty minutes, Ian Cox explained the situation, leaving out certain classified bits, but apologizing whenever he had to do so. I thought that was considerate of him and his government: my own would never be as nice.

The gist of it was that MI5 was indeed investigating the activities of certain Russian agencies that had been operating in and around Scotland in recent months. Cox would not admit that Johnny Cheape, Marquess of Wormwood, was also under investigation, but that inference was placed on the table in such a way as not to allow any doubt.

The British feds had been connecting the dots regarding the REBCCO plan to build a refinery on the Scottish coastline, and Johnny Cheape's desire to sell them some of his land while simultaneously chairing a quasi-official economic development board. It had all been fairly aboveboard, Cox told me, until Colin Kincaid had been killed, followed a few weeks later by the apparent stabbing death of Kasyanov, whose body had been fished out of the North Sea.

Kasyanov, Cox told me, had secretly been reporting to MI5: he wanted to permanently emigrate to the U.K. and was relaying information on the progress of negotiations between the Russian oil company and various local landowners in hopes of being rewarded with a green card, or whatever color of immigration document the Queen prefers to use.

"Most of what he told us was information we already had from other sources," Cox told me. "But he had recently mentioned that negotiations were heating up here in St. Andrews. We were waiting for a new report when he disappeared."

"And my friend Swiftie here witnessed his killing out on the rocks near Crail," I finished.

"Apparently so," Cox said, nodding.

"Apparently, nothing," Swiftie said. "I saw what I saw. They knifed that poor laddie in the back, cut his throat and threw him in the sea, they did. And they'll do the same to John Swift, given half a chance. I demand to be relocated to Australia, preferably Bondi Beach. Or maybe Jamaica. Either one works for John Swift."

I cut a sideways look at my friend. "Bondi Beach?" I said, unable to stop a smile.

Swiftie leaned over and whispered. "The lassies dunna wear tops there, Hack," he said with a wink. "Be like dyin' and bein' in heaven, except I'd be alive."

I shook my head to clear out the cobwebs that Swiftie's logic had created, and looked at Cox.

"How does the Kincaid murder fit into all this," I asked. "Running the golf courses in this town does not seem to impact a Russian-built oil refinery in any meaningful way. And the police seem to think Kincaid had reasons to help the Russians purchase the Leuchars land."

"Yes," Cox said, pacing back and forth. "That gave us pause as well. And to be entirely transparent, we don't really know who actually killed Kincaid. We don't think it was the same Russian actors who killed Kasyanov ... the method and the act itself does not match any previous murder profile we've seen from them. We've deferred to the local police on that investigation. And it is my understanding that they are quite flummoxed as well."

"Flummoxed," I said. "Great word."

"Means they don't have a feckin' clue," Johnny chimed in helpfully.

"I know what it means," I told him. I looked at Cox. "Again: what do you want us to do?"

He stopped pacing and grasped the back of one of the plush armchairs lined up along the conference table.

"We have a plan," he said. I heard Johnny groan softly next to me, but ignored him. "The Russian parties—whoever they are—seem quite anxious to get their hands on Mr. Swift here – "

"Yer damn right they do," Johnny shouted. "They want to slip a *sgian dubh* in me back and toss me to the fishies. Any bloody fool can see that."

"Our plan," Cox continued as if he had not been interrupted, "Is to allow them to do so."

"No feckin' way!" Johnny shouted, jumping to his feet in alarm. The two guards took a step towards him.

"He will be fully wired and tracked, with two teams of our men following him wherever they take him," Cox continued. "He will be as safe as we can make him, although there is a slight element of risk involved."

"Risk he says," Johnny began pacing, but, cognizant of the two goons on the door, he went back to his seat and sat down again. "All the risk is on Johnny Swift. There's nae risk for the likes o'you."

"We'll inject a tiny GPS transmitter in the back of your neck so we'll have an exact location at all times, and our special forces teams will keep you in sight at all times, if possible."

Johnnie threw his hands up in the air in disgust.

"We believe that they will take Mr. Swift to wherever their leadership is quartered," Cox said. "They will likely want to debrief him first…"

"Before they slice his tongue out," Johnny muttered.

"And that will give us time to both record their planning and get in position for a rapid response extrication."

"Rapid resp…'ave ye gone daft, man?" Johnnie said. "Unless you're standin' in the next room, John Swift is a dead man. Dead as a mackerel."

"Mr. Swift," Cox said patiently, "We do this kind of thing all the time. Rarely does it end badly for the undercover operative."

"It's 'operative' now?" Johnny said. "A bloody operative I am. I'm glad me dear ole mum is dead and gone these many years. She did not raise her boy to be a bloody operative."

Cox sighed and looked at me.

"Well, Swiftie," I said, "You are absolutely correct. If you do this, you will be walking right into the bullseye."

"Feckin' right I will," he said.

Cox looked daggers at me. I ignored him.

"There probably will be some dangerous parts, if you decide to go through with it," I continued. "On the other hand, these guys are generally pretty good at what they do." I nodded at Cox. "And while you should keep in mind the risks of helping these guys, there is also a reward part."

"Now you're talkin', Hacker," Johnnie said. He turned to look at Cox. "Let's hear what I'm getting' paid for putting me poor old self in the bullseye," he said. "And then you can start adding zeroes."

I held up a hand to stop him.

"Not exactly what I meant," I said. "Right now,

you can't walk freely about town without looking over your shoulder to see if the Russkis are coming for you, right?"

He thought about that. "Well, them and the coppers," he said.

"Yeah, well, I'm not sure we can do anything about the police, but if you do this thing, you can help get rid of the Russians. Clear 'em out of town, once and for all. You'd be free again."

He pondered that for a few minutes. We could hear muffled cheers from the fans outside as the last groups made their way down the 18th fairway and putted out on the green just beneath the porch.

He looked at me, his eyes sad.

"Don't suppose you'd like to come with me, eh Hacker?" he asked hopefully.

I looked at Cox, who shook his head slightly.

"I don't think that would work," I said. "But I will stay with these guys while it's all going down, make sure they don't fuck it up somehow."

"I'm sorry, Mister Hacker," Cox said at once, his arms outstretched. "That would be quite impossible. Security regulations and all that. I'm terribly sorry but ..."

"Just say 'no,' Johnnie," I said, looking Cox in the eye. "They can't make you do anything against your will."

"Nae," John Swift said, crossing his arms determinedly. "Nae feckin' way."

Cox looked at the two of us and shook his head.

"Fine," he said. "Hacker can observe from our mobile control vehicle. After first signing about a million non-disclosure and indemnity documents."

I nodded my agreement. Johnnie sighed, deeply, from the depths of his soul.

"I'm a dead man, I am," he said to no one in particular.

Chapter Twenty-four

It was after eight o'clock that night when I finally finished my work—game story, notes, column—and sent it all back to the newsroom in Boston. I allowed myself a brief meditation on just how many more years the Boston *Journal* would be willing to send an actual reporter like myself across the ocean to cover a major sporting event; my over-under best guess was about five more years. Then they would replace me with a robot or a fresh-faced newbie writer in his twenties with zero sense of the history, tradition and background of the Auld Grey Toon and it's centuries-old relationship with the royal and ancient game. The 'bot or the newbie will crank out six characterless graphs on who is ahead and who is behind and leave it at that. All the romance, all the sense of connection with Jones and Snead and Hogan and Palmer and Nicklaus, not to mention Morris and Vardon and Ray and Thompson and Player and Faldo and Langer and Ballesteros, will be totally absent from the copy. Old ginks like me would remember those names, of course, but the younger generation—those born in the last twenty years—would never know about the men who came before. All they will report is that Smith is leading Brown by two shots at St Andrews, a flat old golf course in an old dingy town hard by the cold and angry North Sea. They will completely miss the context, and thus, the story.

Pity party over, I collected my stuff and walked back through town to the flat as the sun sank somewhere beyond the Hebrides and the long lingering summer twilight painted the sky a pretty shade of beige. Mary Jane had a bubbling casserole of some fragrant kind in the oven, and was tossing a green salad. She had opened a bottle of Chianti and poured two glasses which were busy breathing on the counter.

I kissed her and asked where the roomies were.

"They went up to Dundee for dinner," she said. "Mario heard of an Italian place there that came highly recommended. He's apparently a tomato-sauce crackhead."

I sat down with a sigh and took a sip of the Italian red. It tasted like dark cherries, with some herbal undertones and a rich smoky tannin finish. Very nice.

"What's up?" Mary Jane asked.

"Why do you ask?" I said.

"You look like something's bothering you," she said. "The way your forehead wrinkles and the corners of your mouth go all twitchy."

"That's kinda spooky," I said, sipping more wine. "The only way I can ever tell if something is bothering you is when you hurl something heavy at my coconut."

She laughed and took the casserole out of the oven. Chicken, broccoli, pasta and some creamy cheese sauce. It smelled wonderful. She put it on top of the stove to cool, picked up her glass of wine and came and sat down with me at the table.

"Tell me," she said.

So I did. Cox had decided to prep Johnnie overnight and release him into the wild in the morning, when the crowds began to gather for the final round of the Open. His squad of special forces troops, all undercover, would surround Swiftie and wait for the Russians to find him and take him away…to wherever.

"And your roll in all this?"

"Strictly an observer," I said. "Cox is going to call me when the Russians grab Johnnie, and I'll ride along in the command vehicle that will follow. I'll be able to listen to whatever they say. But I'll be inside the van, totally protected, away from any action."

"And you're doing this because…?"

"Well, mainly because I promised Johnnie I would," I said. "So he wouldn't feel like he has to do this all by himself."

She smiled. "And secondarily…?"

"And it'll make a great story, if they let me publish any of it."

She reached over and took my hand, and held it.

"And …?"

I was silent for a moment. Or two.

"It's what I do," I said finally. "I follow the story to the end."

"No matter the danger?"

"There isn't any danger," I said, quickly. "For me, anyway. Johnnie has to go into the belly of the beast, not me. I'm just along to watch."

She smiled.

"Neither one of us believes that," she said. She got up and served our dinner, which we ate mostly in silence.

In the morning, the roomies slept in, again, so Mary Jane and I had some toast and coffee and then walked down to the golf course. There was a different atmosphere in the town, the air felt heavier, more weighted. The tension of the final round of a major championship was in the air and everyone breathed it in and then exhaled another layer of excitement. The weather was good: the sky was thick with clouds, but the air was dry. The wind was brisk out of the southwest, but so far not brisk enough to cause the golfers too much concern. The forecast was for generally clear, with a chance of increasing breezes late in the afternoon. In other words, a perfect Scottish golfing day.

The crowds gathered in and around the grandstands in Golf Place were heavy, even though the first golfers in the final-day field would not start until around ten. People jockeyed for position to take selfies: along the picket fence overlooking the eighteenth green, or posed with the R&A clubhouse façade in the background. Facebook, Twitter and Instagram were going to be overloaded later in the day with these "*Hey! Lookit me*!" shots.

I managed to sneak Mary Jane into the press tent, past the security guards who really didn't care at this point who got inside, and we got some coffee from the press canteen and sat down at my desk space to watch the bank of television screens. Without any golf to show, they were tuned to talk shows from London, where the usual array of pundits was holding forth on the political issues of the day. Thankfully, none of them were discussing the American President. Probably for the first time all week.

It was about ten-thirty when my cell phone rang. I startled, even though I had been waiting for the call.

"Yo," I said, "Hacker here."

"Ian Cox," the voice said. "The package has just been picked up. Meet me outside the back entrance to the R&A."

I rang off. And looked at Mary Jane.

"Johnnie's been scooped up," I said. "It's show-time." I paused. She looked at me. "Come with me."

I grabbed her hand and we ran out of the press tent and made our way through the press of the crowds to get around to the back of the R&A building. I saw the big black SUV idling next to the blue door and approached. The rear door flew open and Cox's head poked out.

"Morning, Mister Hacker," he said. "Who is this?"

"Mary Jane Doe," I said. "She's with me."

He didn't like that and moved to block the way into the back of the truck.

"Most irregular," he said.

"Too fucking bad," Mary Jane told him. "I'm coming."

Cox sighed the sigh of a man who knew when a woman had made up her mind about something and would brook no further discussion about it. He ducked back into the vehicle and motioned us to follow.

The entire back part of the SUV was filled with a bristling array of electronic monitors and other equipment that gave off a slight hum. Cox reached down and flipped a few switches that caused two narrow stools to rise hydraulically from the floor. "Sit," he said curtly. "And hold on."

The SUV pulled away from the clubhouse and slowly moved through the crowd. The windows were all tinted black, and we could see people staring at us as we passed, wondering who or what was hidden inside our ominous looking vehicle. Eventually, we made it back to the main road and began to pick up speed.

"Do you know where they're going yet?" I asked.

Cox checked one of the screens on the console. A blinking green light was moving across a map showing the city streets in St. Andrews.

"I'm guessing he's headed for the Gold hotel," he said. "Ah, yes, indeed. They've just turned in the drive."

He clicked a button and spoke. "Red Team One, Red Team One: package is proceeding to the Gold Standard Hotel. Positions please."

"Roger that, Team Leader," came a disemboweled voice from a speaker in the ceiling.

"Red Team One, let me know when you have visual. Blue Team, set up perimeter on all roads, wait for my signal to intercept traffic."

"Blue Team, roger that," came the response.

"Can you hear Johnnie?" I asked.

"Negative," Cox said, tight-lipped. "They tossed him in the back of a delivery van. I've heard some grunts, but that's about it so far."

"Oh, poor Johnnie," Mary Jane said, wringing her hands.

"Swiftie's a fighter," I told her. "He'll be OK."

"Red Team: report," Cox barked.

"Van has parked outside service entrance," came a voice over the speakers. "Looks like two…no, check that, three placeholders have emerged. They are checking the grounds."

"You haven't been spotted, have you?" Cox said.

"Negative, Team Leader," the voice responded. "And I'm a little offended that you asked."

Mary Jane and I chuckled softly to ourselves.

"Team Leader, Red One here. The package has been unwrapped. Repeat, package is unwrapped. They're taking him in through the kitchen."

"Roger, that, Red One," Cox said. "Red Two, what is your location?"

"In the lobby, Team Leader," came another voice.

"Stay there...keep the elevators in visual," Cox ordered.

"Roger that, Leader." There was a brief pause. "Team Leader, Red Two here. Package and handlers have appeared. They're getting into elevator three. Over."

"Roger that, Red Two," Cox said. He punched some buttons on his console, then pointed to another small computer screen in the console. "We've got the elevators surveilled."

Sure enough, we could see the four figures crowding into the elevator cabin: three large men dressed in black surrounded Johnnie Swift, who looked even more emaciated and fragile than ever. He was blinking and looking around, trying to figure out where in the world he was.

"Red Two, Leader here," Cox said. "They're going up to six. That's the luxury suites, right?"

"Roger that, Leader," said Red Two. "Those rooms go for a thousand quid a night. And up. Do we have eyes on the inside?"

Cox punched a few more buttons on his console. "Affirmative," he said. He looked over at Mary Jane and me. "Conrad Gold was very good about working with us," he said. "Most of the rooms in this hotel have hidden security cameras."

"Memo to self: do not stay in a Gold Standard suite," Mary Jane said under her breath. "Guy's a pervert."

"Red Teams, package and handlers have arrived on six. They're going into 620, repeat, room 6-2-0." Cox worked his keyboard furiously, and soon, a grainy black and white image of the inside of the hotel suite appeared on a console screen. The three handlers led Johnnie over to a plush sofa and pushed him down onto it. Two of them took positions at either end of the sofa, while the other walked out of range of the camera shot.

"Sound?" I asked.

"Not from the camera system, I'm afraid," Cox said. "But Mr. Swift is wired."

On cue, Johnnie Swift began waving his arms. "What the feckin' hell do you yobs want of John Swift," he said. "Grabbin' meself off the street and tossin' me in a van like a sack o'clothes. What the hell is going on?"

We could hear a door open: the hardware clicked somewhere off camera. Johnnie turned to look off to the left, where I figured the door to the bedroom part of the suite was located. We watched as a large man, dressed all in black and with a large, glistening bald pate, stepped into view. He walked over to Johnnie and slapped him hard across the face with the back of his right hand.

"Shut the mouth," he snapped, as Johnnie fell backwards against the cushions of the sofa.

He turned to look at one of the handlers standing next to the couch. It was Yuri, Lord Cheape's Man Friday.

"Ah ha, I said. "A clue. That's Yuri. He works for Cheape."

"Quite," said Cox, still pecking away madly at his keys. "Except his name isn't Yuri. It is Sergey Kovalchuk. He's kind of a fixer for the biggies of the Kremlin. Solves problems. Breaks legs. Whatever it takes."

Mary Jane reached over and took my hand.

"Red One, Leader here," Cox said, his voice calm. "Prepare Hand Grenade."

"Roger that, Leader,"

"Hand grenade?" I said. "Really?"

Cox managed a smile in my direction. "Just wait," he said.

"Now then," said Yuri/Sergey as he stood over the form of Johnnie Swift, who was bent over, holding his hands against his face where he had been slapped. "You will kindly tell us what you saw on ocean shore that night please."

"I don't know what the hell you're blabbering on about, Russki," Johnnie said through clenched teeth.

Yuri bent over, took Johnnie's hands away from his face and slapped him hard, twice, backhand and forehand. Johnnie's head snapped left and right from the blow.

"Do not play stupid with us," Yuri said. "We know all about you. Where you live. Where you work. We can kill you at any time. So, again, what did you see at ocean that night?"

"Take a bloody jump from the pier, ya Russki bastard," Johnnie growled.

Yuri nodded, and the two men at either end of the couch stepped forward, yanked Swiftie to his feet and began working him over, punching him in the kidneys and the stomach, the later of which caused him to double over with an exhalation and a low groan."

"Stop this!" Mary Jane said, insistent. "You can't let them hurt him like that!"

"He's actually doing quite well," Cox said calmly. "He's followed my orders to drag this out as long as possible. Give them more time to indict themselves and give us more time to get into position."

He checked his watch. "Which should be any second now."

Almost on cue, we heard a sharp knock at the door to the room, followed by a muffled voice. "Room service."

The men in the room, other than Johnnie, who was bent over at the waist and groaning piteously, startled at the sound. Yuri nodded at one of the other goons, who drew a pistol from his waistband and headed over to the door to the room.

"Red One," Cox said. "Approaching door. Firecracker in right hand."

There was no answer from Red One. But as the Russian goon reached for the door handle, the door crashed open with a loud splintering sound, and the man with the gun went flying backwards, head over heels. Two special forces soldiers, wearing camo fatigues, boots, and full black helmets that covered their faces, came charging into the room, semi-automatic rifles at the ready. At almost exactly the same moment, two more soldiers came crashing feet first through the large windows, tearing down the drapes that had been pulled closed in front of them. They, too, were fully outfitted and armed to the teeth.

The Russians immediately put their hands in the air. Except the one on the floor, who was unconscious. One of the soldiers kicked his handgun away anyway.

"Room is secure, Leader," came the report. "Red Team has the situation in hand."

"Roger that, Red One," Cox said. "Good work, gents. Let's tidy this up."

I watched, fascinated, as the soldiers began handcuffing the Russians with plastic flex ties. Johnnie Swift slowly got up from the couch. He walked over to

Yuri, who was being cuffed by the Red One team leader. Johnnie looked the man in the eye and grinned at him. Even with the fuzzy black-and-white image, I could see the evil in that grin. Then Johnnie kneed the man squarely between his legs with a quick, hard and painfully accurate motion.

Yuri went down hard and began writhing in pain.

"Do not fuck with John Swift," Johnnie said to the man, his voice calm and sure. "And do not fuck with Her Majesty's troops, ya bloody Russki wanker."

Chapter Twenty-five

IAN COX DROPPED us off back at the R&A clubhouse. Johnnie Swift had gone with the Red Team soldiers to be debriefed. He seemed to be in his element now, the center of attention and something of a hero. At least, that's what he thought, and he was going to play that role for as long as he could. Which I suspected was going to be months, if not years.

"What about the Russians?" I asked Cox as we drove back into town. "What will happen to them?"

"In the end, we'll expel the lot of them back to Moscow," Cox told me. "We'll interrogate them first, of course. I doubt if any of this lot will roll over and admit to killing Kasyanov."

"What about Cheape?" I asked. "You gonna raid Wormwood the same way? Special forces and guns drawn?"

He chuckled. "We wouldn't be in business very long if we went around raiding the homes of peers of the realm," he said. "No, I expect Mr. Cheape will understand that his attempted business transaction has come to a close when he notices that his partners are all either in jail or expelled from the country. He'll likely get a call from Sir Jeremy." He was referencing Sir Jeremy Hatton, the head of British intelligence, who was himself a member of the House of Lords.

"In the next week or two, Sir Jeremy will take Cheape to lunch at some club or other in London and let him know that we know what he was up to," Cox continued as he maneuvered the SUV slowly through the increasing traffic close to the golf course. "All very calm and stiff upper lip. Cheape will get the message: he was lucky to get out of this alive."

"No scandal, no press, no weeks of fuss on TV," I said. "Amazing."

"We call it civilized," Cox said as he pulled in next to the R&A clubhouse. He held out his hand. "Thanks for your help with convincing Mr. Swift to participate. Her Majesty appreciates your effort."

Mary Jane and I got out of the truck.

"I don't suppose there's an extra O.B.E. lying around?" I started to say. The door of the SUV slammed shut and the black car sped away.

"Guess not," I finished.

Mary Jane and I went back inside the press tent. She grabbed my hand and led me over to the canteen area. She found someone wearing the white jacket of a server and went right up to him.

"What do you have that's alcoholic?" she asked.

He looked at her, and glanced at his watch. It was still morning.

"Well," he said, "We have beer and wine in the back. But we're not supposed to put it out until noon."

"Not strong enough," Mary Jane said to him. "What else?"

He looked at her with a bit more attention and saw a woman on a mission who was not going to be denied. He nodded like a man who had seen this before. "A moment, please, madam," he said and disappeared behind some curtains into the back of the canteen. He came out a minute later carrying two bottles.

"Brandy or scotch?" he asked, holding up the bottles.

"Scotch," Mary Jane said. "Two fingers, neat."

The server found a glass and filled it halfway. He gave it to Mary Jane, who downed it in a gulp.

"Damn," she said, her voice a little strained. "Hit me again, please."

He did. Then he looked at me, eyebrows raised in a silent query. I shook my head.

Mary Jane only drank about half of the liquid in her glass this time. Then, looking around, she walked over to an empty table nearby and sank down heavily in a white folding chair.

"Jeezus H. Christ," she said, to no one in particular.

I sat down next to her and grabbed her hand in mine. I didn't say anything, because I had no idea what to say. She had just had a glimpse of what happens in this big, bad old world every day; the intersection between good and evil, things that she had heard about, envisioned, watched on TV – but had never actually seen unfold live and in living color. Or scratchy black and white, as the case may be. I could understand how profoundly unnerving the experience must have been for her. So I just held her hand and hoped that she would get herself under control.

She knocked back the last of her second whiskey.

"Can…can I get you something to eat?" I asked.

She turned her head and looked at me, but said nothing in reply. I kept hold of her hand. It was the only thing I had.

"They were going to kill Johnnie, weren't they?" she asked.

"Yes," I said. "But they didn't."

"They were going to find out what he knew about them, then they were going to stick a knife in him and throw him in the sea." Her voice was flat and emotionless.

"But they didn't," I repeated. "The good guys won, this time, at least."

She nodded, but didn't look any happier.

"What kind of people would do something like that?" she said, shaking her head. "It was like they were going to kill Johnnie … end his fucking life with the same attitude that you would have if I asked you to go down to the drugstore and get me some tissues or something. Like oh, OK Mary Jane. I'll be right back. How can they be like that? How can *anyone* be like that?"

I paused for a moment to think. She was asking an important question, and I wasn't going to joke about it to try and relieve her mind. That would have been insulting.

"Somone wrote a book once, I think it was about that Nazi guy Adolph Eichmann, called 'The Banality of Evil,'" I said. "Basically, it said that evil people are not demons or unusually bad human beings, but in fact they are just mundane, everyday people doing what they're told or what they think they're supposed to do. They never even consider that their actions could be considered evil or bad by others. Never enters their consciousness. Just part of the human condition."

Mary Jane thought about that, turning her whiskey glass over and over in her fingers as she thought. Finally, she reached over and carefully placed the glass on the table and took her hand away.

"Well, I don't want to be like that," she said. "Whatever 'banal' means, I don't want to be that."

"You are the furthest thing from banal that I know," I said, and I meant it.

She nodded, then turned to me, and I took her in my arms. She began to sob, quietly, softly, her face pressed against my shoulder. I held her until she stopped.

Chapter Twenty-six

ONCE MARY JANE was back in control, she disappeared into the women's loo to freshen up and make herself presentable again. When she came out, we walked, hand-in-hand, back into the main press area of the tent. We ran into our roomies, Mario and Brad, who were following a mad rush of reporters and cameramen heading for the exit doors.

"Hacker!" Mario said as they pushed past us. "You gotta come see this!"

"What's up?" I asked.

"The E-Go guy is back!" Mario called over his shoulder. "He's taken over the first tee!"

"No way!" I said, and I fell in with the crowd, still holding onto Mary Jane, who came along with us.

Outside, we pushed our way through the crowds to get close to the ropes around the tee box. There was an unusual crush of people standing on the tee—uniformed bobbies, blazered golf officials and at least four golfers with their caddies. The latter were standing off by themselves looking fairly bemused. Ivor Robson, the R&A's official starter, was red-faced and was trying to wrestle his wireless microphone away from the grasping hands of Dr. Cecil Knox, who finally managed to grab it. Eluding both Ivor and a half dozen cops, Knox managed to flick the button and began speaking, his voice, trembling with excitement, echoing through the loudspeakers set around the tee and down the first hole.

"Now on the tee, now on the tee," he said, almost yelling. "The most Honorable Marquess Cheape of Wormwood is now on the tee. Play away, play away…" Knox kept dodging around, staying out of the hands of those trying to make him stop.

"As the landowner of the linksland, the Marquess has the right to play on this course at any time," Knox continued shrilly. "He is entitled by Parliament to play, and he wishes to play right now. Make way…make way. The Marquess Cheape is on the tee."

Sure enough, I saw that Johnny Cheape was indeed one of the many figures milling about on the tee box. He was dressed in a navy windcheater and a snappy pair of black corduroy plus-fours, with woolen socks in a green-and-blue plaid design. He looked calm and almost regal as he stood there, holding a driver in one hand.

"Gawan, ye tosser," came a snarling voice from the people crowding around next to the tee. "Git off the course and let the men play." There were a few boos and whistles coming from the surrounding spectators as well.

Cecil Knox was tackled by one of the uniformed police and the microphone was pried from his fingers. He began shouting something about police brutality.

But the people watching applauded loudly when he was yanked back to his feet and handcuffed.

"This is an illegal police action," he yelled, his face now red. "The Marquess has the legal right to play golf on this course at the time of his choosing … in perpetuity! It is the law of the land."

Ivor Robson was given his mic back. He clicked it on and his calm, reassuring tenor came through the speakers.

"Actually, sir, the law was changed many years ago in the House of Commons," he said. "The claim the Cheape family has to this land was amended. The Links Trust has legal authority and Mr. Cheape is trespassing. If he does not leave the tee at once, he will be arrested."

All eyes turned to the patrician profile of Johnny Cheape. The marquess looked around, smiled, turned and began to walk away. He did not look disappointed to have been denied a round at the Old Course.

The police began to clear all the others off the tee and two of the bigger ones hauled Cecil Knox away. Robson regained control.

"This is Match Number 14," he said in his usual calm tones. "Now playing, from Sweden, *Albert Petterson*!" A smattering of applause burst out from the spectators.

I caught sight of Sir Hamish. He was standing just behind the tee box and was surrounded by a gaggle of officials and policemen. He was red in the face and gesticulating madly. I nudged Mary Jane and nodded over in that direction. She saw him too. We began to push our way through the crowd to get closer to him. When we got there, Sir Hamish was still upset.

"… I had no earthly idea what Johnny Cheape was planning to do here this morning," he was saying. "We rode over together to watch the golf tournament.

At least, that's what I thought we were doing. He had a parking pass for the R&A Members' lot. When we arrived, he told me he had something to do, and would see me later." Sir Hamish was still red-faced and his eyes wide with amazement. "The next thing I knew, he was standing on this tee with that Knox fellow and all hell broke loose!"

Someone asked him a question and he turned and pointed a finger at the questioner.

"Absolutely not!" he practically yelled. "I have no sympathy whatsoever for that madman Knox's movement, and I had no idea that Johnny Cheape would believe any of the man's utter nonsense. I am a respectable businessman, Sir, and I have been knighted by her Majesty the Queen! To even think that I could be somehow involved in this tawdry little incident is, frankly, highly insulting!"

Sir Hamish turned back and saw Mary Jane and I standing there, and he waved, giving us a wan smile. He nodded in our direction. "There is one of the foremost golf journalists from the States," he said. "He will tell you that I had nothing to do with this. Nothing!"

The gaggle of officialdom surrounding poor Sir Hamish slowly broke up and went away, and he was finally able to approach us, shaking his head sadly.

"What an utter cock-up," he said, taking out a handkerchief and mopping his fevered brow. "I may never speak to Johnny Cheape ever again for getting me into this mess. Bloody arrogant aristo!"

Mary Jane gathered him in a big hug and held him tightly for a long moment.

"The world is full of evil," she said to him when they broke apart. He looked at her with raised eyebrows. It wasn't a sentence he expected to hear from her.

"Thank you, m'dear," he said, as if she had said something sympathetic. "And you, Hacker…I appreciate your support and understanding."

"So, you were ambushed a bit, eh, Sir Hamish?" I said.

"A bit?" He started to get upset again, but Mary Jane grabbed his hand reassuringly. "Yes, well, I guess you could say so. We had a lovely breakfast at Wormwood, talking about all kinds of things. Then he offered to drive me over here to watch the golf. He said nothing about his plans to try and sabotage the Open Championship. I mean, I might have taken the ride—the Members' Lot is very convenient—but I would have immediately notified the authorities!"

I laughed. "Yeah, a good parking place is worth its weight in sterling," I said. "Was that Knox guy waiting?"

"I didn't see him in the parking lot," Sir Hamish said. "And then Johnny just walked away. Said he had something to do. Have no idea what their plan was."

"I think they accomplished it," I said. "Made a scene at the Open. It will probably make all the highlight reels later today. 'Mad Marquess Attempts Round on Old Course During Open.' Great story. Will get great play. Mission accomplished."

"Bloody, bloody hell," Sir Hamish said, muttering under his breath. "And that means my name will come out in all of it too. I was his houseguest. I must have known all about it. My board will have questions. So will the press. The Cavendish name will be dragged through the mud."

"I wouldn't worry too much about that," Mary Jane said. "The people I've met who know you will believe your story. Everyone loves Sir Hamish, the Whiskey Man!"

He smiled at her. "Thank you, dear heart," he said. "I hope that is true. I fear it won't mean much once the press juggernaut is launched."

"Hacker will help," she said. "Won't you?" She turned to me. I shrugged. I could write what I knew about the situation, and that might help Sir Hamish a little. But I also knew the other members of the press, and the countless idiot TV pundits around the globe who knew nothing about either Sir Hamish or golf would be all over this story for the next 24 hours.

"Did he really think he was going to be able to play a round right in the middle of the final round of the Open?" I asked. "Is that even possible?"

"No, no, of course not," Sir Hamish said, shaking his head sadly. "Years ago, the Cheape family did have the statutory right to play the course at any time of their choosing. But Parliament rescinded that right when they formulated the Links Trust in the 1970s. I think both Johnny and Cecil Knox knew that to be true. But they decided a nice juicy scandal would get the press' attention, so they went for it. Utter madness!"

I looked at Sir Hamish and Mary Jane, standing there side by side in the morning sunshine. They both looked absolutely miserable. I couldn't help myself. I had to laugh. Neither of them looked at me with either understanding or any desire to join in on the hilarity.

"Sorry," I said, getting myself quickly back under control. "But I don't think I've seen two sadder sacks in my entire life. For good reason, of course," I added quickly, as Mary Jane, for one, looked like she was ready to spit fire and let loose the hounds of hell upon me. "I think you two ought to find the nearest bar and have a couple of stiff bracers."

Sir Hamish looked at me for a long moment, and then nodded.

"That, my dear Sir, may be the most intelligent thing I have yet to hear you say," he said, reaching over and squeezing my shoulder with affection. He turned to Mary Jane.

"Young lady, it would be my highest honor and privilege to escort you to the Members' Bar and stand you to a glass of Cavendish Distilleries finest 40-year, single barrel malt," he said with a gracious bow in Mary Jane's direction. "Shall we?" He held out his arm.

She looked at me again, eyes flashing angrily for one brief second. Then she smiled.

"I believe we shall," she said, and took Sir Hamish's offered arm.

They strolled off toward the side entrance of the R&A Clubhouse, ignoring the jostling crowds, the sounds of cheers echoing across the golf course, and one slightly abused, exhausted and yet amused golf writer.

I went back to work.

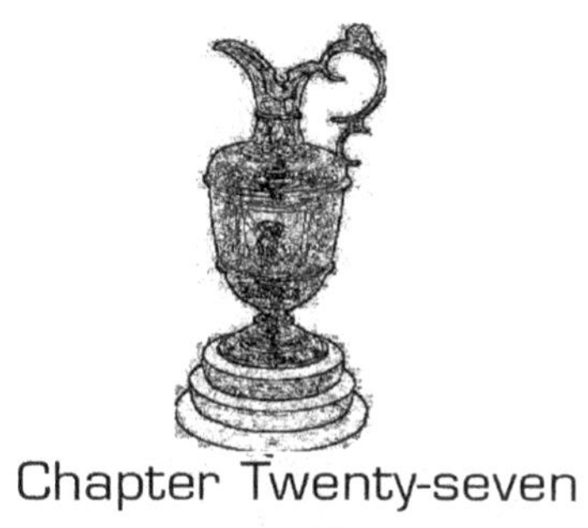

Chapter Twenty-seven

THE GAME OF golf is a cruel and fickle mistress. Anyone who has ever played the game can tell you that. So can anyone who has watched professional tournaments unfold; and as one who has done that for more than twenty-five years now, I can certainly attest to it. Sometimes you have a final round that shapes up to be one of the greatest of all time, yet it turns into a runaway victory; and runaway victories tend to make for unexciting watching. Of course, sometimes it's just the opposite: you wake up on Sunday with a yawn because Joe Whoever has a seven-shot lead, the weather is perfect, and there's no reason to imagine that the final outcome will be anything but Joe Whoever in a walkabout. And then he goes and throws up all over his golf shoes while Sam Whoknew comes out of nowhere, shoots a 63 and enters the hallowed, marble-and-gilt halls of The Greatest Final Round of All-Time. That's golf. Flog spelled backwards.

This final round had been predicted by all to be the former: a shootout to the end with a wealth of golf talent striving to claim the Claret Jug. The German Heinrich Gruber had a one-shot lead. He was paired in the final twosome with the Spaniard Rikki Paz, one of the young guns who had lit the place on fire in Saturday's round. Playing just ahead was the other gunner, the Irish kid Conor Kelly. He was paired with American Zach Johnson. And there were another six or seven golfers within six shots of the lead, and at St. Andrews, anything can, and usually does, happen.

But today, the Golf Mistress was a cold-hearted, indifferent bitch. Like most of the rest of the press corps, I stayed put in the media tent, sitting at my tiny desk and watching the events unfold on the many big-screen TVs, commentary and pictures courtesy of the BBC. Peter Alliss, certainly by now well into his eighth decade, was commenting, along with his usual breathy intakes and muttered "dear, dears."

The weather was good: sunny, not too chilly, and the wind at a manageable howl of around fifteen to twenty miles per hour. The course was in great nick. The crowds were massive and excited. The stage was set for greatness.

But greatness took the afternoon off and went fishing. Gruber birdied the first: everyone else parred and he was two ahead. He then reeled off seven straight pars before he birdied the eighth and ninth. Paz began driving the ball erratically and struggled to finish the front nine in two-over. Kelly played his usual poetic game from tee to green and then putted like someone with six Guinness drafts under his belt: he three-putted three times on the front side. Zach Johnson found three bunkers on the first five holes. Buh-bye!

By the time Gruber made the turn at ten, way out by the River Eden, the crowd had been anaesthetized into near silence. Then the wind died completely, leaving the Old Course vulnerable. He birdied that short hole, then made a great par save on eleven from the front bunker. And that was about all she wrote. He coasted in, playing steady if uninspiring par golf all the way to the end, and there was nobody behind him to step up and make it exciting. Not only could I hear television sets clicking off all across the world, but I watched as some of my buddies organized a stud poker game during the long back nine sludge. And most of us in the press corps spent far more energy and time watching the card game than the golf.

After it was finally over, they trotted Gruber in for his post-victory presser. The German was tall, blond and his face was reddened by the sun. His wife, also tall and blond and sun-streaked, stood nearby smiling the broad and satisfied smile of a woman about to be handed two million dollars to spend. Their two-year-old daughter chewed furiously on a squeaky toy and made us all laugh. Heinrich told us how proud he was that his game had held up all weekend. We asked him about four questions. What was there to ask? He went out with the lead, extended it, and protected it coming home. Nobody tested him and he didn't throw up on his shoes. Good for him, but not much of a headline for the morning paper. *German Gruber Doesn't Puke; Captures Open Before Bored Crowd.*

I did my best to write some excitement into my game story, but there just wasn't much there. The pre-round scuffle on the first tee between Ivor Robson and Cecil Knox was the most exciting part of the day, I wrote. Both Rikki Paz and Conor Kelly expressed disappointment, but each one told us that they had learned a lot during this weekend and that they expected to be back competing for a major tournament in the near future. They were probably right in the assessment, but that, too, did not lend itself to a great headline for the morning paper. *Two Young Golfers Fail; Promise to Be Better Later.*

I got the story written and sent it off to Boston along with some more notes. I knew that today's Red Sox game—the last of a four-game set with Cleveland—would suck up most of the available column inches in the sports section, along with a report of the OTA by the Patriots down in Foxboro. Frankie Donatello, the executive sports editor and walking heart attack waiting to happen, would maybe carve out six or seven inches for my piece; certainly the unexciting final round would mean I'd get no more than that. There was no local, much less any *national* angle. And that meant I'd have to tap dance twice as hard later in the year when it came time to submit my proposed travel budgets for next year. When the R&A signkeepers posted their usual final message on the huge yellow scoreboard at the last hole ("Congrats Heinrich Gruber! See you next year at Turnberry!"), I wondered if I would be included among the cognoscenti travelling to the Ayrshire coast the following July. In this age of rapidly falling newspaper revenue, it is hardly a tap-in.

But I shook off my foreboding, packed up my stuff, bid farewell and thanks to Bernie Capshaw the press guy, and went to find and reunite with my honey bunny.

I stepped inside the R&A entrance and spoke to the security guy sitting at his desk in the foyer. "I'm looking for my girlfriend and Sir Hamish Cavendish," I said. "They came in here earlier this morning."

The security guy looked over at one of his buddies, standing in front of the stairway door, and they laughed. *Uh-oh* I thought.

"Sir Hamish, is it?" the guy said, smiling up at me. "He is no longer on the premises."

"He isn't?"

"No sir," the security guy said. "He was asked to leave some time ago. He, err, found himself a bit under the weather. Not exactly sick, mind you, as in ill. But not quite well functioning. Also, he was attempting to get the members to, err, sing an old college song."

"He was drunk on his ass," I guessed.

"Quite so," the guy said, and his buddy chuckled from over by the door.

"We had to semi-carry him out," the door guy said, his voice deep and gruff, as one would expect from a muscle-bound bouncer at the R&A.

"What about the girl?" I asked.

"Sir?"

"There was a lovely young American woman he came in with," I said. "Did she go out with him or is she still up in the Members' Bar?"

"Oh," the guy said. "The bird."

"The bloody bird," said the doorway guy, laughing his deep bass-note laughs. "No she's gone as well. Funny…the whole time we were, umm, escorting them down the stairs, she was telling us her father-in-law was some organized crime chappie from Boston who would come over here and 'kick our ass sideways' is the way she put it, I think."

"She informed us that he would 'seriously fuck us up,' I believe was the phrasing," said the desk guy. The two gents thought all this was hilariously funny and burst out in great heaving guffaws.

I laughed too. How could one not?

"Do you know where they went?" I asked.

The two men shook their heads. Great, I thought, now I have to search every pub and kebab shop in town, looking for two sloppy, falling-down drunks. I thanked the guys and turned to go. Then I stopped and looked back.

"By the way, Mary Jane was right about her father-in-law," I said. "You get on his wrong side, legs get broken. Luckily for you, he doesn't leave Boston much anymore, and then only to attend the annual East Coast tough-guys meet in Newark. But don't worry…I'll put in a good word for you, if I ever find her again."

"Try the Criterion," the doorway guy said. "They feature Cavendish whiskey there. I know Sir Hamish likes to support his customers."

I saluted them and went off into town.

Chapter Twenty-eight

I FELT FORTUNATE when I walked in the door of the Criterion to see my targets sitting together at the end of the marble-topped bar. Making me feel even better: they were both deeply engaged in slurping down soup and sharing a warm baguette. The bar, one of the smaller places in town, dating from the late 19th century but well restored and modernized, was surprisingly empty. I guessed most of the golf fans who had been following the action out on the course had decided to go home instead of finding a watering hole like the Criterion for some post-game drinking. There were a couple of large-screen televisions dotting the walls in the place, but one was showing a cricket match from Sri Lanka and the other a football game between two African Under-18 teams. Both of which matched the general feeling of sleepiness which seemed to have affected the entire town. I blamed the day of boring golf.

I slipped onto an upholstered leather chair at the bar next to Mary Jane and she looked up at me from her soup bowl with red, unfocused eyes.

"Hi, honey," she slurred. "Want some soup? It's very good." She pushed her bowl, which was empty save for a spoonful of liquid and one slice of carrot, over in front of me. Beside her, Sir Hamish Cavendish didn't even acknowledge my presence: he just kept mechanically lifting his spoon to his mouth. After intaking six spoonfuls, he took a bite of bread, then a sip of his pint of lager. Then he went back to his soup.

"You guys been here long?" I asked. Neither one answered. The pretty young bartender approached from behind the bar and smiled at me. "They behaving themselves?" I asked her. She smiled more and made a wavy motion with her hand: *comme ci comme ça.* I nodded, figuring that was better than *no, get them the hell out of here.* I ordered a shot of Bowmore, my favorite malt from Islay. The bartender took down the bottle from the dozens displayed in the wood-and-glass shelving unit on the wall behind the bar, poured me a finger or two and set the glass down on a round cardboard coaster.

"Utter rotgut," Sir Hamish grunted, pausing briefly from his soup exertions.

"Tastes good, though," I said and took a sip, welcoming the warm fire of the dark caramel-colored whiskey as it burned its way down the back of my throat. Maybe my guts were about to be rotted, but the sharp peaty undertones of the whiskey made me feel good about the risk.

"So how has your day gone?" I said, trying again with Mary Jane.

"Has the day gone?" she replied, looking around with surprise. "It was morning just a minute ago." She sighed, deeply. "I miss Victoria," she said.

"I know," I said. "I miss her, too. We'll see her soon. Going home tomorrow."

" "Thass good," Mary Jane said. I patted her hand gently. She turned and leaned against me, arms thrown around my neck, turning her head to fit it into the crevice between my shoulder and neck. A few seconds later, I heard her soft, rhythmic breaths as she fell fast asleep. Sir Hamish turned and looked at us. His eyes were red and unfocussed as well. But he smiled.

"You know, my dear boy, that there is something you have to do, don't you?" he said.

"Figure out how to get Mary Jane back to the flat?"

"No, sir," he said gruffly.

"Figure out how to get you back to Wormwood?"

"I am not going back to Wormwood, ever," he said. "And, no, that is not the matter I am addressing here."

"OK, then," I said. "I give up. What it is I have to do?"

He leaned over Mary Jane's sleeping form and grasped my forearm, holding it tightly in his hand.

"You must make an honest woman of this dear child," he said, looking me directly in the eyes.

"I must?"

"You must," he said, nodding decisively. "You and she…she and you…the two of you together…" He was casting about for the foundation of a sentence and, deep in his cups, finding it hard to locate. "You simply must."

I thought about that silently for a moment or two, while Mary Jane's moist breath created a sweaty patch on my neck. She wasn't exactly snoring, since women don't exactly snore, but she was making little groany sighs that any snore impressionist would quickly agree qualified as the real deal.

"Actually, Sir Hamish, that thought has occurred to me," I said. "More than once. It is in fact a very good idea. There's only one little problem."

"And that is…?"

"We've never really discussed it, Mary Jane and I, and I don't have the slightest idea what she would say if I popped the question," I said.

Mary Jane stirred and sat upright. I imagined a sucking sound as her mouth pulled away from the skin at the corner of my neck and shoulder, but I was probably hallucinating. She shook her head, as if to clear away the mental cobwebs that had gathered while she napped, and then she turned to me.

"Yes, Hacker," she said. "I will marry you. You are the love of my life."

"How…?" I wanted to ask her how she had heard all that while in a deep drunk sleep, but there was no time to do so. Sir Hamish let out a bellow like a wounded but happy bull, stood up from his chair and began hugging Mary Jane and pounding me on the back at the same time, which was dangerous for both of us. In short order, he had demanded a large bottle of Moët and Chandon, which was loudly popped open by the bartender and soon all ten of the other customers in the Criterion was handed a flute of the bubbly. Rounds of toasts were followed by speeches of salutations and more drinks were ordered and before I knew it, it was late and night had fallen.

Life had begun moving at warp speed. Mary Jane had borrowed Sir Hamish's telephone and placed a call back to Boston. I could hear the squeals of delight when she told her daughter Victoria the news. Then there was a long, sotto voce conversation with Carmine Spoleto, Poppy, her father-in-law, the aged gangster who controlled most of Boston's organized crime network.

"They're coming across tomorrow," she told me when she had hung up. "Private jet. Victoria is over the moon. Poppy Carmine is very pleased."

"Thanks be to God for that," I said. And meant it. It was always a better thing, and a long-term healthier one, to remain on Carmine Spoleto's good side.

Sir Hamish, meanwhile, had also been busy. He had wandered outside for a bit while the party was at its height—everyone in the bar had been unofficially recruited into our engagement celebration—and came back inside a few minutes later with a broad smile on his face.

"Success!" he said, a huge smile wreathing his jowly face. "I have found just the right place for your ceremony. It will be perfect!"

Mary Jane looked at him with a frown on her face. "Hamish, I will not be married on the bridge over the Swilcan burn," she said sternly. "Nor anywhere near a golf course, especially here in Scotland. I will not be rained upon during my wedding."

"Nae, child," he said. "I have found an indoor location. And an apt one, too, I think."

"OK, Hamish," I said. "Let me have it."

"My very good friend, Dr. Charles Benedict, is the Provost of the University of St. Andrews," he said. "I just called him and he agreed to make Younger Hall available for an hour on Tuesday afternoon. And, for extra bonus points, the Reverend Dr. Benedict himself has volunteered to conduct the service. Signed, sealed and delivered!" He looked very pleased with himself.

"Wait a minute," I said, as the people around us in the bar oohed and ahhed at this news. "Younger Hall? Isn't that the place where they made Bobby Jones an Honorary Burgess of the city, just a few years before he died?"

"The very same," Sir Hamish said with uncharacteristic glee. "Bobby was only the second American in history to be so honored," he continued. "The other one was somebody named Benjamin Franklin. I'm afraid I don't know what his golf handicap was."

We all laughed, but I was touched. That ceremony had been one of the last public events attended by the great man, Jones, where he had said "I could take out of my life everything save for the experiences I have had here in St. Andrews, and still I would have had a rich and rewarding life." Jones had connected with the people of the Auld Grey Toon during his competitive years. Indeed, six years after he retired from competitive golf in 1930, after winning the Grand Slam, Jones had returned unannounced to St. Andrews with some friends and signed up to play the Old Course. Somehow, the word got out that the great Bobby was playing, and the entire town shut down and thousands came out to watch his round.

Years later, they gave him the honor of citizenship in the town. And, when the ceremony had been completed, the crowd had sung "For He's a Jolly Good Fellow," and as the great man was slowly and painfully making his way outside the hall, arranging his withered legs into a golf cart so he didn't have to walk or be pushed in a wheelchair, someone in the assembled crowd had spontaneously begun to sing the mournful dirge "Will Ye No Come Back Agin?" and everyone had joined in. It had been a four-hanky moment.

"Thank you, Sir Hamish," I said, and I meant it.

It was at about that point that Mary Jane, fighting her way through layers of alcoholic fog, suddenly realized that she was going to be married in two days. I watched as she jumped to her feet and all the blood drained from her face. She turned to look at me with sheer panic in her eyes.

"Jesus H. Christ," she said. "We're getting married on Tuesday. Do you know how much stuff I have to do between now and then?"

I didn't know, of course, because I am a man and we just assume that things will happen as required for an event like a last-minute wedding to occur as planned. I was going to make some *there, there* sounds and tell her it would all be OK, when, looking again into the depth of the crazy in her eyes, some prehistoric fight-or-flight reflex kicked in and saved me from making that huge mistake.

"Yes," I said instead. "We've both got a ton of things to do. I suggest we go back to the flat, get a good night's sleep and begin working on our lists in the morning when we're rested."

Eminently reasonable, right? Well, it was touch and go for a few moments while *her* prehistoric female brain processed my words, kicked them around in her grey cells for a bit, searching all the while for something sarcastic and biting to say back, something that would enable her to blow off some steam and relieve the sudden stress she felt by attacking dumb ole me, couldn't come up with any—no doubt due to the layers of alcoholic fog still in control—and, in the end, resulted in her smiling, embracing me lovingly and saying "Yeah, that's a good idea. Take me home."

But it was close. And I knew it.

Chapter Twenty-nine

It was closer to noon than dawn before we got really moving the next morning. The roomies, Mario and Brad, had packed their bags and were picked up by a van service to shuttle them down to the airport at Edinburgh for an early afternoon departure for New York. They both expressed their happiness at our impending nuptials and said while they wished they could stay and attend, the change fees in their airline tickets argued against it. "We'd love to stay and celebrate, Hacker," Mario said. "But not for an extra $300." I told them I understood, and I did. I wasn't all that keen about forking out some hefty change fees for Mary Jane and myself, and was hoping that Mary Jane's father-in-law would offer to fly us back to Boston on his private jet.

I did go out and buy a few newspapers, to see how the British media had played the tournament just ended. Most of them were as underwhelmed by that final round as I was, though everyone managed a few words of praise for Heinrich's steady final round. The sidebars were amusing, all featuring an embarrassed-looking Johnny Cheape running away from cameras and issuing a forthright statement: "No comment!" Poor old Professor Knox got nary a word: the press was much more interested in a miscreant aristocrat than another wacky college professor spouting obvious nonsense.

Sir Hamish had arranged for a room for himself at the Gold Standard Resort and taxied over the night before. He called after breakfast to tell me that Conrad Gold himself had offered us two nights in the honeymoon suite, plus a room for Carmine, my father in law, and a hotel-catered dinner for our wedding feast. I started to argue with him on the basis that I could not afford two hours at the Gold property, much less two nights, but he stopped me. "Dear boy," he said, "Conrad made it perfectly clear that his offer was gratis. He knows who you are and no doubt wishes to curry some future favor with you. My advice is to take it, and worry about the quid pro quo later. Life is much too short, dear boy."

So I agreed, and Mary Jane and I planned to move over to the hotel later in the afternoon. We learned that the private plane carrying Carmine and Mary Jane's daughter Victoria, would be landing about five in the afternoon at the private airfield in Dundee, and I arranged for a car service to pick them up and bring them over to the Gold hotel outside St. Andrews.

"OK," I said when all that had happened. "We've got the honeymoon suite, the ceremony location and presiding official, and a place for dinner. What else do we need?"

Mary Jane made a face at me, a face which said "*you stupid man-person. How could you* possibly *not know the bazillion and three things we need to accomplish before our wedding?*"

"I need something to wear," she said. "*You* need something to wear. I've got to get my hair done. And we need flowers."

"Flowers?"

"Yes," she said. "You know what flowers are, right? Colorful little things that grow out of the ground? It is traditional for a bride to have some. And to have others decorating the place where the vows are spoken. I don't know why. Some pagan symbolic thing related to fertility or something."

"Great," I said. "You planning on being fertile with me?"

She sighed. "Hacker, if you don't go find me some nice flowers right now, the chances are excellent that I will never sleep with you ever again."

I found that hard to believe, but nonetheless, I took it as a signal that it was time for me to leave the flat and give Mary Jane some space to prepare herself. Which I thought was proof positive that I am not a stupid man-person.

So I found myself a half hour later wandering aimlessly around St. Andrews trying to find a florist. You would think that a small town like St. Andrews would have at least one. Maybe two. I wandered down the length of North Street, almost all the way from Rusack's to the Cathedral, then cut over onto Central. I was beginning to feel an emotion that seemed to be coming close to panic when I heard my name called.

"Hacker! Wait up!"

I turned and saw Mike Morton come striding up the street, his arms pumping like he was on the treadmill at Gold's Gym. I waited for him to catch up.

"You staying on for a while?" he asked me when he walked up. "Most everyone else seems to have headed out to the airport."

"Yeah, we were supposed to fly out tonight," I told him. "But our plans changed."

"Then it's true!" he said, clapping his hands. "You really are getting married!" Congrats, Hack-man!"

"How did you know that?" I asked. "We only decided last night."

He touched a finger to the side of his nose. "Ve haff our ways," he said mysteriously.

"Yeah, well, I'm impressed," I said. "Listen, do you know any good florists in town? Mary Jane sent me out to find some flowers for the wedding."

"Absolutely," he said, and pointed over towards South Street. "I know a very nice lady who can probably get what you need. Follow me."

We walked a couple of blocks north, then cut down a cross street and meandered past a bank, a betting shop and a coffee place before arriving at a narrow storefront with a large front window. The sign in the window said "Fife Flowers and Gifts," which sounded close enough to me, and in we went, a little bell over the door tinkling prettily as we entered.

A lady in a gingham dress, about sixty, with puffy waves of white hair and a round, red face came out of the back room.

"Hullo, Mister Morton," she said, smiling at Mike. "It's so good to see you again. We're getting up an expedition to the Flats for Saturday if you're of a mind to join us."

"Ah, thanks Betty," Morton said, "I'll let you know. This is my friend Hacker. He's getting married tomorrow and he needs some flowers."

She turned to me with a big smile, showing a mouthful of teeth, some of interesting colors and shapes. "Congratulations to you, sir," she said. "You haven't left us much time, but tell me what you are looking for and I'll see what I can cobble together."

"Haven't got the slightest idea," I said. "My…fiancé sent me out to get flowers for the wedding. So here I am." It was the first time I had thought of Mary Jane as anything but my boon companion, love interest and friend, and thinking of her in a more permanent way gave me a bit of a start. A good one, though.

"I see," Betty said, although I could see by her frown and arching eyebrows that she didn't see at all. "Well, let's start at the beginning. Where is the ceremony to be held?"

"Younger Hall," I told her.

"Oh, that's quite a lovely spot," she said, nodding her approval. "We'll need some taller stems for the ceremony—that room is so large it tends to be a bit overpowering. The University holds many of its graduation ceremonies there. Is it tomorrow, you said?"

"Yes," I said. "One o'clock."

She made a note on a pad. "Right then, I will be able to order some things in from Edinburgh. Lovely, lovely." She looked at me. "Bridesmaids? Groomsmen?"

"No," I said. "Just the two of us. And her young daughter." I told Betty about Victoria, age ten, and she made a few more notes.

"And the bouquet for your wife," Betty said. "What kind of woman is she?"

I pondered that question, not sure exactly what kind of answer Betty the florist was looking for. She noted my confusion.

"Is she more of a traditionalist?" she asked. "Long white dress and veil? Or perhaps a bit less conventional? What is she wearing?"

"No idea," I said. "I think she's determining that as we speak. But I'm guessing more of a less-conventional thing. Really can't see her getting all brided up."

"I see," Betty said. "Well, let's plan for something holistic and nice, then, shall we? Perhaps a nice mix of traditional Scottish things: some thistle, some gorse, some lavender, all tied up in a nice ribbon. The thistle is supposed to bring good luck. " She reached up on a shelf behind her counter and pulled down a thick notebook. She flopped it on the countertop and opened it. Inside were photos of various arrangements she had done for other customers. She flipped through the pages until she found a shot of a bride's bouquet: it was a pretty arrangement of indigenous Scottish plants, magically arranged and tied with a Scottish plaid ribbon. I knew immediately that Mary Jane would love it.

"Bingo!" I said. "That looks perfect."

"And you'll need a luckenbooth, of course," she said, reaching behind the counter again.

"A what?—"

She smiled at me kindly. Rooting through a drawer, she pulled something out and placed it on the counter in front of me. It was a brooch, made of gold metal, in the shape of two intertwined hearts, with a pointed royal crown on top of the hearts.

"The luckenbooth brooch is a traditional token of love between the bride and groom," she said. "It is usually given along with the engagement ring, but since you've foreshortened that, you'll have to give it to her tonight instead, so she can wear it hidden within her dress during the ceremony. It's called a luckenbooth because these things were made in the booths and storefronts outside St. Giles' Cathedral on the Royal Mile in Edinburgh."

"I like it," I said.

She began to bustle around behind the counter, pulling out forms and order blanks, and I reached for my credit card. Mike Morton, who had been standing there watching, glanced at his watch.

"Hey, I gotta go, Hacker," he said. "Got someone I need to meet for lunch."

"Hey, thanks a bunch," I told him. "You saved my ass by bringing me here."

He smiled, pleased, and waved his hand as if to say, no probs.

"Would you like to come to the wedding?" I asked.

"Really?" he said.

"Why the hell not," I said. "Gonna be a small affair anyway. One o'clock, Younger Hall. Be there or be square."

He stuck out his hand and we shook.

"Thanks, Hacker," he said. "I'd be honored."

He took off and I went back to finishing up with Betty the Fife Florist.

"Nice guy," I said to her.

"Yes, quite," she replied, fussing with her paperwork. "Bit of an odd duck, though."

"Yes, I suppose," I said.

"When I first met him, he said he was interested in learning more about the land and the people here in Fife," she said, absently filling out blanks in her forms, occasionally reaching up to brush some strands of white hair out of her eyes as she worked. "We run nature hikes and explanatory rambles through the countryside almost every week," she continued. "Identifying various plants and their native habitats, some birding, some geology. Some come for the walking, some for the fellowship, others to learn new things."

"And Mike?"

She looked up from her work at me, and frowned. "Well, when I first met him, about five months ago, he seemed avid to participate with our weekly expeditions," she said. "He told me he was trying to find ways to fit it with the people here, as he had come over from the States to live here for a time. My understanding was that he was taking odd jobs around town and joining various clubs and civic associations as a way of meeting people and fitting in. He came hiking with us for at least four, maybe five weeks in a row, but then he stopped coming and hasn't joined us since."

"Well, I understand he's working on a book now," I said, "So he must be busy with his research and all," I said.

"Perhaps," she said. "But during that time we hiked with us, he seemed to be very interested in getting to know Colin Kincaid, who was one of our leaders."

"The Colin Kinkaid who was killed?"

"Yes, the same," Betty said. "Such a shame. Colin was a wonderful man. He was active with our group, and even led several of our hiking trips. After he died, Mister Morton never came back with us."

I remembered DC Wallace telling me that forensics had found traces of local plants and seeds in Kincaid's trouser cuffs and pockets.

"That place you're going to this weekend," I said.

"The Flats?"

"Yes," I said. "Where is that?"

"It's on the other side of the River Eden," she said. "A bit downstream from the A91 towards the sea. It's a primeval woodland, rolling terrain. Lovely collection of wildflowers, fungi. Always interesting things to see along the way. Some standing stones and what we think is a prehistoric burial ground. One of our more popular walking tours."

"Sounds great," I said.

Betty promised to send the bouquet to the Gold hotel in the morning, and promised that the flowers for the ceremony would be placed in Younger Hall in time for the wedding. I paid the bill, thanked her, and left.

Chapter Thirty

MY LAST NIGHT as a single man did not work out exactly as I had planned. Which is assuming I actually had a plan, which I really didn't.

In any case, Carmine Spoleto, his granddaughter Victoria and two goons arrived right on time in Dundee late in the afternoon and soon arrived at the Gold Standard Resort. Mary Jane kissed her father-in-law, wrapped Victoria up in a bear hug and swept her off to the bridal suite, telling me to get lost.

"The groom is not supposed to look upon the bride before she walks down the aisle," she told me solemnly. "Victoria is my maid of honor and she is the only one who can see me in person between now and tomorrow at one o'clock."

"What about the great Scottish tradition that the bride and groom go off and drink a bottle or two of single-malt whiskey the night before, and then have madly passionate relations until the sun comes up?" I asked.

"Really, Hacker," she said, rolling her eyes.

"Really," I said. "It's called the Ceremony of the Rumpy Pumpy. You can look it up. I think it was started by Robert the Bruce. Or was it the Wolf of Badenoch? Be bad luck not to keep the tradition alive."

Nonetheless, she cancelled the ceremony on me. So I was left to have dinner with Sir Hamish Cavendish and Carmine. We took a booth in the hotel's smaller steak house dining room, and Carmine's two goons took up their positions at the door. They were dressed in black sports coats and pants, white shirts with Italian collars and black ties. They got a lot of strange looks from the other patrons coming and going.

"Is your life in danger over here in Scotland?" I asked Carmine when we had settled in, nodding at the body guards.

He smiled his toothy smile at me, which made him resemble nothing so much as a rabid wolverine deep in the Maine woods.

"Do you know how old I am, Hacker?" he asked me. I shook my head. Even if I did, I was not going to hazard a guess.

"Eighty-seven," he said, a touch of pride in his voice. "And the reason I am still on this side of the grass, even on this side of the pond, is because I always have someone watching my back. Always."

He turned his beady little animal eyes on Sir Hamish, who was uncharacteristically quiet. I had told Hamish what my father-in-law to be did for a living. I think he was impressed. Maybe curious. Maybe frightened. But impressed.

"What line of work are you in, Cavendish?" Carmine now asked.

"My family has made whiskey in this country for two hundred and twenty-seven years," Sir Hamish replied.

"Whiskey!" Carmine repeated the word with a cough. "I suppose you know all those Kennedy bastards. They took over the whiskey market right after Prohibition. That's how old man Joe was able to buy Jack's ticket into the White House."

"Well, yes, I understand that the Kennedy family was involved in the importation business," Sir Hamish said. "But I've never dealt with them directly..."

"Involved!" Carmine laughed, which turned into a coughing fit. He took a sip of water from his glass to recover. "Hey, can ya drink the water over here without getting the trots?" he asked no one in particular. Then he remembered he had started on a story about Kennedys and the whiskey trade.

"Yeah, old man Joe—he was as crooked as they come—he came over here just before the end of Prohibition. Ya know who he brought with him? Little Jimmy Roosevelt, FDR's boy. First thing they did, meet with Churchill himself. The three of them set up a company called Somerset Importers—old man Joe named it after some fancy social club in Boston that had blackballed him. They didn't let the Irish in to places like that back then. Or us wops, either. Anyway, he signed up all the big whiskey makers over here, got the exclusive importation rights. Little Jimmy set up another company to sell insurance to these guys. Y'know: hey, it would be a damn shame if your ship full of Scotch would hit a goddam iceberg or something, y'know? Pretty good little racket, they had. And that Churchill fellow was an investor. They all got filthy rich. And they call me 'organized crime.' Hah!"

A waiter wearing a stiff, starched long apron tied around his chest at armpit level came and took our orders. We all went for the Angus steak. Sir Hamish opened a bottle of one of his aged Cavendish whiskies and poured us all a glass. Carmine took a sip.

"Not bad, there Cavendish," he said, nodding his approval. "Better than the rotgut crap we smuggled down from Canada during the Depression. That crap'd take the hair off an owl."

Sir Hamish thought that was funny and laughed. He asked a few more questions, and Carmine spent most of the dinner regaling us with tales of old Fords packed full of hootch driving across a frozen St. Lawrence River, and then, chased by the revenuers, making their way down through the Green Mountains of Vermont and into Beantown. There were gun battles with the Customs boys, and tales of betrayal and thieves' honor and a lot of bloodshed. Old Joe Kennedy the movie mogul could have made some good films out of the stories Carmine was spinning. But of course, Kennedy's experiences were quite different: he mostly sat in warm, comfortable offices and listened to the sound of his money compounding quarterly; and when he did run a Hollywood studio, he spent most of his time banging starlets instead of encouraging storylines.

Dinner over, Carmine excused himself and went upstairs to bed. The goons went with him. I took Sir Hamish into the clubby hotel bar, all brass, leather and polished wood, and bought him a brandy.

"This is the time when I am supposed to ask you if you harbor any lurking regrets or second thoughts," Sir Hamish said as we clinked glasses. "Better to admit to them now, rather than once you're officially married."

"None," I said truthfully. In fact, I was ecstatic that Mary Jane was agreed to become my wife. I had no idea what it would be like to be a married man, but I also had no doubts that Mary Jane was the best possible person on earth to be my lifelong partner. "But there is one small regret I have."

Sir Hamish sighed. "Out with it," he said, waving his hand at me impatiently.

"It's Colin Kincaid," I said.

"Ah," Sir Hamish said, sounding relieved. "Unfinished business."

"Well, somebody killed the man," I said. "And so far, that somebody has gotten away with it. I don't like that."

"And if I remind you that it is the business of the Fife Constabulary to investigate all such crimes and to bring the criminals involved to the bar of justice ...?"

"Yeah, I know," I said. "But it still bothers me."

"I had been of the opinion that it was one of those fearsome Russian chaps," Sir Hamish said. "They may never be formally charged with the crime, but I think everyone suspects that one of them killed Kincaid."

"But why?" I asked. "Kincaid had nothing to do with the Russians' plans to develop the airbase, at least as far as we know. Even so, the Russians had no motive to kill Colin Kincaid. In fact, it would have been counter-productive: killing Kincaid would bring unwanted police attention to them and their plans."

"Yes, I suppose that's right," Sir Hamish said.

"And there's another problem."

He took a sip from his brandy and waited.

"Why would the Russians dump Kincaid's body in the Bottle Dungeon?" I asked. "That makes no sense at all. If the Russkis killed someone, like they did that poor fellow the night Swiftie was out fishing on the rocks, they'd just dump the body in the sea and hope it floats away to Norway. The last place on earth they'd stash the body of someone they just killed would be in the dungeon where the police would find it and examine it and uncover all the clues it held."

"Well," Sir Hamish said, "Couldn't you say that about any prospective killer? Why would anyone dump the body down the dungeon?"

"It was a message," I said. "The killer was saying '*I did it.* Here it is. You can't figure out why I did this.' He was taunting us. Leaving a calling card. Telling the authorities that he, the killer, was several moves ahead of them. And smarter."

"Interesting," Sir Hamish said, nodding. "I had not thought of that possibility."

"That made me think of Dr. Knox, the Eliminate Golf fellow," I said. "He would have loved nothing better than to stick it to the police. Perform an unsolvable crime right under the nose of the St. Andrews police. Make them look like fools. All part of his campaign to make this town look stupid, and just when the eyes of the world are focused here. But he apparently is not a suspect."

"No," Sir Hamish agreed, nodding. "He was at a conference in London when Kincaid was murdered."

"So, ruling Knox out, and a political motive for the crime, we're back to Kincaid himself," I said. "Who wanted him dead? As it turns out, a lot of people. Well, to be fair, a lot of people might have been torqued at the guy…that was Kincaid's job, after all. But who wanted him gone? Is there anyone who would be angry enough about a tee time to kill the man?"

"Hard to believe that would be the case," Sir Hamish said.

"Right," I agreed. "Someone angry enough to kill him, then to dispose of his body like he did, which was also a big middle finger to the police. That's a lot of layers of pathology. Most murders are spur of the moment bursts of emotion. This one has a lot of strange motivation behind it."

"Hmm," Sir Hamish said. "Quite a mystery."

"Which I haven't been able to solve," I said. "Which makes me a little regretful. And crazy."

"Only one thing to do," Sir Hamish said.

"What's that?"

"Drink up, my boy, drink up. Get a good night's sleep and start in afresh tomorrow."

It wasn't the most satisfactory advice I'd ever received, but it was probably the best I would get.

Chapter Thirty-one

THERE WAS A firm rapping at the door early the next morning. I moaned and rolled over to look at the alarm clock on the bedside table: 7:30 a.m. I heard snoring and looked over at Sir Hamish, fast asleep in the other bed in the room. I had called Mary Jane after Sir Hamish and I had finished our drinks the night before, but Victoria answered.

"Hi, sweetheart," I had said. "Is your Mom there?"

"Yeah," Victoria had said. "But she's crying."

"Oh," I had said, "How come?"

"I don't know." I had heard her say to her mother: "Mommy, why are you crying?" Then she had come back on the line. "She says she's crying because she's so happy," Victoria had said.

I had covered up the phone and whispered to Sir Hamish: "Is there a spare bed in your room I could use tonight?" I had said. "Sounds like a tsunami of emotion in Mary Jane's room."

He had nodded, and I had told Victoria to tell her mother to be ready at noon tomorrow.

Now it was tomorrow and that rapping was repeated at the door to Hamish's room. I rolled out of bed, threw on a robe and opened the door. Johnny Swift stood there grinning at me like someone who had just won the lottery.

"Do you know what time it is?" I said.

"I know what day this is, Hack-Man," he said. "An' your friend John Swift is here to make sure your happiest of days is a perfect one. Come along, then, we have things to do."

I sighed, and tossed on some clothes. Sir Hamish rolled over and pulled the pillow over his head, which I took as a sign he wanted to be left alone.

"First, a good breakfast," Johnny said as we rode down the elevator. "A man canna be happily wedded wi'out a good breakfast inside him."

The main dining room offered a lengthy breakfast buffet, so we headed there. I grabbed a cup of coffee while Johnny made a beeline for the buffet line. I was almost finished with my coffee when he came back to the table with a groaning plate of food, and began to tuck in with relish.

"Where's the missus?" he asked.

"In the bridal suite," I said. "Where no man is allowed."

"Aye," he said, nodding. "Tis bad luck to lay eyes upon the bride before its time. Have ye made plans to wash her feet yet, Hack?"

"Wash her feet?"

"Oh, aye," he said, nodding while he shoveled in eggs and sausage and pancakes, like a man who hadn't eaten solid food in a month or more. "Traditional. The bride's feet must be carefully washed afore she dons her stockings. Usually it's another woman what does the job, but the groom is allowed to do it as well."

"Ah," I said, "Well, being uncouth Americans and all, we haven't planned for that."

"Too bad," Johnny said. "Do you know how many marriages end in divorce? It's because they don't follow the traditions."

"Yeah, well, I think we'll risk it," I said.

"And what is it you are wearing, then?" he asked.

"I don't know," I said. "I haven't been allowed into my room so I have no idea what clothes I have that are not dirty and wrinkled. I brought my blue blazer with me, and I think I have a necktie."

Johnny dropped his cutlery with a clatter against the plates in front of him. "Blue blazer … necktie–? Ye Gods. That is complete rubbish, Hacker. I am surprised at you. No matter, I've got us a plan."

"If you've got a plan, I'm going to need more coffee," I said, and I went to fetch some.

An hour or so later, Johnny led me into the narrow glass doorway of the Kirk Wynd Kilt Shop on one of St. Andrews' narrowest streets. The doorway was framed by two large picture windows, criss-crossed by white sashes, which set off the greenish tint of the stucco walls. Inside, a young man greeted us with a smile, and Johnny and him exchanged some words in a language that seemed to be English, but of which I understood nothing.

"Very good, sir," the sales guy said to me. "Let's get a few measurements done and I'll fix you right up." About an hour later, I had been fixed up with a kilt in a nice blue-green plaid, along with the black velvet Argyll jacket, matching waistcoat, a furry dress sporran, shiny black lace-up shoes, white woolen knee socks, colorful flashes to keep them up and a sword-shaped pin to keep my kilt from flying up over my head in the wind. We talked about adding a *sgian dubh,* the short-bladed knife that tucks into the top of one of the knee socks, but we all agreed that perhaps my personal safety was not going to be threatened inside Younger Hall. I was a little hesitant about the sporran, which is really just a man-purse, but Johnny told me it was a required part of the kit.

"Where else ya gonna keep your money?" he asked. I thought about it, realized he was right, and nodded my approval.

"Do I have to go commando?" I asked next.

"Sir?" the kilt man said.

"You know, under the kilt," I said, feeling my face turn a bit red.

"Ach, of course," he said, smiling. "That is entirely your personal preference," he said.

"Unless ya wanna be a total wanker," Johnny said with a guffaw. "Real men wear the kilt the way it's supposed to be worn."

I decided to postpone my decision until later. The kilt man promised to send my rental over to the hotel within the hour and Swiftie and I left. It was a bright, sunny day, with a bit of a breeze cooling the air. Enough of a breeze, actually, to make me think going commando would be inadvisable.

"Coffee?" Swiftie suggested. There was a Starbucks shop across the street and down a bit.

"Nah," I said. "Let's take a walk down to the sea. A little fresh air would be good right about now."

We wandered down towards the towering ruin of the old cathedral transept, now surrounded by the ancient churchyard at the edge of the town. From there, we followed the road downhill, catching glimpses of the flat rocky reef exposed at low tide, pools of seawater shimmering in the bright morning sun. Beyond, the North Sea stretched out to the horizon, deep blue and cold looking. Once on The Scores, the road that skirted the cliffs above the sea, we eventually arrived at the entrance to the Castle, its pale stone façade and tower rising above a grassy verge. We walked across the wooden bridge spanning the old moat and entered the inner courtyard, now a perfectly manicured greensward ringed by ruined walls all around. There were benches spread around the courtyard, and we sat down on one, basking in the warm sun.

“Nervous, Hacker?” Swiftie asked, looking at me with some concern.

“Nah,” I said. “Not a bit. Have you ever been married, John?”

“Me? Oh, aye. Twas many a year ago, of course,” he said. “Dinna last. Agatha did not like me when I was on the drink. Can’t say I blame her.”

A woman came out of the doorway that led into the gift store and interactive area of the museum. She saw Johnny and me sitting there and came over.

“Is that you, John Swift?” she called out. “I hope you’re sober, this time o’ the morning.”

“Aye, shut yer gob, Winnie,” Swiftie said, smiling. “I’m as sober as a judge, I am.”

We stood up and Johnnie gave the woman a hug. He turned to me. “Winnie McCray,” he introduced her. “She’s some kind of relation to me, although I have no idea how. Winnie, this is my Yank friend Hacker.”

We shook hands. She was a small woman of about fifty, with a weathered but pleasant face, wreathed in a smile. Her reddish hair was pulled back and pinned at the rear. She was wearing a reddish blazer over a black skirt, and there was an official looking badge of some kind pinned over her heart.

"Winifred is the manager here," Swiftie told me. "Been here for years and years."

"It's a lovely spot," I told her. "Love the views from the walls. Quite peaceful."

"You are most welcome," she said. "I am glad to hear that some find peace and rest here, a place where there was not much of either over the centuries."

"I suppose the incident with Colin Kincaid was troubling for you," I said.

"Oh, aye, a terrible thing," she said, shaking her head sadly.

"Do you have any idea how Kincaid's body got into the dungeon?"

"Not a clue," she said. "The grating over the entrance hole is always tightly locked."

"Who has the key?"

She rummaged around in her jacket pocket and pulled out a Day-Glo keychain made of twisty plastic. A small handful of metal keys dangled in the sunlight.

"Anyone else?"

"Nae, nae," she said, exhaling. "Only the janitor, Old Willy. He has a set of keys to the all the doors as well. But he's nearly eighty years on now, and only works two days a week at most." She paused and looked at me askance. "May I ask why you are asking me all these questions?"

Johnny Swift laughed and slapped me on the back.

"Ach, Winnie, y'dunna ken Hacker," he said. "He's a reporter fella back in the States. Askin' the questions is what he does for a livin', he does."

"I see," Winnie said. She smiled at me again, but with a bit less warmth. She glanced at her wrist watch, made some gotta-go sounds and bid us good day.

Johnny and I watched her go.

"Did I piss her off?" I asked.

"Aye," Johnny said. "But that's no hard to do with our Winnie. Bit of a stick, she is."

"Do you know this Old Willie guy?" I asked.

"Of course, Hack," he said. "I know everyone. At least, everyone worth knowin'"

"Do you think he's at home?"

"Unless he's gone and died on us, that's exactly where he'll be," Swiftie said. "Follow me."

Swiftie led me back down The Scores toward the Cathedral. We skirted around behind the churchyard and followed The Shore road that turned inland along the route of the Kinness Burn. Near the sea, the burn was wide enough to be called a harbor, but further upstream, it turned into a narrow and somewhat stagnant waterway. We turned onto The Glebe, a narrow little road and Swiftie turned into a smallish parking area surrounded by three or four gray stucco buildings with slate roofs and metal drainpipes running down the side.

"Council flats," he told me, meaning these were public housing units. "Have to be an old body to live here."

Swiftie led me to the door of one of the units and knocked on it, loudly. When there was no answer, he knocked again and leaned in to the door, listening. "Aye," he said, nodding to himself. "He's there all right." He opened the door and led me into the apartment inside. It was very warm, as if all the windows had been tightly shut, not allowing any fresh air or breezes from the nearby sea to air the place out. The unit was small:

a very small kitchen to the left of the door, and, down a short hall, a single room with a dining table on one side and two easy chairs facing a telly on the other. Beyond, I saw a doorway leading to a bedroom. The television was on and the sound was loud, and sitting in one of the easy chairs was a very old man dressed in slacks and a casual shirt buttoned all the way up to his neck. He had a few wisps of white hair arranged artfully atop his head. His feet were stretched out in front, towards the TV screen, and propped atop an ottoman. He was a hefty man and his jowly face was red, with age marks dotting his chin and cheeks.

He looked up when we entered and, seeing Johnnie, the old man's face broke open in a happy grin.

"John, lad," he said, his voice gruff and tremulous. "Good to see ya."

"Hullo, Will," Johnnie said, his voice overly loud, and went over to give the old man's shoulder an affectionate squeeze. "How goes the battle?"

"Ach," the old man said, waving a hand in the air. "Same shite, different day." He looked at me. "And who's this, then?"

"Me friend Hacker," Johnnie said. "He's a newspaper man from the States. Came over to report on the Open."

"Oh, yes," the old man said. "They're playing that this week, then?"

"Nae, Willie," Johnnie said. "They just finished Sunday."

"Aye, I knew that," he said nodding to himself. "And who won, then?"

"The German," Johnnie said. "Gruber."

"Never heard of 'im," the old man said. "Did Peter Thomson play? Ach, what a man was he. Did I ever tell ye the time I caddied for him, Thompson? Grand man, he was, grand."

"Aye, Will, you've told me," Johnnie said, sneaking a quick look and half smile at me. He raised the volume of his voice again, so the elderly ears could pick it up. "Old Will here caddied for many years. He once had the bag of Peter Thomson, and I don't think he's forgotten a shot the man made."

"True, true," Willie said nodding. "He was going to hit an eight-iron on the eighth hole," he said. "I told him it was the seven. He didn't want to, but he took the seven. Laid it dead. Two feet. Ach, but that man could golf his ball."

"How many times did he win the Open?" I asked.

Willie held up his hand, fingers spread open.

"Count them, sir," he said. "Five wins. More than any other man, save for Vardon. He won it here in '55. Beat Johnny Fallon by two. Johnny was from Lanarkshire, y'know."

We could tell that Old Willie was about to launch into a trip down Memory Lane, so Johnnie cut him off.

"Say, Willie," he said, "Are you still working some, over at the Castle?"

"Aye," the man said. "But not so much anymore. Me legs are a bit weary and they don't take me as far as they used ta."

"Growin' old is a bitch, and that's a fact," Johnnie said. "Listen, do you know where the keys to the Castle are? You still have a set, right?"

"Oh, aye," Willie said. He pointed towards the kitchen. "They're on a nail by the icebox."

I went over and looked. Sure enough, a keychain rested on a nail, four or five keys dangling from the clasp.

"Anyone ever ask to borrow these?" I asked.

"Borrow? The keys?" Willie looked at me as though I was daft. "Whatever for? So they can go sweep the steps and empty the bins for me?"

I laughed. "That would be a nice surprise, wouldn't it," I said.

"Is there anyone comes in to help you, Willie?" Swiftie asked. "Helper from the council maybe? Friend or relative?"

"Oh, aye," he said. "The council people have a girl stop by once the week to make sure I haven't died. I think they want the flat for someone else. But I keep disappointing her by being alive when she calls." He chuckled to himself.

"Anyone else?"

Willie shook his head. "Nae, can't think of anyone," he said. Then he sat up. "Wait…I just remembered. There was a nice young fella that stopped in for tea and biscuits from time to time," he said. "Come to think, I haven't seen him back in a while." He turned and looked at me. "In fact, he was a Yank, like you. Maybe you know him?"

"Maybe I do," I said, smiling at the man. "Do you remember his name?"

Willie took a minute to ponder that. He stroked his chin and pulled on his ear. He smoothed the lace doily on the arm of his chair. Finally, he slapped his hand down hard.

"Yes!" he said, his gravelly voice triumphant. "Michael was his name. Michael Morton. Said he had come over to live a spell with us, and had found a little flat not far from here. Nice young fella. Knew a lot about golf, as I recall. He knew who Peter Thomson was, I remember that much!"

"I don't suppose you gave him the keys to the Castle, did you?" I asked.

"Now why would I do a thing like that?" Willie looked at me like I had lost all touch with the real world. Then he paused. "But I do remember when he helped me find them."

"He found your keys?" I asked.

"Aye," Willie said, nodding. "I'm a bit forgetful these days," he said. "I always keep those keys on the nail by the fridge." He nodded in that direction. "But once, I couldn't find them. Looked everywhere…under the chairs, under the bed, in my closet. Young Michael stopped by while I was looking and he found them right away! They had fallen in behind the icebox. He's a good lad. I hope he comes by again. Enjoyed talking with him."

Johnnie and I looked at each other.

"Johnnie," Willie said. "Put the kettle on. Let's have some tea. I think there's some biscuits in the cupboard."

I shook my head and Johnnie took over.

"Thanks, Willie," he said. "But my friend Hacker here is getting married in two hours. We have to go. Can we take a rain check?"

"Sure, sure," Willie said, waving us off. "I'm not planning on goin' anywhere!" He looked at me. "And as for you, sir, let me say what they said to me afore I was wed these many years ago: May there always be work for your hands to do. May your purse always hold a coin or two. May the sun always shine upon your windowpane. May a rainbow be certain to follow each rain. May the hand of a friend always be near to you and May God fill your heart with gladness to cheer you."

I shook his hand, which was cool and dry in mine, his skin papery and thin.

"Thank you," I said.

Chapter Thirty-two

IT WAS ABOUT noon, and I was standing in the front courtyard of the Gold Standard resort chatting with Sir Hamish. His gold Mercedes had been washed and polished and sat gleaming in the bright sun of the day, the top down and Queenie the sheepdog, who had also been washed and groomed for the occasion, was curled up asleep in the front seat.

"Ye look like a bloody native," he told me, brushing some lint off my shoulder and straightening my lapels. He sounded like he approved, though.

"It's my first time in a skirt," I said. "Feels a little weird." I adjusted my kilt for about the millionth time since I first put it on about twenty minutes ago. "It's like learning how to walk for the first time."

"I suggest you take some lessons from her," Sir Hamish said, and nodded toward the elegant entrance door to the hotel. Coming out was Mary Jane, holding the hand of her daughter Victoria. They were wearing matching dresses. Mary Jane had somehow found a simple, off-white long dress with a sophisticated halter-top that left her arms bare. At the waist and neck, there was a contrasting band of tartan plaid that came close to matching the design of my kilt. Her hair was swept up atop her head and pinned with a floral crown, and she held the Scottish bouquet of Queen Anne's lace, sprigs of lavender, purple heather and a couple round globes of prickly thistle. Victoria, dressed much the same, was beaming.

"Wowza," was the best I could come up with at short notice. I had no breath in my lungs for anything longer or more profound.

"Isn't Momma the most beautiful bride you've ever seen?" Victoria said.

"Without question," Sir Hamish said, obviously able to form words with more than two syllables. "My dear girl, you are a resplendent sight to behold."

"And beautiful," Victoria added.

"Totally," Sir Hamish said, smiling down at the girl. She nodded in satisfaction.

"Shall we go?" Mary Jane said. "We're supposed to meet the vicar at 12:30."

Mary Jane and I climbed into the back seats, and Victoria took Queenie on her lap in the front. Sir Hamish drove us slowly back into town.

"Where's Carmine?" I asked.

"He went into town on his own an hour or so ago," Mary Jane said. "He was getting antsy waiting around."

"You haven't commented on my, err, outfit," I said.

"It is taking every ounce of self-control for me to keep from running my hand up your skirt to see if it's true," Mary Jane said.

"If what's true?"

"What they say about Scottish men and kilts," she said with a slightly evil grin.

"Oh, aye," I said, in a mocking brogue. "That's for me to know, and you to discover, woman!"

We arrived outside the impressive Neoclassical façade of Younger Hall on North Street, and Sir Hamish found a parking spot right outside, where a line of metal bollards marched down the sidewalk. The sooty limestone building, with its four distinctive rectangular columns towering three stories above the street, conveyed a feeling of stolid accomplishment and established power, both appropriate either for a graduating class of college students or a couple about to embark on matrimony.

We climbed out of the car and adjusted our clothing. I saw Johnnie Swift waiting near the granite stairs that led up to the entrance of the Hall. He was chatting with DCC Wallace, who was wearing his full uniform. Swiftie came over to greet us. He was wearing an actual suit of clothes: slacks, white dress shirt, narrow black necktie and a sportcoat. When he got close, I noticed that the color of slacks and jacket were close, but not exact.

"Swiftie," I said in greeting. "I don't think I've ever seen you all dressed up before."

"Aye, Hack," he said with a grin. "Tis me wedding and funeral suit. I found the jacket in a bin about two months ago. This is the first time I've had 'er on."

"Well, you look nice," I said. He kissed Mary Jane and gave Victoria a tweak on the chin.

Carmine Spoleto, flanked by his two goons, came around the corner on Castle Street. He was wearing a dark black suit and a dark shirt with a contrasting white tie, and wore a red rose pinned to his lapel. He came over and kissed the bride, and gave his grand-daughter a nice hug. Then he looked at me.

"You're wearing a dress," he said.

"It's a kilt, actually," I said. "What they wear over here."

"In Boston, it's a dress," he said.

"So, what do you think?" I asked, twirling around a little. "Looks good on me, huh?"

Carmine sniffed.

DCC Wallace came up to us and saluted smartly.

"Chief Wallace," I said, "This is my soon-to-be father-in-law, Carmine Spoleto. He is one of the leading figures in organized crime back in Boston."

They shook hands.

"You are welcome in St. Andrews, sir," Wallace said with a slight smile playing at the corners of his lips. "I would remind you that, unlike in Boston, we have cameras on almost every corner here. Word to the wise, and all that."

"I came here for my daughter's wedding," Carmine said. "You think I'm gonna knock over a bank just for fun while I'm here?"

"I certainly hope not," Wallace said. "But if you do, it would be my honor to arrest you."

Carmine Spoleto doesn't laugh. At least, I've never heard him do so. But he did smile a little. Which made me relax a bit.

Sir Hamish came up with Queenie on a leash at his heels. "I believe we should go inside," he said. "I think I saw Rector Benedict in the lobby."

He handed Queenie's leash to Victoria, who bent down and let Queenie lick her face in excitement. We all headed inside. DCC Wallace walked with us.

"Are you coming to the wedding?" I asked. "Not that you're not welcome of course. Glad to have you, in fact."

He smiled at me. "No," he said. "I am working. But thank you for the invitation."

Carmine Spoleto hung back a bit and, with a slight gesture with his head, indicated that he wanted to speak with me in private. I let the others walk inside and waited.

He grabbed me by the elbow, not with a hard grip, but enough to make me focus my attention on him. As if I wouldn't anyway. He peered up at me, his eyes clear and hard.

"I like you, Hacker," he said.

"Well, thanks Mr. Spoleto," I said. I wondered if I would ever be comfortable calling him Dad, and decided not to think about that right now. "You've always been good to me. And Mary Jane and Victoria both think the world of you."

He waved his hand and my compliments away.

"I like you, Hacker, and Mary Jane likes you, and Victoria likes you, and that's good enough for me," he said. "But if you ever hurt that girl, or cause her to be hurt, I will not like you anymore." He paused and we locked eyes. "And you know what that means, don't you?"

"That I will sleep with the fishies?"

His hand on my elbow tightened. Just a bit. But tighter.

"I am not joking, Hacker," he said. "Mary Jane was good to my boy, and he mostly didn't deserve it. She never complained, never said a word to me about all the things he did: the other women, the slapping, the drug abuse. But I knew what went on in their home. And I will know what goes on in your home as well. And I am telling you that I will not allow that girl to be hurt again, by you or by anyone. Am I clear?"

I looked into his eyes, which were clear and unblinking. And knowing what things those eyes had seen over the years, I understood completely what he was saying.

"Mr. Spoleto...Carmine," I said. "Mary Jane means the world to me. Victoria, too. I promise you that I will look after both of them as long as I live."

He let go of my elbow and patted me on the shoulder.

"Good," he said. "But that's the first time I had to have a serious talk with a man in a dress."

I laughed, and gestured for him to precede me inside the Hall.

He started to walk in, then stopped suddenly.

"I almost forgot," he said, and began patting his pockets. He reached into his left-hand pants pocket and pulled something out: a small, black jewel case.

"This is the ring worn by my wife," he said. "I think it was worn by her mother before her. Maria never knew Mary Jane, or Victoria, which is a damn shame. But then, she also did not have to see her son die, either, so maybe that good balances out the bad. I don't know. But she would have wanted Mary Jane to wear it. I hope it fits."

It took me a moment or two to recover my voice.

"I'm sure it will fit perfectly," I said. "Thank you so much."

We walked in to Younger Hall together.

The Reverend Doctor Charles Benedict was a large and effusive man who exuded confidence and authority, as befits a man who was head of the University of St. Andrews and an ordained minister of the Church of Scotland. He was wearing his long white priestly robes draped with a colorful vestment draped around his shoulders. He quickly made everyone feel at ease and led us into the rectangular space of the large Hall. The floor tilted gently towards the front and there were a dozen rows of theater seating installed on both sides of the central aisle. At the far end, the stage area rose above the floor and the wall at the end of the hall contained the full set of pipes for a church-size organ that was hidden from view. The Hall contained a balcony on three sides which contained more seating both on the sides and the back section, where the loge seating was quite large.

A simple table had been set up at the front of the stage, covered in a white cloth and set with two vases containing a colorful spray of summer flowers. It was simple, not particularly denominational, and just about perfect for our purposes.

Doctor Benedict was pointing out some of the architectural highlights of the room, when Mike Morton entered, and began to approach us. I saw DCC Wallace move to intercept, and saw another uniformed policeman enter the hall behind Morton. I excused myself and went to greet Morton.

"Hacker," he said, holding his hand out to shake mine. "Hope I'm not late for the fun."

"No," I said, "I think the fun is about to begin. I think DCC Wallace here has a few questions for you first."

"Oh?" Morton stepped back a step and then looked behind him at the other officer standing quietly at the door, hands folded in front, eyes locked unblinkingly on him. "About what?"

"About the death of Colin Kincaid, Mr. Morton," Wallace said to him.

"Ah, yes," Morton said. "That was very sad. I knew him, you know. We had talked about doing a project together. A history of the Links Trust."

"Yes, we know that," Wallace said. "We also know you had been hiking with Kincaid on several occasions, and had the opportunity to attack him and kill him when nobody was around to witness the crime."

"Wha–?"

"We further know that you had access to the keys to the St. Andrews Castle, keys that you took from the residence of the Castle's custodian, Willie McTavish. That would have enabled you to gain access to the Bottle Dungeon in the Castle, and to dispose of Mr. Kincaid's body there."

"How–?"

"And we know that you and Kincaid had discussed a writing project that fell through, and because you were short of funds, that rejection gave you the motive to end Mr. Kincaid's life."

Morton looked at me, his eyes now wild with panic.

"Hacker!" he said. "Tell him this this is nonsense! You know me. Would I ever do something like this? C'mon..."

I looked at him sadly. "Actually, Mike, it sounds a lot like something you might do," I said. "I think you should go with the chief here and tell him everything."

We had been standing at the end of the rows of theater seating, while the rest of my wedding party was waiting down at the front of the hall. I heard a sound, kind of a snort, a gasp, a forceful exhalation of breath.

"Aww, fuck you," was what Morton said and then he lunged. His hands came up to my chest and he pushed me, hard, back into the last row of seating. I began to fly backwards, catching my legs at the knees on the seatbacks and tumbling head over teakettle backwards. Just before I lost visual focus, I saw Wallace reaching to grab Morton. And then I was flying through the air, hoping my head wasn't going to connect with anything hard, reaching blindly out with one hand for something to grab onto.

But there wasn't anything to grab, so I completed my backwards somersault, feet flying up in the air, back arching, a slow motion tumble that wasn't so slow. Somehow, miraculously, my head missed the next row of seat backs and the arm rests and I managed to fall awkwardly between the rows of seats. That was the good news. The bad was that I was momentarily wedged there, legs akimbo, kicking furiously in an attempt to get right side up again.

And of course, in my upside down, wedged between the seats position, my kilt flopped down over my face. It took me a few seconds to extract myself from my predicament. When I stood up again, I saw Mike Morton being led out of Younger Hall by the two policemen. I turned to look at my wedding party at the front of the hall.

Mary Jane's mouth had formed a perfect O, and her hands had flown to her face, her face drained of color. Carmine Spoleto was shaking his head in disgust. Johnnie Swift was grinning at me from ear to ear, and he held up his thumb in a "Yah, mate" signal. Sir Hamish was struggling not to burst out laughing. The reverend doctor and Carmine's two goons just stood there, mouths agape, as if unable to process what they had just seen.

Victoria, holding the leash of Queenie the dog, looked at me sadly.

"Oh, Hacker, can't you be serious for once?" she said. "It's your wedding."

I straightened my cuffs, smoothed out my kilt, whose pleats had quickly fallen back into the proper position, and threw back my shoulders.

"Right then," I said to them all. "Let's do this."

ABOUT THE AUTHOR

James Y. Bartlett is one of the most-published golf writers of his generation. His work has appeared in golf and lifestyle publications around the world for more than thirty years. He was a staff editor with *Golfweek* and *Luxury Golf* magazines, and edited *Caribbean Travel & Life* magazine for several years during his "golf hiatus" period.

Bartlett was the golf columnist for *Forbes FYI* magazine for the first fifteen years of that publication and wrote a similar column on the golf world for *Hemispheres,* the in-flight magazine of United Airlines for nearly twenty years under the pseudonym of "A.G. Pollard, Jr."

His first Hacker Golf Mystery, *Death is a Two-Stroke Penalty,* was published by St. Martin's Press in 1991. *Death from the Ladies Tee* followed soon thereafter, and Yeoman House Books proudly continued the series with *Death at the Member-Guest* and *Death in a Green Jacket.*

With the publication of this new title, Bartlett is now halfway home to complete his planned "major series" of Hacker Mysteries. Look for his planned novels on the U.S. Open and the PGA Championship, coming soon from Yeoman House!

Add these other Hacker Golf Mystery titles to your library!

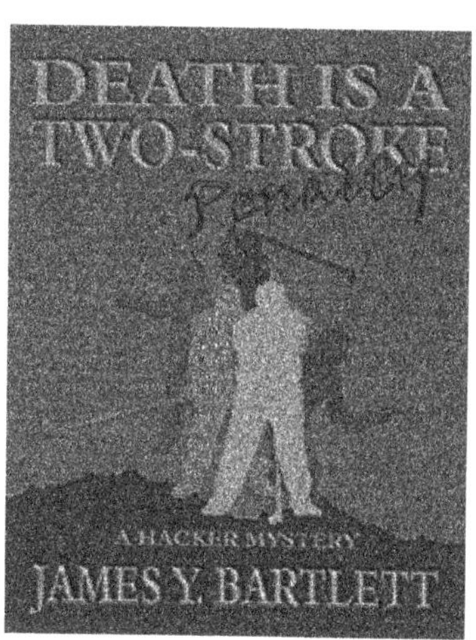

Golf reporter Pete Hacker is covering the PGA Tour event in Charleston, S.C., when an up-and-coming Tour star is found dead on the course. Or, was he murdered? Hacker digs into the case, tracking a drug-dealing caddie, a bevy of golf groupies and a strange, Bible-thumping chaplain before he finds the killer.

Doing a favor for an old friend, Hacker agrees to cover an LPGA event in Miami. There, he finds that one of the Tour's stars holds an unhealthy degree of control over the Tour and its players. When he begins to dig in, bodies turn up everywhere and his own life is threatened before the explosive final round!

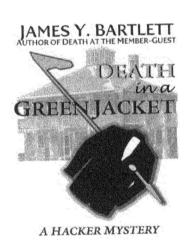

CPSIA information can be obtained
at www.ICGtesting.com
Printed in the USA
BVHW05s1134090718
521160BV00030B/1473/P